DEATH FLIGHT

George Kennedy liked to pilot airplanes as much as he liked to make movies. So he had no fear of flying until the private jetliner of Arab sheik Prince Ibrahim turned into an airborne hearse.

One body had already turned up on a prayer rug in a most unholy position. Another had made the sign on the plane's washroom read "occupied"—for eternity.

It wasn't long before Kennedy and his best buddy, cop-turned-actor Mike Corby, figured murder was going to empty more seats than a skunk in a movie theater... unless they figured out who on board was playing the part of the killer. And anybody could be the next victim: Jimmy Stewart or his lovely wife Gloria, Bobby Troup or Julie London, top model Candy Vandermeer or even George Kennedy himself if a bullet turned his famous *Airport* role of Joe Petrone into a farewell performance.

Other Avon Books by
George Kennedy

MURDER ON LOCATION

MURDER ON HIGH

GEORGE KENNEDY

AVON
PUBLISHERS OF BARD, CAMELOT, DISCUS AND FLARE BOOKS

AVON BOOKS
A division of
The Hearst Corporation
1790 Broadway
New York, New York 10019

Copyright © 1984 by George Kennedy
Published by arrangement with the author
Library of Congress Catalog Card Number: 84-91102
ISBN: 0-380-88062-8

First Avon Printing, September, 1984

AVON TRADEMARK REG. U.S. PAT. OFF. AND IN OTHER COUN-
TRIES, MARCA REGISTRADA, HECHO EN U. S. A.

Printed in the U. S. A.

WFH   10 9 8 7 6 5 4 3 2 1

This book is dedicated to Jennings Lang.

BEFORE WE BEGIN

When I wrote *Murder on Location*, the predecessor to this book, I imagined certain distinguished actors and other public figures as present in some of the scenes to add flavor to the story and make it realistic. None objected and some called to say thanks for remembering them. One even asked why I didn't give him a bigger part.

So I've done it again. The real people you'll meet in this book have my admiration and respect. They were never there, of course, but they could have been.

I want to give credit to Walt Sheldon, novelist and longtime friend, who as creative consultant supplied advice and encouragement. Also, I'm most grateful for the assistance of Mr. John R. Wheeler and Mr. Kevin C. Austin of the Boeing Commercial Airplane Company, who cheerfully gave their time, documentary material, and considerable expertise to this project.

G.K.

CHAPTER ONE

The taxi Mike Corby and I were in careened down the dusty brown road from the heart of the hazy brown city toward the powdery brown airport.

Qram is brown. Most of the countries in that portion of North Africa are. It isn't just the color brown, though it seemed to me the sunsets, pool water, my string beans, and lemon Jell-O were all brown. There's sort of an ambience about it. In Qram, one is personally free of the layers of dust only after taking a fresh shower.

Taxis in Qram, I had discovered, careened wherever they went, whether down the palm-lined boulevard of the foreign quarter, through the narrow alleys of the Medina, or over the several roads that led out into the desert, eventually dissolving into nothingness. It was as though the drivers felt they could be profligate with the small principality's plentiful oil reserves.

That oil underscored everything: the politics, the dazzling wealth, the grinding poverty, the foreigners who had flocked in, the motion picture we had just made, and yes, the murders that were to be, though we hadn't even begun to dream about them yet.

Beside me in the back seat, Corby looked as though he'd rather be dreaming about almost anything. He definitely didn't want to be awake facing the sun-baked morning. On the screen, Mike Corby comes across as tough— a man in firm control of everything. It's that beat-up bullterrier look of his, which, I have no doubt, was an asset when he was a lieutenant of detectives in New York City. It continued to be an asset when he accidentally became an actor in *Badge of Honor*, a film based on some of Mike's exploits. Al Pacino played Mike and Mike played a bit part. By now he'd played minor roles—always a tough cop—in a number of pictures, including *Airport: Middle East*, which we'd just finished shooting here in Qram. But don't let that stubby, rolling walk of his, or the mashed middleweight's nose and penetrating cop's eyes fool you. When Mike's in the grip of a crushing hangover, as he was this morning, he's a mewling babe who needs someone to take care of him. I was again acting as his nursemaid, corner man, and Dutch uncle—and, frankly, getting a bit fed up with it.

Groaning out the words, Mike said, "George. Tell this clown to turn around and take us back to the city. I need ice water. I need sleep. I need oblivion."

"Hang in there, for pity's sake," I said. "We all promised the prince we'd watch his nice new airport get dedicated. Got to keep him happy. Got to keep those funds flowing. We may have finished the location shooting, but there's still a few million to go before the whole project's really wrapped up."

Hearing that, Mike merely groaned.

I had to admit that the back seat of this jolting taxi was not the ideal place to recover from a hangover. The driver was a short, heavy Arab who dangled a foul-smelling cigarette from the corner of his mouth. It filled the cab with thick clouds of smoke. I'd tried to open the windows of the old Chevy but hadn't been able to budge them. The driver must have fixed them to prevent all that precious smoke from escaping.

Outside, heat waves rose shimmering from the desert. The molten sun was higher now that it was mid-morning. In the near distance, I saw the pumping arm of an oil rig rocking slowly, out of sync with the hiccuping mobile radar range we were trapped in.

"Last night was stupid," said Mike.

"It must have been," I said, knowing the best thing to do with a hung-over Mike was to agree with him.

"She was a little *zaftig*," he said. "These Arabs like 'em *zaftig*. You know—kinda plump."

"Uh huh," I said.

"At least she asked for her money in American dollars, so I didn't have to figure out the exchange rate in my head."

"Considerate of her," I said.

"She took me to this small hotel with splotched wall-paper and a creaky bed and one of those propeller fans slowly going whump-whump on the ceiling. I remember telling her I'd take a nap for a few seconds first. When I woke up again it was morning and outside somewhere this muezzin was making like Pavarotti in one of the towers. He could have been singing to her for all I know, 'cause she was long gone and so was the rest of my money."

"Very inconsiderate," I said. "Did she leave a receipt?"

"Lay off, George," he said grumpily. "I had to walk all the way back to our hotel."

"Maybe you're lucky," I said. "You didn't pick up a souvenir from her you wouldn't have wanted."

"Maybe," said Mike. "But I blew it again. When it comes to women, respectable or otherwise, I always blow it. I wonder what Meredy's doing right now?"

I shrugged. "Find out when we get back, Mike. Go on down to Mexico and root her out. Tell her you're sorry if you have to."

"But what am I sorry for? I didn't do anything to bust us up. She didn't either. It just happened."

"So you've told me. A hundred times."

"Yeah," said Mike, frowning. "I guess there's just no answer."

If there was, I certainly didn't know it, though Mike seemed to think I would come up with something every time he poured out his miseries to me. In case you don't follow movie gossip, Mike had met Meredy Ames in Mexico when we'd filmed *The Godless* there. Meredy was a fine artist, and they'd been married for a while, but it hadn't worked out and now they were both in what amounted to a trial separation. Mike was back in the acting business, keeping himself busy, trying to numb himself on hard work and the sauce, about in that order.

So here we were in Qram, one of these new nations, like the Yemen or the Emirate states, created by recent political shufflings. It's roughly the size of Rhode Island and has a population of about one million. Its currency is the Qram dinar, and everyone in the country has either too many or hardly any. There's nobody in the middle. Qram has oil that everybody wants. Their side, our side, and all its neighbors. Fortunately, so far the U.S. has been getting most of it, to say nothing of military cooperation, because of the benevolence of its beloved hereditary ruler, Prince Ibrahim, Lion of the Desert, Son of the Prophets, Protector of the Faith, who likes everything American, including the legendary quarter-pounder with cheese.

Ibrahim had bankrolled the movie. He figured it would be good publicity for his emerging nation, and also, in all likelihood, a profitable investment. Each *Airport* movie had made more money than the one preceding it. They did particularly well in foreign markets, and there was no reason to suspect that another with a cast that included Jimmy Stewart, tall and magnificent Candy Vandermeer, Bobby Troup and Julie London, comic Stubby Dawson, and the pulse-quickening new pin-up star from *The Godless*, Blossom Foster, wouldn't do at least as well.

And something else.

There's something about Middle East nations that makes them build totally unnecessary international airports the way some women wear too much makeup, or some entertainers flaunt too many diamonds. They all do it. It deters them not in the least to know that their busiest terminal would handle less traffic in a year than the tiny Van Nuys airport would routinely dispatch in a week. Qram International would be second to none. And producer Jennings Lang, as shrewd a dealer as ever donned an eyeshade, had convinced the prince that filming *Airport: Middle East* on and about Qram's white elephant would be a public-relations coup.

With all this going through my mind, I somehow suf-

12

fered my way through the rest of that hot, spine-jolting taxi ride across seemingly endless miles of sand. On his late-night show, Johnny Carson once asked comedian George Gobel how things were going. Gobel replied, "Did you ever feel like life was a tuxedo and you were a pair of brown shoes?" He may have never been there, but Gobel really understood Qram.

And then there it was. More people were expected today than perhaps would pass through all year. The dedication ceremonies this morning were to be held in the one completed building. Oh, the others were there all right, fifteen of them, but as on any movie set their insides were filled only with echoes. Ibrahim could get all the native spectators he wanted by ordering them out, but with distinguished foreigners he had to say "Please." And he had said please to a lot of people, from Barbara Walters to the night man at the Associated Press desk in Cairo. It was a nonevent, and everyone had politely declined. So he turned to the movie company, which was ready to go home as soon as its charter plane arrived. Though many were busy packing, some of us sighed and agreed. What the hell, he'd been more than okay to all of us, and there wasn't much left to do now that we'd all bought our obligatory hookah pipes in the bazaar.

The taxi let us off in front of the huge, ferrocement terminal building with the manufacturer's stickers still on the plate-glass doors. Either we were early or the prince and his people were late—hardly anybody was there yet except for the crowd which had arrived on buses. It was now gathering along the cyclone fence near a temporary reviewing stand that had been built on the flight line.

Mike and I walked into the high-ceilinged building, both surprised and relieved to find the air-conditioning working. In Qram, anything mechanical seldom did. There were fifty thousand phones here and all worked like the one in my hotel—rarely if at all. The ticket counters and the lounge seats for waiting passengers were virtually empty, a portent of things to come, I thought.

"Water," groaned Mike. "Ice water."

"They ought to have some somewhere," I said. I spotted a booth in a far corner, just open for business. "You can get some *gazoz* there, I think."

"Not that stuff," said Mike, shuddering. "When I was a kid my mother used to try and disguise the taste of castor oil in orange juice. I never forgave her until I tried *gazoz*. Maybe a Coke somewhere. I'll look around."

"Go ahead. I'm gonna check flight operations and see what kind of weather readouts they have available. We'll be flying out tomorrow or the next day, and I always like to see what Mother Nature has coming up."

"I'll save you a trip," said Mike, slowly shuffling away. "Hot and dry and more hot. Is it ever anything else?"

He paused to swing the Nikon camera he was carrying off his shoulder and positioned it properly at his eye. For Mike's purposes a twenty-dollar Kodak would have been just fine, but no, he had to have this professional model with a lens as big as the bottom of a wine bottle. After a moment, he looked at me quizzically.

"Perhaps if you remove the lens cap."

"Oh. Yeah. Naturally," he mumbled. "I'll probably be out on the flight line taking pictures."

"I'll find you," I said, though I half-hoped I wouldn't. If I heard any more about Mike's problems of the heart I'd probably look for the nearest wall and claw my way up it.

Flight operations for World International Airlines, which would soon have a route to Qram, was down a couple of corridors in a part of the terminal that overlooked the flight line. I entered and ambled past an untended counter. I was only somewhat surprised to find working weather-data printers against one wall. World International was big league. If it had been left to the expertise of the locals, a small boy would have answered my questions by wetting the end of his finger and sticking it out the window.

In any case, as I started to examine the charts, I heard voices from the other side of a low bookcaselike partition. You could see through it—and I realized that this other part of the WIA offices served as a crew lounge and that someone was in it.

I just couldn't help overhearing and seeing what was going on beyond the divider. Two Americans were sprawled comfortably in vinyl-upholstered chairs playing gin rummy. Each was in uniform, and each had removed his airline blouse, slid down his knotted tie, and opened his collar. One had his leg hooked languidly over the arm of the chair, revealing a cowboy boot instead of the regulation black oxfords. He was agelessly handsome, like Dean Martin, and appeared even to have Dean's relaxed and ever-good-humored way about him. His long, carefully styled, wavy hair had a few threads of premature gray in it.

"O'Malley," he said to his companion, "I hate to do this to you—but—gin!" He laid his cards down.

"I knew I shouldn't have discarded that queen, god-damnit." O'Malley's voice, though clearly American, had a kind of Irish lilt to it. He was younger than the other man, and his malleable freckled face made him look more boyish than his probable age, which I took to be late twenties or early thirties.

"If you're gonna be a pilot one of these days," said the handsome, relaxed man, "you'll have to learn to play gin rummy better than you do. With all the layovers, it's a requirement."

"Don't be handing me that requirement jazz, Larkin," said O'Malley. "You know I've flown everything up to a C-5A Galaxy. I can fly as well as any pilot anywhere. It's just the bureaucracy of this goddamn airline that keeps me where I am. Ted O'Malley, boy flight engineer. In another few years I'll be the oldest flight engineer on record. Sometimes I think I ought to go back to crop dusting. At least I'd get to kick a rudder once in a while."

"What have you got to complain about?" said Larkin. "I'm still a copilot."

"But at least you fly. You don't just sit there and stare at gauges."

"Shut up and deal," Larkin said.

As O'Malley started to deal, I started to edge away, when a third man entered the room through another door at

15

the end of the lounge. Both O'Malley and Larkin looked around idly.

Who, I often wonder, does the casting for real life? One of God's angels in charge of that department? If the call had been for the very model of an airline pilot, the guy who had just entered was it. Tall, distinguished, silver-haired. Not a wrinkle in his well-tailored uniform with its gold first-officer's stripes on the sleeves. He must have been wearing it out in the heat, but not a drop of sweat stained that cool, marble brow. Nor was there even the beginning of a smile on the rest of his face.

He crossed the room to the card-strewn table, glanced at O'Malley and then at Larkin. "You must be Jake Larkin," he said.

"Right," drawled Larkin. "This is Ted O'Malley. And you must be Captain Fowler. Have a seat, John. You can kibitz while we finish."

Fowler drew a deep breath which, I realized, was to stifle an apoplectic fit. "The first thing I want both of you to do," he said coldly, "is to button your shirts and get your goddamn blouses on!"

"What?" Larkin stared at him.

"You heard me. You both know regulations. Or do you?"

Larkin swung lithely out of the chair and shook his head as though slightly stunned. "Is this for *real?*"

"Let's get it straight," said Fowler. "Right from the start. You're the assigned pilot, Larkin, and you, O'Malley, are the designated flight engineer. They sent you to report to me and you're on duty. I didn't call this get-together this morning so we could socialize. I don't give a goddamn how either of you looks in his spare time, but this is work!"

Larkin kept staring at Fowler. "You're really what they say, aren't you? It's hard to believe—"

"I don't know what you heard," said Fowler icily, "but I can tell you this much. When I get ready to fly, I want everything exactly the way it should be. With the crew, with the airplane. Down to the last detail. That's how I get safely from here to there. Every time. Is that understood?"

Larkin looked at O'Malley. "We're back in ᵤₑ Force. *Hut*-two-three-four!"

"Marines for me," said O'Malley quietly, "but it sure sounds like boot camp at that."

"That's enough!" said Fowler. "Now look, I'm going to explain this once, and if you have any objections you can get home some other way. Your records say that you're qualified, but as far as I'm concerned neither of you has enough time in the 300 model, which we'll be flying. I want my copilot and flight engineer to have everything down so cold they can do it in their sleep if they have to."

"Come on, Fowler," said Larkin. "The 300's the same damn airplane as a regular 747 and you know it. A couple of little differences in the instrumentation maybe—"

"Little differences," said Fowler, "are what make airplanes crash. We're going out there to the prince's private airplane, and we're going to run through every challenge and response in the manual. Here and now. Not somewhere between here and LAX when we've got some emergency!"

I'd heard about Prince Ibrahim's private airplane. I've got a private airplane, too, but what the prince paid for his would buy a zillion A-36 Bonanzas. His Boeing 747-300 was very much like the one modified at the Boeing plant at Everett, north of Seattle, for the king of Saudi Arabia. A palatial home away from home, with everything except a lawn and crabgrass. Looking out the window I could see it, in front of its hangar. A thing of beauty, if you're an airplane freak, as I am. Maybe even if you're not. The prince hadn't been able to hire a qualified flight crew for it yet, so World International Airlines, with an eye to future business, had subcontracted Fowler, Larkin, O'Malley, and even a small crew of flight attendants out to him till he could get his own personnel.

Larkin was frowning at Fowler. "How long is this checkout of yours going to take, anyway?"

"All day, if necessary. Do you have something better to do?"

"Well," said Larkin vaguely, uncomfortably, running

17

carefully styled hair on one side, "they've
___ ceremonies, and the prince is gonna be there."
___ what?"

"Just thought I wanted a look at him. I've got my
reasons."

Fowler drew a deep breath, in and out again. "Find
yourself another parade on your own time, Larkin—if that's
how you get your jollies. Now, both of you. Put your blouses
on and let's get out to that airplane. . . ."

It took me a while to spot Mike Corby. I looked for
Mike first in the VIP's spectator stand, which was separate
from the reviewing platform. Jimmy Stewart and his wife,
Gloria, who goes where he goes, were already in place,
both graciously trying to pretend the sweltering heat wasn't
bothersome. She is like a magnificent piece of Lladro por-
celain come to sparkling life. Gloria is gifted with beauty,
warmth, wit, and a smile so radiant it makes everyone else
look as if they're frowning. I smiled back, both because of
very real affection and because Jimmy was wearing this
huge, straw farmer's hat to keep off the sun. It didn't go
with his neat tropical worsted, but he wore it with his usual
great flair.

My eye finally caught Mike in the press box where a
few persons I took to be Arab reporters had found metal
chairs for themselves. He was sitting beside a woman in a
white dress, and, as I came closer, I saw she was on the
mature side but quite attractive. Maybe close to Mike's age,
or mine for that matter, but she was so carefully groomed
she gave the impression of being younger. She might make
a fair stand-in for Lauren Bacall, I thought.

Both looked up as I approached. "Oh, hi George," said
Mike. "C'mere a minute. I want you to meet Florence
Haverman."

She extended her hand. I took it, and she said, "Mike
said you'd be along. I get the feeling he can't make a move
without you."

"He can," I said, chuckling. "And I wish he would now
and then."

18

"Florence is with the embassy here," said Mike. "The press section. It's her first foreign post and she's been here almost a year. She reads books instead of seeing movies and her favorite color is fuchsia."

Florence's laugh was as well-groomed as the rest of her. "I never saw anybody learn so much about me in five minutes! He walked right up, introduced himself, and the first thing I knew I was being grilled."

"You have to watch out for ex-cops," I said.

"Won't you sit down, George?"

"I think we're supposed to be someplace else—I'm not sure."

"This is as good a place as any," said Mike. He glanced at Florence. "In fact, better."

I sat. Mike started to swing his Nikon around to take pictures of the event—the reviewing stand, the crowd pressed to the fence, the vehicles and soldiers standing by to pass in parade. Like most new camera owners, he had only two rules—photograph anything that moved, or didn't. I said to Florence, "Any idea what the delay's all about?"

"Probably normal. Princes don't have to be punctual. And Ibrahim's staff is less than efficient in setting things up. We didn't get the invitation at the embassy until the last minute, and by that time the ambassador was out of town, so they reached way down on the totem pole and sent me instead—"

There was a stirring near the terminal building. A band of about twenty musicians, all in gaudy, Graustarkian uniforms, began to play somewhat sourly. A group of men emerged from the terminal.

"There they are," said Florence. "The prince and his party."

I knew the prince; I'd seen him from afar, as had most of the members of our movie company. He hadn't socialized with us in spite of his professed admiration for several of the stars. He was a small man, slender and trim, in an air marshal's uniform with several rows of ribbons, and pilot's wings on his chest. His *ghutra*, or Bedouin headdress, held in place by braided black and gold cords, shaded most of his face. The prince kept himself a little apart from his retinue, but close by his side was a rolling butterball in a dark suit whom I recognized as Jabala, his chief of staff. Or whatever his actual title was.

"I see he's got his court jester with him," I said.

Florence looked at me sharply. "Jabala? Well, I know he makes jokes and is very popular with foreigners, but don't underrate him. Yakub Seif al-Jabala really runs everything. That's because the prince prefers to devote his time to airplanes and ladies. He's not callous—he wants his people to be happy and healthy—but he doesn't really know how to bring it about. So there's an underground opposition, as there is everywhere these days. They've had a few riots and terrorist attacks. The secret police are supposed to keep that under control but don't, entirely. It's really kind of a powder keg, but I suppose that's par for the course in the Middle East."

The official party began to walk toward the reviewing stand, Prince Ibrahim and Jabala several yards ahead of the others, leading the way. Mike fumbled to change to a telephoto lens, and then, clicking the shutter, tracked the prince. No one else in the press box was taking pictures, and I wondered if Mike was supposed to. I knew the officialdom here could be touchy, and the last thing I wanted was an international incident.

Florence gently put her hand on Mike's arm. "It would be better if you didn't," she said, reading my thought.

"Huh? Why?"

"Their ground rules. It was in their press release. Only official pictures by their own people. No real reason for it as far as I know, just their own version of bureaucracy."

Mike shrugged and lowered his camera. He turned his attention to Florence. "You really know your way around here, don't you?"

"If any foreigner ever does," said Florence.

"Wish I'd met you before. You could have steered me right. But we're leaving pretty quick now. Our charter flight's supposed to get here soon, and that won't leave much time. For getting to know you better, I mean."

"I thought you'd already made a file on me this morning," said Florence, laughing.

"But it lacks the important details. Marital status, for example. Is there a husband somewhere? If there is, I hate him already."

"Divorced," said Florence. "Quite awhile back. Isn't everybody?"

"Look," said Mike. "How about dinner tonight?"

"Why, that would be very nice," said Florence. I was pleased to see that she wasn't at all being coy about it. As I kept watching the prince mount the reviewing stand, they busily made arrangements for Florence to meet Mike in the hotel lobby, sevenish. I was listening with only half an ear.

A whistle blew.

The band struck up a second march, playing so badly I almost longed for the first one again. The driver of the jeep that was to lead the procession—fire truck, ambulance, follow-me vehicles, all for the new airport—started his engine. Several squads of soldiers in camouflage fatigues with Arab headdresses got ready to pass in review.

I will probably never forget the tableau—the picture that hung there, strangely motionless, before the next few seconds passed. The prince and Jabala were standing at one end of the reviewing stand perhaps ten yards away from the rest of their party, a collection of dignitaries or flunkies in assorted European and Arab dress. Even farther to one side was the VIP stand, with Jimmy and Gloria Stewart on it and a small group of foreigners who, I presumed, were some of the businessmen—all at least vice presidents— who were in Qram City attempting to get their share of the money the prince was throwing around.

The sun, directly overhead now and searing, was but another spectator.

Then a terrible explosion broke the moment—a thunderous blast under the reviewing stand where the flunkies stood. Flame, smoke, broken bits of lumber, and several human bodies were tossed upward in the hot, still air as though from an invisible trampoline. The prince and Jabala,

21

evidently slapped hard by the concussion, staggered sideways and fell.

All I could see were people running chaotically and all I could hear were piercing shouts and wails.

CHAPTER TWO

Mike Corby, Florence Haverman, and I sat in the back of an embassy staff car as it headed toward the city.

"I'm still shaking," said Florence, pressing herself more closely against Mike for reassurance. "The way those bodies flew up. It was horrible!"

"But the prince wasn't right on top of it," I said. "I saw him get knocked aside. I wonder if he's okay."

"Hard to say. Nobody could get near anything after all those soldiers closed in. For a moment I thought it was going to be like the Sadat assassination in Cairo, but fortunately it wasn't."

"It was bad enough just the way it was," I said, shaking my head with bewilderment. Everyone on the flight line, once the initial shock and confusion had died down, had been herded into the terminal building to undergo what seemed like endless questioning by soldiers and secret policemen. It had taken us over an hour to get away from the airport in spite of Florence's diplomatic status and the sedan waiting for her outside. No taxi had been available, and she offered us a lift.

"The prince looked alive when they carried him to the ambulance," said Florence. "At least to me he did, though I'm not sure why. Jabala was on his own two feet, so I guess he wasn't hurt seriously. As for the prince, I think it'll be awhile before we find out anything. They'll be clamping down. It might be days before they make an official announcement."

"Well, it's their country," said Mike, shrugging. "They can run it like they want, I guess."

"They can," said Florence, "but whatever they do sets up vibrations all over the world. Do you realize what might happen if the prince should die?"

"A very expensive funeral," said Mike dryly. "Nothing but the best."

"It's a serious matter, Mike. Prince Ibrahim is the only thing holding this country together. He's the rightful heir, and the people worship him no matter how well or badly he treats them. That's hard to explain to an outsider, but it has to do with their culture, their religion, the bloodline connections the prince is supposed to have with the ancient prophets. The trouble is, he had daughters instead of sons. They're very nice little girls—I've met them. But the Qramis aren't quite ready for female rulers yet."

"Maybe it's time they got into women's lib."

She shook her head. "Never. If the prince should die there would be a huge void. The opposition, who are either Marxists or think they are, would move in at last. Not easily—it'll be a civil war. Qram's neighbors would get into it. The whole Middle East might well go up in flames. And then maybe the rest of the world."

"Lovely," I mused. "You come to make a movie in a place you never hoped to see in the first place. Somehow, it's never specified in your contract that you might be there at the beginning of World War III."

"I didn't count on that, either," said Mike.

"Nobody ever does," said Florence. "Not even the ones who might start it. That's why I'm here, in a way. To do what I can—in a very minor capacity, to be sure—to prevent that kind of thing."

Mike sighed. "I hope the world's still there when I get back. I'm afraid international politics isn't my bag. Not that I don't admire what you're doing, Florence, but I'm just a tourist at heart. Of course, if I could help . . . in any way . . ."

"You might, at that," she said, turning her head to look at him.

"Yeah? How?"

She nodded at his camera. "Those pictures you took. We won't have any at the embassy, and I know the Qramis aren't going to give us anything taken by their own official photographers. What you've got just might be interesting from an intelligence standpoint. We've got cloak-and-dagger types who can pick up all sorts of information from photo analysis. Faces in the crowd—that kind of thing."

"You want my pictures?" Mike looked put-upon, and I wasn't sure he was joking, entirely. "I was going to use 'em to bore my friends back home." Close enough, I thought.

"I'll return them," Florence said. "Just let us develop them at the embassy for what they're worth, if anything."

"Okay," said Mike, as he started to wind the film back into the camera, "I only regret that I have but one roll to give to my country."

The sedan passed through the outer gate of the city and, as the road narrowed, it slowed its pace to avoid hitting assorted Arabs and stray donkeys. A thick smell of charcoal and dung permeated the marketplace. The sun glared on plaster walls. Overhead reed mats threw cross-hatched purple shadows on the dust, stirred up every few moments by cars full of armed soldiers racing who knew where. The populace may not have known of the day's events yet, but someone had sure pressed the right military panic button. It looked like the evening news almost any night of the week at home. Unreal . . . only it wasn't.

"Come on in for a tall cool one when we get to the hotel," Mike said to Florence.

"I'd like to," she said, "but they'll need me at the embassy. Everybody's in a flap there, I'm sure."

"We still have that date tonight, don't we?"

"All things being equal, crisis-wise," she said, smiling. "But no guarantees."

"If that's all I can get," sighed Mike, "then that's what I'll take."

* * *

I was sure Florence, as she'd anticipated, went back to her flap at the embassy, but what I hadn't expected was the flap that greeted Mike and me in the hotel lobby. At least the air-conditioning hadn't been clogged with sand for a few days and it was cool there, cool and very luxurious. The Grand Khayam—almost a palace in its own right—was where any foreigner who could afford it stayed.

Jennings Lang buttonholed us before we even got to the elevators. "Over here," he said, nodding toward an alcove with potted palms and brocaded settees in it. "We're in a fix."

Jennings is tall and gray-haired, and I've never known his face to be without a smile for longer than three minutes. His sense of humor could best be described as robustly contagious, but that would describe his appetite for life, too. His uniform was any good-looking open-necked shirt, and perhaps the best giveaway that he was not altogether on top of things today was that, heat notwithstanding, he was fully arrayed in jacket and tie. He had produced all the *Airport* pictures. The realization that some of the stuff we'd shot for *Airport: Middle East* had been screwed up hit me. We'd have a hell of a time reshooting it now.

"The whole damned country is bottled up tight," he said, slumping into that fifty-dollar-a-yard upholstery. He looked harried, like a mouse just shaken by a cat toying with it. "The charter plane that was to take us out? There are no exits or entries. It can't get here."

"We're stuck a few days?" I asked.

"A few *days?* The people I've been talking to say weeks, maybe. George, I've been dealing with these government types all along, and I believe it when they say weeks. You'd think that the fact the prince has an interest in this picture would clear the way, but it doesn't. They've created a monstrous bureaucracy that has a will of its own. Besides, the prince is in the hospital and not in a position to give orders. They won't let anyone near him or take any messages in or out."

My head came up. "He's okay, then?"

"So they tell me. Injured but alive. I don't know how

26

serious the injuries are. They said he was in surgery." The three minutes for his face were up. It wasn't much of a smile, as vintage Jennings Lang smiles go, but it sufficed. He continued, "You couldn't get shit out of these second-level officials if you hosed prune juice up their ass for a week." The worry returned. "Our friend Jabala seems to be as incommunicado as the prince himself."

"Well, it sounds bad," I said, "but it still isn't a total disaster. Not yet."

"But it is disastrous!" said Jennings, fighting to keep his voice even. "Our insurance has an act-of-God clause for anything of a cataclysmic nature which occurs during the shooting. We ain't *shooting* any more. Do you have any idea what it'll cost to keep this case, this production crew—all top people, all getting well over scale—in croissants for just one day, let alone several weeks?"

"Oh," I said, and it was like a thud.

"It could break us," he said. "The picture might never get out of the can." There was a long pause. "The critics may dance in the street."

"Critics don't pay to get in, Jennings," I said, trying to lighten his load. "Would you like me to trot out the bank statements from the other four *Airport* films you've made?"

He hardly heard. "Look, George, the immediate problem is to get some kind of clearance so we can all leave, and that's where you come in."

"Me?"

"You're a movie favorite of the prince, even if he hasn't met you. You get along with Jabala, too. I've dealt with both of them, but they think I'm just a necessary evil. My gut feeling is that you could get a lot further with either of them than I could."

"What's that mean you want me to do?"

"Go to the hospital. Get to the prince, or Jabala. Explain. Get 'em to give us a special dispensation or whatever it takes so we can all get out of here."

I cocked my head. "This sort of thing's *your* job, isn't it, Jennings?"

"It is," he agreed. "And I'll do all I can if you fail. It's just that I want to try it this way first, okay?"

"Well . . . all right," I said. "But this'll be the first time you've asked Patroni to get the *cast* out of the mud."

"I'll give you a medal," said Jennings.

"Make it St. Jude," I said. "I may need it."

Mike, after half a bottle of aspirin, still had a hangover. I prescribed a raw egg in tomato juice with considerable Worcestershire and even more Tabasco sauce. It did nothing to relieve the hangover, but his throat got so hot he couldn't dwell on his throbbing head anymore, so he decided to go with me to the hospital. He mumbled something about acting as my bodyguard—and, at the time, I thought that was just a joke, too.

The new hospital in Qram City was like the airport—big and beautiful and first-class with hardly anything in it, including enough doctors. We walked into a nice spacious reception room, and a pretty Arab girl who spoke English told us to wait, then busied herself at the switchboard, using her own language.

Presently, what looked like the defensive line of the Los Angeles Rams came down the corridor toward us. The Arab version of it, anyway. It was led by a huge man in billowing *surwal,* or pantaloons, and what looked like a sleeveless T-shirt that could have been tailored for him by Omar the Tentmaker. You could see that his fat had plenty of muscle under it. He had a bald head and sweeping Sicilian mustaches. I've gotten friendlier looks from guard dogs at the Berlin Wall. I wondered immediately if he might not be a eunuch, though I thought those had gone out with harems. Maybe they still had harems—I didn't know—the last one I saw was wrapped around Yvonne DeCarlo.

He halted. The backfield, in loose slacks and sports shirts, halted behind him. We rose. He glared down at me. When somebody can glare down at me you *know* he's big.

"You want see prince?" His accent was thick, and it took a moment for the English words to filter through.

"If you don't mind," I said. "His highness, or Mr. Jabala."

"Cannot see. Nobody can see."

"This is special. It's very important. We're from the movie company." Nothing budged. "Will you at least tell Mr. Jabala we're here?"

He glared for another moment, then said, "Fuck off."

My eyebrows rose. "You know better English than I thought. Where do you fit in around here anyway?"

The fat giant struck his chest with his thumb. "I am Muhanna. Chief bodyguard to prince. They tell me nobody can see. You get broken ass if you try."

"Now, look Mr. Muhanna," I said, in the same reasonable tone you'd use if you ever were forced to say something to a charging rhino, "I know neither his highness nor Mr. Jabala has had time to think about this, but they've got a whole movie company stuck here at thousands of dollars a day and we've just got to get out. All it will take is a moment to explain—"

Muhanna grabbed me. He held me under my arms and lifted me up—all two hundred and seventy pounds of me. He glared into my eyes and I could smell his breath, which was like sour camel's milk. "You no go yourself, *effrengi*, I throw you out!"

Mike said, "Hey! Put him down!"

Muhanna ignored Mike and kept glaring.

Mike stepped in and stamped hard on his instep. Muhanna looked surprised—and pained—at that. He put me down, shoving me back so that I stumbled.

With Mike about half Muhanna's size, I'm sure the giant didn't expect much in the way of opposition and, frankly, neither did I. But Mike came forward with a short, hard right into his bulging midriff. Anybody else, I think, would have gone down with the wind knocked out of him; Muhanna only grunted.

He reached out for Mike, and Mike, bobbing and weaving, danced away. He threw himself at Mike and Mike dodged. Muhanna's charge took him past, off balance. The other tackle and guard simply looked amused. Muhanna was very irritated as he stopped and turned. Very distinctly, very quietly he said, "Garrorpfff." That's the same in English as it is in Arabic.

Who knows what went through Mike's mind when he decided to take on this hulk? All of my life I've owned terriers, and one, my beloved miniature schnauzer Sugarfoot, was still sailing into Irish setters when he was twelve, and always, shredded, sailing out again. Maybe nothing went through his mind. Maybe he short-circuited it. I could have told Mike from the beginning that even if he was very, very good he was going to lose very, very big. In the next instant, Muhanna managed to get hold of Mike and lifted him up with one hand, with Mike's legs kicking. He pulled him in close, wrapped the other arm around Mike, and squeezed.

I've been in a lot of staged fights in movies and gotten hurt in some, but the truth is that, like most of us, I haven't been in a real one since I was a kid. But what could I do? There's a sound the human frame emits when the chest cavity is being crushed that's indescribable and unforgettable. Mike was making it. I stepped forward. If anything was going through my head, it probably had to do with my last will and testament.

A sudden voice, speaking sharply in Arabic, sounded in the corridor. I turned and saw Jabala's butterball figure trotting toward us.

Still glaring, Muhanna put Mike down, throwing his gasping body back as he'd done with me.

It was far from a comical situation, but somehow Jabala, puffing and flustered, managed to look funny. He had that me-against-the-world expression that makes Dom DeLuise so funny no matter what he says or does. His round face, round, surprised-looking licorice disks of eyes, and busy lips always seemed on the verge of trembling. "Gentlemen, please! One is supposed to be quiet in a hospital!"

"That's what I thought," said Mike, "till the big ape came along." He glowered at Muhanna.

"A misunderstanding, I'm sure," said Jabala. "He must

30

have thought you were threatening his highness. Muhanna's very loyal, you know . . . very devoted."

"Goody for him. Look, all we asked was to see the prince. Or you. It's urgent."

"Quite impossible to see his highness. And I should be with him at this very moment. But now that you're here, what is it?"

I found it hard to think of Jabala as a powerful man, actually second in command to Prince Ibrahim. Years of schooling in the United States had evidently erased not only most of his accent but also the somewhat sinister dignity you'd expect of an Arab of the highest rank. He had an easygoing, somewhat casual manner that I think he used to put you off guard. After you looked at him awhile you began to see something in his eyes that was not as comical as the rest of him.

"Your excellency," I said quickly, "the whole movie company's stuck in town and it's costing a fortune. We've got to have permission for our chartered aircraft to land here so we can leave."

"Ah . . . that," he said, nodding gravely. "I sympathize with your problem, Mr. Kennedy. You must understand that everything's been done in haste, and we haven't had time to give close attention to details."

"Can you take care of it? Put out an order or something?"

"Not immediately, I'm sorry to say. There has been an assassination attempt and, naturally, we must have a thorough investigation. I'm sure none of your movie people were involved; still, we can't allow any exceptions."

"But the expense—"

"Perhaps his highness will be able to take care of it. When he recovers."

"Ah. That means he's alive. I'm glad to hear it. Was he hurt badly, or what?"

"His condition must remain confidential. Thank you for calling upon him, Mr. Kennedy, and you, Mr. Corby. Though next time, you might inquire first about visiting hours. . . ."

I only got as far as "But...but..." before Jabala, smiling blandly, pirouetted away and bounced back down the corridor. Muhanna and his bruisers stayed in place, still glaring at us.

"I think they'd like us to leave," said Mike.

"I think I'd like that myself," I said, sighing.

Back at the hotel, Jennings Lang seemed to melt down into the carpet when we told him what had happened. He stared at me and said, "What are we gonna do?"

"I don't know about you," I said, "but I'll be able to give it more serious thought while I'm in the pool."

I'd been looking forward to a swim, a shower, and a siesta ever since that taxi ride out to the airport. A half-day in Qram's heat is like a week anywhere else. I was as worried as Jennings, of course, for somewhat different reasons. Joan had gone home with my daughter Shannon about two weeks earlier, and I'm one of those square dudes who believes family is the only reason for doing anything. I wanted to be where they were. Right now a splash in the concrete pond seemed to offer the best respite from my misery.

When the elevator stopped at my floor, Stubby Dawson got in as I got out. Always the *tummeler,* Stubby called after me, "Hey, George. Do you know why American elevators go up and down?"

I stopped and turned to look into his jovial face as I replied, "No. Why?"

"Because if they went from side to side they'd be Chinese!" he chortled, the elevator door providing a closing curtain.

I didn't like the joke, but I liked Stubby. Though only five-foot-three, he looked life and everyone straight in the eye. He reminded me of Mickey Rooney, not so much physically but rather in his joyful outlook. In my view, Stubby Dawson is young and has a long way to go, but he has that sparkle, that élan, that positive and gleeful respect for every moment of the day that are the very marrow of giants like Mickey Rooney.

After changing in my room, I strode out to the pool in

my terry-cloth robe. The pool area was behind the hotel. Grillwork overhangs and very tall palm trees broke up some of the fierce sunshine. Ornately carved wooden tables and matching wooden chairs, shaded by umbrellas, were decorated by a lot of Hollywood's beautiful people. They were sipping drinks while casually checking to see if they were being noticed. Waiters in fezzes and white smocks that looked like nightshirts glided among them, surreptitiously ogling the exposed ladies. The dress code in this part of the world allows you to see all the skin of a Qramis woman you wanted, as long as it was from the bridge of her nose to mid-forehead. I never did find out how much the waiters paid the hotel to keep their jobs.

A voice called, "George!"

I halted and saw young Ken Dilworth, in bathing trunks, seated at the table. My eyes only rested on him for an instant, then went immediately to the exquisitely lovely woman who was sitting with him. Her bikini covered hardly anything and, esthetically speaking, it would have been a shame otherwise. She was lithe and full-bodied and marvelously well-proportioned. I'd heard that years ago Richard Burton had described Elizabeth Taylor as "okay, but her breasts are too big." It seemed to me Burton might not have been too happy with this lady either. Her glossy black hair cascaded over her shoulders, and her eyes, as she held them on me, were large, lavender, and liquid. I got the impression there was quiet intelligence behind them, which made her more than just some broad with a great bod' and exquisite face, though—Richard Burton notwithstanding—that would have been enough for most people.

"Sit down a minute, George," said Ken. "I want you to meet somebody."

It was not an invitation I was about to refuse. The swimming could wait. As I sat, I paid only the required polite attention to Ken Dilworth. He was a reasonably well-built young man who might have been mistaken for one of our actors—the nice guy who usually gets killed before the end—but he wasn't even in the movie company. Rather he was with World International Airlines. I'd met him and chatted with him several times in Qram, as I had with others in the foreign business community. Ken was young for an airline executive. His father, Carter Dilworth, was WIA's chairman of the board. The old man had brought him up the hard way, starting him out as baggage handler, and now, as I understood it, he was being groomed for the heady levels of top management. He'd been here a month or so, helping Prince Ibrahim set up his own airline, which wouldn't compete with the international franchise promised to World International.

"George, this is Lisa Garcia," said Ken.

"How do you do." Her hand was warm and alive, and as sexy as the rest of her. But her eyes as they met mine were genuinely friendly rather than seductive. I have to admit in a nostalgic, dirty-old-man's way that I almost wish they had been seductive.

"No ring yet—we haven't had time," said Ken, "but Lisa's my fiancée."

She laughed. "That makes it sound so official! It almost takes the romance out of it."

"Well," I said. "Congratulations. Best wishes, and all of that. Do I take it this is something sudden?"

"Practically whirlwind," said Lisa, nodding.

I liked her cultivated diction and wondered if she were American, or somebody's daughter sent to finishing school in the States—or don't they have finishing schools anymore? Anyway, I liked her.

"Lisa's been a governess at the prince's palace," Ken explained, "teaching the prince's daughters how to dress and use the right forks and all that. But she resigned awhile ago and she's been here trying to decide on her next move. Now I've met her and she doesn't have to decide any longer."

"Oversimplified," said Lisa, smiling, "but basically that's it."

"Where are you from originally, Lisa?" I asked.

"What foreign country?" She laughed outright. "Harlem."

"Harlem? Like in New York?"

"Spanish Harlem—an enclave in dirty old New York

City with its own language, customs, and everything else. A little bit of Puerto Rico away from home. Some of us get lucky and manage to emigrate."

"Now *she's* oversimplifying," said Ken. "She worked like hell to bootstrap herself out of it."

Lisa glanced at Ken. "It's still the wrong side of the tracks, I'm afraid." Her face had clouded.

"There you go again," said Ken. "Relax. The old man's gonna love you."

"I hope so." It was quietly said by Lisa, and with some doubt.

"Well," I said, a little uneasy at this glimpse of what was making them uncomfortable, "I wish you all the happiness in the world. When were you supposed to leave for home?"

"We were going on that charter plane that's supposed to fly you people out. Now I hear all arrivals and departures have been postponed. We'll just have to wait, I guess."

I said, "I don't suppose you have enough clout with the prince to get that ban lifted, do you?"

"I might. But I can't get to see him. Nobody can. I wonder what the hell's going on in that hospital anyway."

"Normal conspiracy," said Lisa. "They can't do anything here in Qram unless it's all complicated and secret and roundabout. But you ought to know that, Ken. You've been dealing with them."

He nodded. "Which hasn't been easy. But I think I've got all those exclusive rights for World International, and that was what the old man wanted. He said if I didn't come back with it I might as well go back to baggage handling. You know something? He was only half kidding."

"Nice meeting you, Lisa," I said, rising. "Gotta go get my exercise in that pool, or I wouldn't break it off so quickly." Her smile almost changed my mind.

"Sure we understand, George," said Ken. "See you on the plane—if there is one. . . ."

On certain exciting days you reach a point when you want a good sleep more than anything else, but your motor's

35

still running so fast you know you won't drift off right away. So, perversely, you keep going. I'd had my swim, my shower, my change of clothes. My usual jogging suit, in which I do everything but jog, was too hot for Qram, so I changed into the lightest slacks and sports shirt I could find. I checked with Mike about dinner plans, and he reminded me he had a dinner date with Florence Haverman. I had a chef's salad sent up to the room and ate it while idly reading a script someone had sent me in the hope that I could get it produced for him. The script wasn't any better than the salad. At least I could send the script back.

Knowing I still wouldn't be able to sleep right away, I said what the hell and wandered down to the bar.

The bar was cool and dim. It was oval-shaped and had a place I could sit where, I hoped, I wouldn't be seen by any well-meaning movie fans who just *knew* I was dying to talk to them. I'm a very quiet fella by nature, and unless I know someone quite well, I really don't have anything to say. Unless I'm pretty drunk, in which case I've been known to converse with coat racks.

The bartender, an older, gloomy-looking man in a short red mess coat and a fez, brought me a sugar-free, caffeine-free lemon-lime. It was also almost taste-free, but the sprig of mint on the side of the tall glass saved it.

Looking across the bar, I suddenly saw Rod Larrabee lurch into the room. He was obviously smashed, as usual, and I hoped he wouldn't see me. Any movie fan would have been preferable to Rod, and one hell of a lot less abrasive. I guess you know about Rod Larrabee, especially if you're hooked on the tube. He is large and fat—pudgy, soft fat—and he always wears these huge horn rims that give him his owlish, quizzical expression. He's a talk-show host, and has been compared to Steve Allen, but he lacks Steve's wit and intellectual capacity. Steve's wit is merry and doesn't bite; Rod's wit is aggressive, and does. Yet somehow it had gained him a following and so, primarily for his name value, he'd been given a feature part in the movie.

The bartender stepped toward him. "Your pleasure, sir?"

"Ali Baba," said Rod, bringing the bartender into focus, "if that is your name, and if it isn't it ought to be, because out here every Tom, Dick, and Harry is named Ali Baba, do not ask me what my pleasure is, because I no longer take pleasure in it."

"Sir?"

"Never mind," said Rod. "I'm talking to myself again. And do you know why? I'm the only one that can stand me. Make it a Chivas Regal on the rocks. A double."

"Yes sir," said the bartender, still impassive.

Another man, who had been several stools away, now moved in beside Larrabee. Good, I thought. A fan to bug him. Served him right for calling attention to himself. The stranger wore a bush jacket, was tall, spare, and in his early forties. His neatly cropped light-brown beard with streaks of gray in it kept him from looking like a businessman, though lots of them have beards these days. Typecasting, like everything else in the modern world, just ain't what it used to be. The man smiled and said, "You're Rod Larrabee, aren't you?"

"In the flesh," said Larrabee, turning and blinking. "And of that flesh there is much too much, as you see. I've tried everything from exercise to the drinking man's diet. Nothing works, but I liked the last one best. What is your name, sir?"

"Lowell Hibner. And if you ever came on television fifty pounds lighter you wouldn't be the same. I admire your work as it is." Hibner had a flat, almost nasal, mid-western sort of voice, yet with an undertone of cultivated speech.

"Flattery," said Larrabee, "will get you a drink, but not much more. You here on business?"

"I'm a political-science professor," said Hibner. "I've been helping set up the department in the new university here."

"So the prince has founded one, has he? When the former king of Egypt did they called it Farouk U."

"Sorry," said Hibner with a smile. "I've heard that one before."

"No matter," said Rod. "There was a chance you hadn't. I was saving it for the interview I never got with the prince. Maybe I'll throw it out. Maybe I'll throw everything out. I am, at this point, suffering from absolute and utter frustration, which I would not wish upon a dog, let alone one of the local camels. I know what I think I might do. Get one of those camels and try and put him through the eye of a needle, just to prove it can be done."

Hibner laughed. "You sound just like you do on TV."

"Tell that to my writers. They think *they* give me everything I have to say."

The bartender, responding to Larrabee's gesture, brought a drink for Hibner, too. Hibner said, "Just what is this great frustration of yours?"

"Ah . . . that." Larrabee blinked, sipped deeply, and blinked again. "I want to do a series of interviews with international figures, only with the light touch—bring out their real personalities. I thought I'd kick it off with his highness, Prince Ibrahim. That was partly why I accepted the role in the movie and came out here. I'd thought the prince and I were buddies. We spent a lot of time together in Las Vegas, where he owned the hotel I was appearing in. Banged the same hookers, which is a form of blood brotherhood. But do you think I could get in to see the prince again when I got here?"

"I don't know. Couldn't you?"

"It was don't call us, we'll call you, all the way. I never saw such a defense in depth! I'll bet those flunkies of his never even told him I'd been around. But he must have known I was in the movie. To hell with him. I think I'll fly to Moscow and start the series with Gromyko. He'll be easier to get to."

"And this is the great tragedy that drove you to drink?" Hibner seemed amused.

"The drinking," said Larrabee, with a sigh, "I'd be doing anyway."

Keeping to the deeper shadows along the edge of the

room, I left the two men in earnest conversation. I'd had plenty of Rod Larrabee on the set and didn't need any more, especially now that I was starting to yawn comfortably.

In my room I went through the ceremony of getting ready for downy sleep, death's counterfeit, as Shakespeare called it—off with the shoes, fluff up the pillows, one light on over my right shoulder and the delicious stretch-out on the bed. In Qram, an English-language newspaper or periodical is harder to come by than rain, and I've been known to overtip the bellman on Monday night so he'd bring me Tuesday's international edition of the *Herald Tribune* on Wednesday. Thus, though I'd brought plenty to read with me, I was on my fourth go-round with a dog-eared *Aero* magazine which featured an article on back-up vacuum systems for single-engine airplanes. I had a battery-operated communications radio between the two front seats of the A-36, but no back-up vacuum supply for my gyros. I wanted one. When I'm flying around in the clouds I've always felt it a good idea to know which part of the airplane is up.

And then my eyelids started to droop and I reached out and turned off the bed lamp. I wriggled into comfort and waited for delightful unawareness to settle down over me and blank out all the nonsense the day had brought.

Bangedy-bam-bam, went the door. I groaned and switched the light on again. "Who the hell is it?"

"Mike! Let me in!"

I mumbled an epithet having to do with swine feces and went to open the door. I'd thought Mike would look beat up or worried or something; instead there was a beatific and dreamy expression on his mashed face. "Damnit, Mike, it's late! For me, anyway—"

"Gotta talk," he said.

"What is it now?"

He was already on his way to an easy chair, where he plopped himself down. "She's wonderful!" he said. "She's really something!"

"Who? And what's it got to do with me?"

"Florence. We had dinner. Little French place she knew. Everything perfect—the wine, the candles. Then this nightclub. They had the kind of music you can dance to holding on. We danced. We talked. We talked about everything. She likes the same things I do, including anchovies on pizza. What a marvelous evening!"

"Is this what you woke me up to tell me?"

"I'm getting to that. I think I'm in love with her. I'd know better if we could have—er—rounded out the evening, but she was a little old-fashioned about that. Not averse to it, I gather, but doesn't want to jump into anything too quickly."

"So you think you're in love again. What do you want me to say? That you're too old for it or something? I don't think anybody's ever too old, if that's what you want to hear."

"You don't understand, George. I also think I'm still in love with Meredy. How is that possible? How can a man be *equally* in love with two women at the same time?"

"How the hell do I know? Why don't you write a letter to Ann Landers?"

"I've got to talk it out, George. I can't put it together in my own head. It helps when you listen. You got a drink around here?"

"No. Unless you mean ice water, which you were craving this morning."

"My room," he said, pushing up from the chair. "I've got a bottle in my room."

"I don't want any. I just want to sleep."

"Then come on down and watch me have a nightcap. You're not going to leave me alone with all this on my mind, are you?"

"I ought to," I said. And maybe if I hadn't been on the edge of sleep and a little fuzzy-headed I might have done just that at the risk of another friendship gone down the drain. As it was, I slipped on my robe and followed Mike down the hall to his room.

The granddaddy of all yawns was catching up with me as Mike worked his key in the lock. My mouth was opening like one of those hippos on the Disneyland Jungle Cruise, so I wasn't really looking and didn't catch in any clear detail what happened next.

Something, as soon as Mike pushed the door open, shot out of the room like a cannonball—I remember that. It was a human being—a stocky, kinky-haired Arab in European pants and shirt. He caught Mike by surprise and bowled him aside, then rushed past me and down the corridor before I could do anything. The light in the corridor was dim enough to keep me from seeing him sharply; I doubted I'd recognize him. In a moment, he had vanished in a stairwell far down the hall, leaving Mike and me standing there looking stupidly at each other.

"Who the hell was that?" I said to Mike, in hanging bewilderment.

"I don't know." Mike looked as baffled as I felt. "Some prowler. I thought the crime rate was pretty low here, but I guess not." He turned abruptly to the open door of his room. "Damnit, I wonder if he got anything—"

We stepped into the room and Mike switched the light on. We stared. The room was in shambles—furniture shoved out of place, closets opened, drawers hanging out with their contents strewn all over the floor.

"Christ, that's all I need right now!" said Mike. "I wonder if he got my NYPD cufflinks. They gave 'em to me when I left." He started for the bureau, the upper drawers of which had been removed.

Halfway across the room he halted and stared down at the floor. His brand-new Nikon camera lay there, the back of it hinged open. He stooped, picked it up, and looked at me. "Why would he open it and not take the camera itself? It's worth plenty."

"Mike," I said, "you're asking me too many questions. At this moment I don't have an answer for any of them."

CHAPTER THREE

Many years ago I was in the Army. I won't dwell on all the things I didn't like, but one of the things I *did* like was the travel and all the distant places I got to see. I didn't know that when I became a motion-picture actor I'd still be traipsing all over the world for location shooting. By that time I'd become something of a homebody and would rather have stayed back home most of the time with my wife, the kids, the dogs, the big-screen TV, and the other blessings a homebody acquires. This review occupied my thoughts as I lay again in the hotel room bed with adrenaline pouring, keeping me from sleep.

I tried to think about future pleasures instead of the puzzling events of the past day. My Beechcraft Bonanza A-36, for example—that was a pleasure. I'd just sold a Cessna 182, and moved up to a plane that was more powerful, had more room, and was justifiably referred to as the Mercedes of all single-engine aircraft. Almost before I'd had a chance to try it out, I'd had to run off to Qram. Right now the A-36 was sitting back in California doing nothing but looking pretty.

The pleasant thoughts started to work as an antidote to the adrenaline. A warm, gray, amorphous blanket of sleep began to draw itself over me again.

And for the second time that night—which by now was the dark morning of the next day—there was a pounding on my door.

This time I asked who it was and came to the door cautiously.

The answer was molasses-slow and drawn out. From that alone, I knew who it was. If Jimmy Stewart had been Abraham Lincoln he'd still be in office, because the Gettysburg Address would still be going on. "George . . . is that you? Are you in there, George? Come on . . . open the door!"

He stood there, casually but fully dressed, in the dim hallway. I said, "Don't tell me *you've* got problems you have to talk about."

"Problems, George? Well . . . I guess we've all got a problem here. We—uh—we've got to move real fast, or we'll—uh—be stuck here gosh knows how long—"

"Move fast? How? What? Where?"

"I—uh—I'm getting to that, George."

He looked down the hall toward the stairs and started to point. Then he thought better of it and started to point the other way.

"Jimmy—is there any way you could get to it a little faster?"

A surprised look crossed his face. "Well, uh. There's a lot to explain."

"Right." Jimmy would get to it when Jimmy got to it.

"The—uh—best thing you can do is get dressed and packed right away. The vans'll be downstairs to pick everybody up in fifteen minutes. The plane's waiting right now at the airport."

"It came in?"

"Not the charter plane. The prince's own 747—you know, the 300 model he had done up so fancy." Then I saw the beginnings of a slight smile and a faraway look. "That's a really nice airplane and I, uh, wouldn't mind handling it myself if I got the chance, though probably I won't—"

"We're flying out on that? How come?"

"I don't know exactly, George. But the prince or Jabala or somebody must have relented and cleared everything. They can't take the whole company—the airplane's full of staterooms and things so there aren't enough seats. But about sixty of us can go. Jennings got the word and, uh, well, asked me and a couple of others to help round up everybody who gets a big salary." He rubbed his chin. "I'm having trouble finding *anybody!*"

"I'd better start packing."

"Do that, George," said Jimmy. He started wandering back to his room. "I wonder if Gloria . . ." His voice trailed off. Whatever he wondered, he probably finished the sentence about the time you're reading this.

It was a Chinese fire drill getting all the people out of their rooms, with doors banging open and sleepy eyes clicking awake all over the hotel. Blossom Foster, in lightweight cashmere, and hauling two suitcases, came toward me down the hallway. After her enormous success in *The Godless*, she had become the nation's number-one pin-up, defying her mother. Thus, mother was no longer along, a loss we all felt was something akin to being freed of poison sumac. Blossom also defied gravity with her no-bra look, and when she hurried, as she was doing now, it looked as though two kittens were wrestling under her sweater.

"Oh, damn," she fussed, coming to a halt by my door. She put down the two bags and said, "George, keep an eye on these for just a second, will you, please. My dumb key's still in the door." She was gone even as I nodded, and in seconds was speeding back even faster.

They weren't kittens, they were cats.

I grabbed the bags for her, and she smiled in appreciation as we went to the elevator. "I'm so lucky to be getting out of here," she said excitedly. "My agent has sent me telex after telex pleading with me to phone him right away. Something about Sylvester Stallone's next film. *How* could I call?"

"Beats me," I said. "The manager told me that the last long-distance phone call in or out of this hotel was two years ago. From Honolulu, of all places."

As the elevator clacked downward she said, "Do you know how much I heard Sly Stallone got for his last picture?"

"No," I said, "but he's awful good up there on the screen. And he's hot. They pay a lot for that."

44

Blossom said, "Twelve million dollars?"

I gulped. Quite visibly. I thought twelve million dollars is what you'd pay if you wanted to buy Finland. Our industry has some peculiarities, one of which is that there's very little money around to make low-budget pictures, and what little capital there is is absorbed making made-for-TV films, or big-screen pictures starring nobody you ever heard of, with titles like *Halloween the Nineteenth at Ridgemont High's Amityville Fun House*. But just come up with the right *deal*, and the millions tumble your way like confetti on New Year's Eve.

"You know, Blossom," I said as we crossed the lobby, "there aren't too many stars nowadays who guarantee on their name alone that people will pay to see them in a theater. Bo Derek is one and Sylvester Stallone is another. That's why most of what you see advertised is aimed at the group between ages thirteen and nineteen—they're the ones who are doling out the dollars to the local box office. My feeling is if they gave Rocky that much, it's because he's also pulling a lot of people into theaters who aren't in that age bracket. The money guys must think he's worth every shekel."

We stopped at the front door. Seeing Blossom, forty cabdrivers materialized out of palm trees, but Jennings was signaling me to put her in his car with Candy Vandermeer. I set her bags in the trunk, and as she got in I said, "After *The Godless* and all your magazine covers, you're probably not too far from that category yourself."

She beamed and said, "Will you still coach me like you've been doing when I become rich and snobby?"

"Will you get me Sylvester Stallone's autograph?"

After she'd been driven off, happily waving out the back window, I realized that some of the few selected for our unscheduled flight were still out on the town, presumably in nightclubs or possibly in brothels, and they never did get notified. Fortunately, they were not in the upper-upper brackets, so the loss, while they waited for the charter plane to be allowed in, would at least be sustainable.

I found myself, still half-asleep and wondering what

I'd forgotten to pack, in one of the vans on its way to the airport over that same dusty road out of the city. The crescent moon was low in the west and all the diamonds in Africa had been thrown across the sky. It was hot for anywhere else, but cool for Qram.

In the shuffle I'd drawn a rear seat, and some of the airplane's crew members occupied the rest of this particular vehicle. I'd thought I'd be able to doze off briefly, but they were chattering enough to defeat my attempt.

The first thing was an exchange between two of the stewardesses. I'd noticed both, in passing, and as we'd all mumbled good morning to one another when climbing into the van. One was an older woman whose nameplate identified her as Rita Schmidt. I'd seen that her uniform was getting a bit tight and, knowing all about calorie problems as the years pass, I'd sympathized with her. She'd bleached her hair to a shade too blond, but that hadn't made her look more youthful.

Sitting beside her was a much younger girl, Mary Lou Carmichael. I hadn't noticed her nameplate, but I'd learned her name later. She was pretty in a fresh, wholesome, ingenuous sort of way.

"Oh, my God, Rita!" said Mary Lou, "I think I forgot my passport!"

"*What!*" Rita's voice was stern. "That's all we need! On top of everything else, that's all we need!"

"On the desk back in the hotel room—I must have left it there!"

"Carmichael," said Rita Schmidt, with the air of a drill sergeant, "I thought something like this would happen when I saw you'd been assigned. You're the one who dumped the lettuce and tomatoes all over that senator on the Bangkok run, aren't you?"

"That was an accident—"

"Yes, it was. But flight attendants on my crew toss the salad—they don't *propel* it. And they're usually experienced personnel. This crew must have been put together in an awful hurry."

"But what'll I do about my passport?"

46

"When we get to the airport, you'll have to find a way to go back and get it. If you miss the plane, well, tough turkey. I'll be shorthanded, but that's better than having a tray-dropper aboard."

A male steward who had been sitting in front of the two women now switched around in his seat. He had a hairline mustache and finely chiseled features, and if he hadn't been in a steward's uniform I'd have taken him for a gigolo, a vanishing breed. He spoke with a French accent. "Rita, *ma chère,* you must not be too 'ard on 'er!"

"Bernard," said Rita, "I'm responsible for the flight attendants, and if I have to be hard on them, I will!"

Mary Lou leaned forward and said, "Thanks for your support, M'sieur Fourrier, but it really is my fault."

"It is not the end of the world," said Fourrier. "If you do get on the plane, come to see me. I will 'elp you, if Rita won't."

"She doesn't need your kind of help, Bernard," Rita Schmidt said sharply. "I'm sure she can get undressed all by herself!"

"You do me a grave disservice, m'am'selle!" said Fourrier, all wounded.

"Knock it off," said Rita. "Save your seduction for after hours. We're taking care of a lot of important people on this flight, and I want everybody tending to business—nothing else!"

Having known lots of airline people, I'd seen overage-in-grade stews like Rita Schmidt before. Kind of sad, actually. The airlines didn't really want them because they were no longer young and sexy, but they couldn't fire them because of the union and sex-discrimination laws and their own seniority regulations. Sometimes they manage to kick them up the ladder and get them out of the way. They'd done this to a degree with Rita Schmidt by making her a purser, in charge of the other flight attendants, so that she spent more time doing paperwork than fluffing pillows and serving in areas where the passengers would prefer to see something shapely. But, as Rita must have very well known, they would welcome any excuse to fire her. She had to be

47

twice as efficient as anyone else just to hang on until retirement.

In a way I felt sorrier for her than I did for the flustered kid, Mary Lou Carmichael. As it turned out, Mary Lou didn't get left behind after all. When we piled out of the van on the flight line, near the airplane, with customs and other formalities apparently waived, Flight Engineer Ted O'Malley, who had arrived in another vehicle, came running up, waving a passport.

His eye picked her out immediately. "Mary Lou Carmichael?"

"Why . . . yes—"

"I'm Ted O'Malley. I saw you drop this in the lobby."

"Omigosh. Thank you! Thank you so *very* much!"

"You're welcome," said O'Malley, grinning, his eyes going all over her, crossways and up and down. "Tell me, now. Aren't you going to ask how you can ever repay me?"

And now she was inspecting O'Malley closely. If his face was the map of Ireland, she was taking it in, from Dublin to Galway Bay. "I was afraid you'd say that," she said. But from the way she laughed I could tell she wasn't afraid at all. On the contrary, she was looking forward to further discussion of the matter.

"Let's go, let's go," said Rita Schmidt impatiently.

We all headed for the airplane.

There is always a certain amount of excitement when you board an airplane for a long flight, though the truth is that most of them prove to be more of a leaden bore than an adventure.

I figured this one would be the same—which, as it turned out, was about as wrong a guess as I could make. Anyway, getting on the prince's special airplane that dark, early morning, meant a chance to catch some of the sack time that had been eluding me. So I found a seat and dumped myself into it immediately. When you're my size, and perhaps even if you're not, wide seats which recline *waaay* back guarantee a good, long, uninterrupted sleep, which I sorely needed. Since we'd be flying, roughly, east to west, we'd be chasing the darkness, and it would be many hours before the dawn would catch up with us; this time I planned to turn jet lag to my advantage.

Things hadn't entirely settled down yet, though I expected they would once we were airborne. It seemed the ten staterooms hadn't been made ready yet, and there was some question as to who was going to get them. Rita Schmidt was busily in charge, waving people back to grab what seats they could find for the time being.

Rod Larrabee came aboard, lurching heavily, smelling like he'd been shipped uncorked from some Loch Lomond distillery. He was blinking behind his armor-plate glasses and throwing his forklift weight around. "The bar, stewardess!" he said imperiously to Rita Schmidt. "I want a seat near the bar! There shall be no moaning at the bar when I put out to sea. No moaning, just some very serious drinking!"

"Please take seat G-nineteen on the main deck," said Rita, without a trace of expression. I knew that was way to the rear, and admired Rita's maneuvering him out of the way. He staggered aft, looking for G-nineteen, where, as Rita knew, he'd be pretty much all by himself.

Husband and wife Julie London and Bobby Troup made a low-key entrance in Larrabee's noisy wake. Julie, with her large, clear eyes, was as beautiful as the striking photo on her album, "Julie Is Her Name." In person she's as enchanting as the music inside the jacket. Bobby, gray-haired but still youthful, with his calm, agreeable manner, has a settling effect on anyone near him. Under any circumstances, it would be nice to have them aboard.

Even though I hadn't had a chance to explore yet, I had at least a vague idea of how the airplane was laid out. Some time ago, finding myself in Seattle on business, I'd been treated to a look at the 747-300 the Boeing people had made for the king of Saudi Arabia—the equivalent, I guess you could say, of Air Force One. If you're not an airplane freak you can skip this next part, though the layout did have a bearing on all that was to happen.

The 300 model has the same principal dimensions as

other 747s—a wing span of almost two hundred feet, and so on—but the upper deck, which is like a forward hump on a whale, has been extended more than twenty-three feet to provide extra cabin space behind the flight deck. Instead of the old circular staircase, there's a straight, aft-rising set of steps that goes up to it. On the prince's plane, I understood, this cabin had been converted to an executive office, complete with computer terminals. The bar and lounge Rod Larrabee had been so concerned about was forward on the main lower deck, and there the abstemious Muslims could get their *gazoz* or Coca-Cola, while their foreign guests could lap up booze, if they wished. Extending aft, in an interior twenty feet wide, were sections with extraordinarily comfortable sleeper seats, well-spaced with a sixty-two-inch pitch, and various islands that contained the staterooms, galleys, and storage areas. The entire rear quarter of the plane was a separate compartment for extra cargo space—so the prince could haul along an extra Cadillac or two, I supposed, the way some people take their own golf carts to the course.

There was one unusual feature the prince's plane shared with the one designed for the king of Saudi Arabia: a modulus, as it was called, that was in essence another stateroom, but had been set aside for the prayers and devotions Muslims take very seriously, and practice at prescribed moments several times a day. This, of course, was off limits to us infidels, and if we had any manners at all we didn't need to be told that.

All of which passed only lightly and abstractedly through my mind as the engines began to whine to a start. I settled back and closed my eyes again.

"Oh, there you are, George!" said Mike Corby's gravelly, lower-Bronx voice, about as welcome as the sound of a motorcycle revving its motor on a Sunday morning.

I opened my eyes. Mike stood there in the aisle. And to my complete surprise, Florence Haverman, smiling sweetly, and tastefully clad in a pottery-blue button-front traveling dress, stood beside him.

50

"Guess what!" said Mike, as he and Florence, without even being asked, took seats beside me.

"What are you doing here?" I asked, as graciously as I could.

"Florence has been assigned to go along as State Department representative," he said, beaming.

"Wonderful," I said. "As soon as I wake up you've got to tell me all about it."

For all the good it did, I could have been hinting in an unknown Basque dialect. Now it was her turn to chatter—everything I'd never wondered about and didn't really want to know about why she was on the plane. "It had to be top secret till we were all aboard," she said, "but now that the lid's off, you might as well be the first to know. Prince Ibrahim is flying to the States with us!"

This did wake me up. "He's okay, then? His injuries, I mean."

"Well, no," said Florence, frowning slightly, "he's still in critical condition. They've got him in the master stateroom—smuggled him aboard in the dark before anybody could notice. Jabala's in there with him, and Dr. Fayez, his personal physician. I didn't hear all this till the last minute when his advisors got everybody in the embassy out of bed to enlist their cooperation, which, of course, they gave. U.S. policy here is to give the prince anything he wants and don't ask questions. Nobody else could get ready on time, so they sent me along to 'monitor the situation,' whatever that means."

"Isn't it great?" said Mike, patting Florence's hand. "I thought I'd never see her again!"

"If the prince is in critical condition," I asked Florence, "why are they moving him?"

"Arab whim as much as anything," she said. "As I understand it, there's a bomb fragment in his brain or close to it. It's a job for a neurosurgeon, which they haven't got here. They could probably fly him to Zurich or London or someplace, but they've decided on Los Angeles. That's because they own a hospital there."

"They do? I know they've got hotels and businesses and things, but I didn't know they had hospitals, too."

"Well, the prince founded it or took it over or something years ago. I think it was part of the benevolent image he wanted to project. He likes to keep the American public happy so they won't object when the U.S. sends him armaments. Anyway, he owns it, and that means complete comfort and security for him when they do the operation. You're lucky it went this way, and that Jabala decided to give you all a ride home. All we have to do now is keep our fingers crossed and hope the prince survives the trip."

I looked at her sharply. "You think he might not?"

"I don't know. They're anxious to get him to L.A., though, without the slightest delay. We're flying nonstop."

"We are? Fourteen or fifteen hours? That's close to the maximum range even on this half-loaded airplane. They'd do better to make at least one stop somewhere."

Florence shook her head. "They're stubborn about that, and I don't know all their reasons. Medical, maybe, or perhaps for the sake of security. The more stops we make, the more vulnerable the prince is to another assassination attempt. Anyway, it's their paranoia, and the State Department is going along with it. The cables have been humming, clearing the way. They're waiving all kinds of regulations, like having a spare crew aboard and that sort of thing."

"Well," I said, "I'm sorry the prince got hurt, but I have to admit the rest of us lucked out. I wonder who's gonna get those staterooms?"

"George," she said, "I know you don't mean to be insensitive, but the big worry, for all of us, is whether or not the prince makes it. If Qram has a rebellion...if war breaks out in the Middle East...if it spreads...we'll be thinking about bomb shelters instead of staterooms."

"I know, I know," I said, scowling. "It's just too big to seem real. Maybe if I got some more sleep I could think about it clearly."

Now she was the one who was being insensitive; she didn't pick up this hint any better than she'd picked up the earlier one. She was turning her head this way and that, looking at the other passengers who were scattered among the many empty seats around us. The pilots, anticipating the nonstop flight, had obviously insisted on a light load, and that was why only part of the movie company had been invited aboard.

"Jabala must have had an unexpected attack of kindness," she muttered. "I see he gave Minister Kebir a ride, too."

I didn't care who Minister Kebir was, but Mike picked up the cue, though I wished he hadn't. All it could mean was more chatter to keep me awake. "Who's Minister Kebir?" he asked.

Florence nodded toward a man who sat by himself a few seats down the aisle. He was a small, middle-aged Arab in a quiet gray business suit; I had a vague idea I'd seen him on the reviewing stand before the bomb blast, but I wasn't sure about that. He was swarthy and slender and had a way of fading into his seat so I'd have never noticed him if Florence hadn't pointed him out.

"He's been the prince's finance minister," said Florence. "The rumor is he got caught with his hand in the till. In the old days they'd have cut it off, but the prince is enlightened, so all he gets is exile. To some luxurious villa in the States, I suppose, where he'll have nothing to do but enjoy himself the rest of his life. They need another line on the Statue of Liberty. 'Give me your rich...'"

"Florence," I said wearily, "sometimes I wish you weren't an expert on Qram. Sometimes I wish nobody was an expert on anything."

"I'm sorry, George," she said, quickly. "You want to sleep, don't you?"

"Hey, that's not a bad idea," I said, snuggling back down as they finally moved off.

Sweet, sweet sleep, and such stuff as dreams are made of was not to be, alas. Not quite yet. I did manage to snooze a little during takeoff. Mike and Florence, probably a little apprehensive, were mercifully quiet for a while, but after we had leveled off and could unfasten our seat belts, part of what Florence had said kept gnawing at me until I was up and out of my seat. My motor, like one of those diesels you can't shut off on a hot day, was running again.

That was why the faint strains of music I now heard acted more as a stimulant than a lullaby. They came from the lounge forward, in the nose of the airplane, and I knew at once that Bobby Troup was at the tiny spinet there, playing and singing "Girl Talk." I couldn't resist. I rose and lumbered that way.

The lounge was bubbling and full of people making like a bunch of GIs joyfully returning from combat duty overseas. Bobby was singing his original composition in a tender whisper, delivering it as though he'd just thought of it for the very first time. Julie was happily ensconced in a bridge game, tapping her foot and looking up every once in a while to enjoy what amounted to a spectacle on the floor.

There, very short Stubby Dawson was dancing with very tall ex-model Candy Vandermeer. Unlike many statuesque cover girls, Candy would not be called a string bean by anyone in his right mind—she was perfectly proportioned. She and Blossom Foster had become great friends, and together they were the female version of Mike Corby's and my Mutt-and-Jeff twosome.

Stubby was milking the dance for all it was worth. A short guy and a tall doll may have been involved in the very first burlesque bit there ever was, and with Candy laughing helplessly, Stubby kept swinging away from her and then swinging back so that his nose went straight between her boobs. Then he'd make a silly, leering face, do a Groucho with his eyebrows, and growl something like, "It's a great place to visit but I wouldn't wanna live there!"

I waited until this marvelous impromptu schtick finished to a round of applause, then, not wanting to be drawn too deeply into the party, climbed the stairs to the executive office in the long hump just aft of the pilot's compartment. It contained everything an efficient office ought to have, from desks and computer consoles down to wastebaskets

54

and pencil sharpeners. I took it all in as I worked my way forward to the flight deck.

I don't really think I expected the door to the pilot's cubicle to be open. Regulations require that it be kept closed and locked while en route, except for authorized crew members. Any little deterrent you can place between you and a hijacker is welcome. But open it was, and the question in my mind could best be answered by the man in charge of this flying hotel.

Ted O'Malley was at his panel of gauges on the starboard side. Forward of him, Jake Larkin was in the copilot's seat. Both looked up and smiled at me, but Captain Fowler, in the pilot's seat, swiveled his head around and scowled in annoyance.

"Look," I said, "I hope I'm not interrupting anything, but I just wanted to find out if we're really going nonstop to LAX, the way I hear."

"That's the flight plan," said Fowler curtly.

"No reason why we shouldn't, is there?" I asked.

"You're a pilot, aren't you, Mr. Kennedy?" said Fowler, inspecting me a little more closely. I felt like an officer candidate in front of the board all over again. That had been many years and several wars ago. "Maybe you'll understand this."

"Understand what? And my name is George, if you'd care to use it."

"All right, George. You might as well know. We had everything set for a long flight, except for one little detail. Those camel drivers in Qram gave us all the Kero-50 they had at the new airport, and that wasn't a lot. The damn tanks aren't as full as I like 'em to be."

"Oh? Just how much fuel is there?"

"Enough, if we don't run into a really strong jet stream. I just don't want to run out over the wilds of northern Canada or someplace."

Jake Larkin, relaxed and languid in his seat, saw my troubled expression and grinned. "Don't let it bother you, George. Our hospital has never lost a baby yet."

"You're damn right we haven't," snapped Fowler. "And while I'm captain we're not going to!"

"I'll get out of your hair," I said quickly. I didn't want to witness another dogfight between Fowler and his copilot. I turned and started back out.

"Leave that door open," growled Fowler. "I want immediate access to that computer." So much for my other question.

At my seat, Mike and Florence were still chattering and sending moonbeams back and forth with their eyes. I wasn't sure I could take any more of it in my present mood, so I muttered something about having to go potty and continued aft.

I went past the staterooms, which were lined up along a corridor, a little like those in European trains. The door to one of them was open and a couple of flight attendants were inside, making up the beds. I'd heard flight attendants complain that they were nothing but glorified waitresses, and on this flight, apparently, they had to be chambermaids, too. No job, I thought with a sigh, is all it's cracked up to be. Not even being a movie actor.

In front of the master stateroom towered Muhanna, the prince's chief bodyguard, looking like something you'd meet at the top of a beanstalk. He glared at me as I went past, and, not wanting to be picked up and breathed upon again, I gave him a wide berth and decided to return by the other corridor, where he wouldn't see me.

Past the master stateroom was another island with a galley not in use for the moment. Beyond that was the modulus, which had been inserted into the airplane like a prefabricated house. When I saw the gilding and elaborate curlicue decoration on its doorway, I knew that this must be Ibrahim's airborne mosque, or prayer room. The door was open and hung at about forty-five degrees, concealing most of the interior, which was illuminated by a dim glow. Had it not been partly open I would not have bothered to look inside. But a prayer room was something I'd seen aboard an airplane only once before, at the Boeing plant, so I was naturally curious to find out if this one was about the same.

I was careful to slip my shoes off before I entered. I'd been in enough Arab countries not to forget that custom. In some of them you risk getting your head off if you don't take your shoes off.

I pushed the door all the way open and took one step inside. And that was all. I froze. Sprawled on an exquisite, wine-colored prayer rug in the middle of the tiny room was a pile of still flesh that was—or had been—Rod Larrabee. His glasses had fallen off and lay near his head. One of his chubby cheeks was on the thick nap of the rug. His eyes were open and popped halfway out of their sockets, and somehow they still had that quizzical look they'd had in life, the puzzled stare so familiar to millions of TV viewers.

There was a small round hole in the back of his head, right where the neck met the skull, and the blood around its edges was glistening.

CHAPTER FOUR

Dr. Fayez was a small man who, unlike most Arabs in European dress, wore bright, clashing clothes. His slacks were of Madras patches and his sports shirt, full of tropical blossoms, could have been used on a tourist poster for Hawaii. I don't know, maybe he was color blind. He had a spade beard with a cropped mustache. His eyes were intelligent but curiously disinterested, wandering, withdrawn. It was as though he'd long ago found out that everybody in the world is absurd, so to hell with it.

By this time some of the confusion had settled down and several of the distasteful chores had been done. I'd notified Captain Fowler immediately upon finding Rod Larrabee's body, using one of the phones scattered throughout the airplane. After that Fowler, and those he'd caused to be notified in turn, had flocked to the prayer room to stare at the body and ask me the same questions over and over, as though I knew anything about it. I kept giving the same answer: I'd wandered there, pushed the door open, and seen Rod's corpse.

At Fowler's direction, the flight attendants had removed the body, wrapped it in a blanket, and taken it to the cargo space in the rear, laying it out among the dogged-down pallets of crates and boxes. There was blood on that beautiful prayer carpet, and the job of scrubbing it out fell to Mary Lou Carmichael. She obviously didn't like it. Jabala, seeing the body, had looked flustered and put-upon and had kept wiggling his gelatinlike jowls and asking helplessly who could have done such a terrible thing. In the prayer room, too. This was worse than murder—it was sacrilege.

Mike showed up. I learned later that Fowler, on his way back to the flight deck, had quietly told Mike what had happened and asked him, as a celebrated ex-policeman, to go back and take a look. Mike now had hold of Dr. Fayez's arm to keep him from returning to the master stateroom where he was supposed to be taking care of the prince, and was drilling him with his cop's eyes. "Come on, doc, what did you find?"

"Find? He was dead. Instantly, I would say."

"Why instantly? I've seen people shot in the head before. Sometimes they live for hours."

"Not if the medulla oblongata is destroyed. That is why it is well protected behind the topmost vertebra and the lower process of the occipital plate. There is a procedure called cisternal puncture and it is always very difficult to insert the needle properly."

"What's all that mean in layman's language?"

Dr. Fayez shrugged. "Someone put a bullet into his skull in exactly the right way to cause instant death. A rather small-caliber bullet, I would say. You will notice that there was no exit wound . . ."

Mike and I finally headed back to our seats. In the main deck area, everybody was looking apprehensively at everybody else. Several cast members tried to stop Mike to find out what he knew, but he put them off rather gruffly, saying he knew no more than they did. Rod Larrabee had been shot in the head by person or persons unknown for reasons that were anyone's guess. Captain Fowler had said that much over the aircraft's speaker system when he'd admonished all passengers to stay out of the rear of the fuselage.

"My God—Larrabee!" said Stubby Dawson, looking shaken. "He was a funny guy! Funny guys aren't supposed to get killed. Bad guys and sweet, innocent guys, but never funny guys. Does that sound stupid? I guess it does. It's just that—"

"I know, Stub," I said, and kept going.

Candy Vandermeer, with her shocked stare, looked almost spiritually beautiful as we passed her. I would have rather seen her beautiful in her usual way.

When I worked with Bo Derek in *Bolero*, my initial thought before our introduction was the same as yours: Is she really a "10"? In that film, I played her chauffeur, father-figure, guardian, confidant—and just about every place she went, I went. I saw about as much of Bo as there is to see, dressed and undressed, and in great measure so does the film audience. Folks, Bo is a "10," easy.

Candy Vandermeer had those same qualities distributed on an exquisitely formed six-foot carriage. She all but looked me straight in the eye, though I had trouble staring back. There's something about delicately slanted jade-green eyes that unnerves me. "George," she said softly, touching my hand, "do you think we'll be all right?"

"Honey," I said, "you and Blossom are sharing a stateroom. Just as a precaution, when either of you wants to come out, pick up the phone and have one of us that you know come and escort you." She squeezed my hand and flashed a smile which would unstick an Arctic ice-trawler.

We took our seats again and Mike filled Florence in on what he'd seen in the rear. Florence was pale. "May I say the obvious? I've got to say it—take off the pressure. There's a murderer on this plane. Among us."

"Yeah," said Mike, "I guess everybody's thinking about that. But just because somebody apparently had a mad on for Rod Larrabee doesn't automatically mean that the rest of us are in danger. And I hate to badmouth Rod Larrabee now that he's dead, but we know he rubbed a lot of people the wrong way."

"Enough to get killed for it?" asked Florence.

"Who knows? People get strange reactions sometimes. Maybe he really upset somebody who was very devout by entering that holy room."

"Not likely," said Florence. "I don't think anyone on this plane is that devout."

"Maybe not. And the way he was murdered doesn't look like anger or sudden impulse. A small-caliber weapon, probably silenced. Placed in exactly the right spot, the doctor said, so death would be instantaneous. That suggests special knowledge—planning. As though whoever did it was some kind of professional. Or had some kind of medical training."

"Or looked up what he had to know," I said. "Became an instant expert. Like this script writer, Walt Sheldon, who did the screenplay for this *Airport* movie. Known him for years, since my Army days in Japan. He once told me someday he was going to write a book called *The Story of Everything*."

Mike shrugged. "Well, he's not aboard. The only other guy who's a writer type and looks things up is our eminent producer, Jennings Lang, and he *is* aboard."

"The only thing Jennings has been known to kill is a fifth of vodka. Why would he want to kill Rod Larrabee?"

"Why would anybody? Unless we go into every passenger's background, we'll never know. And maybe not even then. Anyway, we're just beating our gums. After we land there'll be an investigation and that ought to turn up a thing or two. All we can do is wait."

"I know," said Florence, frowning, "but that's the hard part."

At this point one of the stewardesses came up the aisle and stopped where we were seated. "Mr. Corby? Mr. Kennedy? Mr. Dilworth wonders if you could come up to the executive office for a minute."

Young Ken Dilworth was in the swivel chair at the fancy desk, frowning and looking earnest as we emerged from the stairway to the upper deck. "Sit down, sit down," he said. "I can have some drinks sent up if you like."

We both shook our heads.

I reflected that Ken, with his youthful and unpretentious air, didn't look like an executive, but maybe after a few more hassles like the one we had on our hands he would. He'd made a stab at it, anyway, by dressing in a button-down collar and a tie with regimental stripes—the kind of duds you get from the Brooks Brothers representative when he has a hotel showing on the West Coast. That way you make yourself look East Coast.

61

It's kind of a reverse snobbery. I avoid the whole problem by traveling in a jogging suit.

"If you gentlemen will forgive me," said Ken, "I've just got to talk to somebody about this whole damned situation. Like a board meeting, only I haven't got a board. What's happened is kind of down Mike's alley, and I know that you, George, are pretty familiar with airline procedures."

"Okay. Meeting called to order," I said.

"The first thing," said Ken, "is that the body ought to be landed and offloaded. Frankfurt would be good—lots of U.S. officials there. But I've been in touch with LAX and the word I get there is that the State Department wants us to keep going. I understand how they feel: nothing's too good for our staunch ally, Prince Ibrahim, and he's got to get to Los Angeles without delay. But can you see what this does to World International Airlines?"

"What does it do? This is the prince's airplane, not WIA's," I said.

"But the crew's WIA. The public won't make a distinction in their minds. What's happened is kind of like a hijacking. Maybe you don't know it, George, but whenever there's a hijacking, or any disaster for that matter, ticket sales fall off appreciably till the public forgets about it. If we dump the body and have a nice, normal flight the rest of the way, it takes the sting out of it."

"So land," I said. "Dump the body."

"Then the State Department's mad at us. We need all the good will we can get with the government. We spend millions lobbying for favorable legislation, and we need more regulation like we need a hole in the head. Every time something like this happens Congress slaps on new regulatory legislation. That's *their* way to solve problems. First, they'll investigate the nonstop flight without a spare crew, which, frankly, is of questionable legality."

I shrugged. "It's your decision, Ken."

"It is," he admitted, looking harried. "And either way I go the old man's not going to like it. Just when I'm trying to keep him in a good mood, too. I'm bringing Lisa home for him to meet, and I'm not sure how he's going to react to that. Now this mess on top of it."

"The thing to do with messes," I said, echoing a speech I'd made to myself many times, "is roll up your sleeves and clean 'em up."

"Exactly," said Ken. He turned his attention to Mike.

"If we could somehow nab this murderer, that would look very good for the airline. You know—make it seem we take care of our passengers, no matter what. This may be the prince's airplane, but it's under our operational control, so it's practically the same as if it were one of our own flights. We get blamed for whatever's bad, but we also get credit for whatever's good. Catching the killer would really smooth things over."

"Are you looking at me why I think you're looking at me?" asked Mike gruffly.

"I certainly am. You're a detective, Mike—or used to be. A damned good one, if I'm not mistaken. I realize it's a long shot, but you just might be able to zero in on this guy if you looked into it."

"Stop right there," said Mike. He shifted in the plush chair. "I run into this all the time and have to explain it. You don't solve murders smoking a calabash pipe and staring at the wall while you make deductions. You have a whole organized setup behind you and the help of a lot of experts. Files, crime lab, people to do all the boring legwork. A good stable of snitches. You dredge through the backgrounds of everybody involved and in time—sometimes a very long time—things begin to pull together. If you're lucky."

"You've got the executive office here," said Ken, casting his eyes over it. "Radio communications anywhere you want, and these computer terminals that can be tied in to anyplace. This ought to enable you to dig up *some* information, if you need it."

"Well, I don't know," said Mike, frowning.

"And there's something else you'd be just the man to handle. We need security measures on this airplane. That alone would calm the passengers down. You'd know how to organize them. I'd pay whatever fee you name, of course—we can do the paperwork later. The old man probably won't like the extra expense, but to hell with him. I'm in charge here, and he might as well get used to it."

Mike was still frowning. "I can't make any guarantees—you realize that, don't you?"

"Of course. I said it would be a long shot. But just having the passengers know that you're in charge of security will be worth it, whether you get anywhere or not."

The phone on the desk buzzed. Ken answered it and said, "Yeah, yeah" several times, and then said, "Okay, patch him in." He rose, went to the communications console, picked up a microphone, and flipped on a speaker.

"This is Ken, Dad," he said. "How do you read me?"

"Not bad for halfway around the world," said a deep, incisive voice—the kind used to giving commands. I'd met Carter Dilworth, chairman of the board of WIA, before, and I could visualize him standing in his shirt sleeves as he called from flight operations. Tall, well-built, vigorous. White hair cropped short, like in his Navy days when he flew fighters and wore crash helmets. No pretensions. Mechanics on the line first-named him and he preferred it that way—as long as they hopped to when he gave an order. "Now, tell me," he said, "just what in hell's going on aboard that airplane?"

"I thought you knew everything by now. Somebody shot Rod Larrabee, the TV comedian—"

"I know that much. And so does the whole world by now. The reporters have been bugging me. What I want to know is *who* shot him and what are you doing about it?"

"We don't know who, but we're looking into it. I've got Mike Corby aboard—you know, the actor who used to be a famous cop—and I've just put him in charge of security."

"What the hell good does that do? Look, you'd better land that plane and put this in the hands of the proper authorities."

"We can't. The State Department wants us to keep going."

64

"The State Department? I knew I shouldn't have fooled around with Middle East politics! But that Qram run will produce lots of revenue eventually, so I had to play footsie, at least, with his highness. I'll call State. The secretary himself."

"You do that, Dad. But meanwhile I'm inclined to cooperate with State and keep going. Look, you're a real John Wayne–type patriot, aren't you? Maybe some of that rubbed off on me. The United States needs Qram and Prince Ibrahim. If he should die, all hell breaks loose——a Marxist government could take over. If you ask me, this supersedes any of WIA's selfish interests."

"What the hell's selfish about our interests? I never should have sent you to college where all those bleeding-heart professors teach you to hate corporations. Do you know what corporations are? They're little old ladies and plain people all over the country who own stock. Backbone of the nation——"

"I know all that," said Ken patiently. "But if the next war comes along there won't be any corporations——"

"Look," said Dilworth, "this is no time to argue about it. I think you ought to land that plane, but I will check with State first and get their side of it. From the horse's mouth. Meanwhile, see if you can find out who did the killing so he can be arrested. That will help. A little, anyway."

"We'll do what we can," said Ken. "But I want you to let me handle it. You said I'd be in charge, and I'm holding you to it."

"We'll see about that." Dilworth must have been glowering——it was in his voice.

"There's one more thing, Dad," said Ken.

"Yeah? What's that?"

"Remember? I wrote you about Lisa Garcia——"

"You mentioned the name. Look, your love life's okay with me. Had a pretty good one myself in my day. Get it out of your system and we'll find the right one for you one of these days when you're ready to settle down."

"That's the point," said Ken. "Lisa's the right one."

"What!" I thought the speaker would explode.

"I'm bringing her back with me," said Ken. "You'll love her when you see her."

"*Lisa Garcia?* Who is she—some Chicano?"

"Puerto Rican," said Ken.

"Same thing!" snapped Dilworth. "Now, look here, Ken—"

"Save it for later," Ken said. "I've got a lot to do right now. Over and out, okay?"

He switched off the radio and turned to us and said, "Now. Where were we?"

Where we were wasn't much of anywhere. While Ken was on the radio, Mike must have been thinking about his security plan, because he now started to outline it. The first thing to do, he said, would be to set up a regular series of patrols by the flight attendants. He'd work out routes from the floor plans of the airplane and they'd cover them at irregular intervals, keeping their eyes peeled for anything untoward—anything out of place, any suspicious behavior among the passengers. His command post would be the executive office and they would immediately report anything offbeat that they noticed to him. They weren't to take action, unless it was an emergency—just report. They weren't to let the passengers realize what they were doing. He'd get them all together in here, as step one, and brief them on what he wanted.

"That'll cut into their regular duties," said Ken, frowning.

"It'll have to," said Mike. "Let the passengers wash their own diapers for a change. Tell the pilots about it, but nobody else."

"I think we'd better coordinate with Jabala," Ken said. "He's probably got his own security people aboard. There's at least one—that bodyguard at the stateroom door."

"Okay. But the fewer who know, the better."

"That makes sense," I commented—not sure whether or not it was my place to comment. "But it could turn out that somebody taking part in the security drill is the person we're looking for. It would give him a tremendous advantage in covering his tracks."

"We'll have to risk that," said Mike, shrugging.

Ken was thoughtful. "We can't keep it from the passengers entirely," he said. "After all, the object of this whole game is reassure them—calm them down. If it's okay with you, Mike, I'd like to have Captain Fowler make an announcement to the effect that you've been put in charge of security and that it's all in your good hands, and now they can rest easy."

"If you have to," said Mike. But he was frowning and I could see he didn't like it. He looked at me. "I'd like your assistance in this little chore, George."

"Have gun, will travel," I said. "What am I saying? I haven't got a gun. You haven't, either. Or have you?"

"No, I haven't. But let's not forget somebody aboard this plane has. After all, we didn't go through the security gate back at the airport."

I sighed. "All I wanted when this day started out was a little sleep."

"So drink lots of coffee," said Mike.

"Coffee keeps me awake," I said.

Ken, using the phone to send one of the flight attendants as a messenger, now got in touch with Jabala. When he had him on the phone, he tried to explain the situation briefly and asked him to come to the executive office to discuss it. When Jabala arrived, bobbing up out of the stairway, all rubbery smiles, I was surprised to see that he had the huge bodyguard, Muhanna, with him. Muhanna hung back, looking hostile and stupid, glaring at all of us in turn. He was in a plain suit now instead of his muscle-shirt and pantaloons, but it fit like Boris Karloff's had in *Frankenstein*.

"Ah, gentlemen, gentlemen!" said Jabala, in that amiable voice he always put on for foreigners. He often succeeded in giving the impression that he was a most reasonable man who could be dealt with. "It's a terrible state of affairs we have here, is it not? A deplorable tragedy!"

"Yes," said Ken. "And what we're concerned with now, your excellency, is the safety of the passengers—and especially of Prince Ibrahim."

"So I understand. You said you had a security plan and that Mr. Corby was to implement it?"

"That's right. And we want your people in on it, too. If you'll direct them to cooperate with Mike."

"That shouldn't be difficult," said Jabala. "Especially since there aren't any except Muhanna here. The flight was arranged in some haste, as you know, and we were unable to put a full complement together. There'll be some to meet you at the airport, but we really didn't expect trouble aboard the plane. It's another reason I don't want to land anywhere en route. The opposition is well-organized and they have agents everywhere. There's been one assassination attempt, and there *could* be another—"

Mike cocked an eyebrow and gave him that cop's look of his that said he didn't necessarily believe what anyone was saying until all the returns were in. "Has it occurred to you, Mr. Jabala, that there *might* be a connection between the attempt on the prince and what happened to Mr. Larrabee?"

Jabala looked baffled. "What possible connection?"

"I don't know. Mistaken identity, Larrabee witnessing something he shouldn't have—something along those lines. It's just that intended violence sometimes has a way of hurting innocent bystanders."

"Are you sure you aren't reaching for straws, Mr. Corby?"

"Right now," said Mike, "that's all we've got to reach for. And no possibility, no matter how wild, ought to be ignored at this stage. The important thing is that you're with us in what we're trying to do. And since it means the protection of the prince as well as everybody else, it's in your interest."

"Oh, absolutely!" said Jabala, bobbing his head up and down, making his several chins appear and disappear. "I will instruct Muhanna here to cooperate fully. But he's to remain in place, of course, guarding the stateroom. He should be back there right now. So should I, for that matter."

"Just tell him not to interfere if anybody comes snooping around," said Mike. "Ken will advise you as to who is authorized."

"As long as they make no attempt to enter the stateroom," said Jabala blandly, even a little primly.

"Tell him not to pick anybody up and squeeze them, like he did me," said Mike, with an acid look at Muhanna.

"That was unfortunate," said Jabala. "I want you two to be friends."

"Yeah. Sure. Real buddies," said Mike sarcastically.

"You should forget the little misunderstanding in the hospital. You should both shake hands right now."

"Huh?" said Mike.

Jabala spoke to the huge bodyguard in Arabic, and Muhanna looked surprised for a moment, then knotted his brows for another moment and finally pulled his heavy lips into a cold grin, stepped forward, and extended his hand. Or was that a first baseman's mitt he was wearing?

"Go on. Shake," said Jabala to Mike.

"This is crazy," Mike said.

"Humor me," said Jabala, beaming.

Mike gave his hand to Muhanna. Muhanna's hand engulfed it. I could see the squeeze, and I could see Mike trying to limp up on him so he wouldn't have his fingers crushed. I could also see him trying not to twist and turn or grimace with the pain of it.

I didn't know what Jabala said in Arabic then, but I was ready to bet it was something like, "That's enough." Muhanna dropped Mike's hand and stepped back, still grinning.

After Jabala and Muhanna left the stateroom Ken stared at Mike, watching him shake his swollen hand, and said, "What was *that* all about?"

"A message," said Mike. "It said, 'Don't push us.' It said, 'We're in charge here, and don't forget it.' The bastard."

"Well, at least you didn't have to do it Arab-style," I said.

"What do you mean?"

"He might have asked you to kiss him."

CHAPTER FIVE

Mary Lou Carmichael told me about it later, so I think I've got it right. The details are reconstructed, but more or less everything happened the way I'm going to give it to you now.

Busy setting out snack trays in the galley, Mary Lou became gradually aware of a male presence in the narrow space with its banks of food-warmers and storage compartments. She smelled a musky after-shave lotion first, and then, when she looked up and around, she saw Flight Attendant Bernard Fourrier standing there showing her a delicately twisted smile. There were some, she supposed, who would call his finely cut features handsome, but to her they were excessively refined, bordering on the feminine. Not that he swished, or anything like that. There was plenty of masculinity in the look he held on her— the masculinity of a prowling wolf.

"I 'ave not yet 'ad a chance to say 'ello to you," he said.

"All right. Hello," said Mary Lou flatly. She continued to lay out food on the trays.

"It is a shame we are so busy, always," said Fourrier. "There is no chance to get acquainted."

Mary Lou shrugged. "I don't mind being busy. It makes the time go faster."

"But why make time go fast, eh? It passes . . . it never

comes again. The moments should count. We should seize them when we 'ave the chance!"

"Uh huh," said Mary Lou, the way you agree with somebody so you won't encourage them to keep it up.

"I will be laying over at LAX. You are based there, *ne c'est pas?* It is not one of the more civilized cities of the world, but I 'ave found some places there that will do. There is one little restaurant, *La Belle Epoque,* where the cuisine is more than passable. The wine is correct, and there is candlelight. Afterward...ah, well...afterward...we shall see, eh?"

"I'm sorry, Bernard," she said. "But I'm already dated up. Thanks anyway."

"Dates can be broken—"

"Some other time, maybe," said Mary Lou. She hoped she wasn't blushing as she often did when she lied. She didn't have any dates, though she might have after they landed. There was even a possibility that cute flight engineer, O'Malley, might try to arrange something. Unless he turned out to be married and settled down like so many of them. He didn't *look* married—

Fourrier sighed in exaggerated fashion. "You do not give me the chance to make your acquaintance. You leave me desolate!"

She smiled a little. "You don't look desolate."

"But you 'ave no idea 'ow it is! Sometimes I wonder what I am doing on this airplane—on any airplane. It seems very exciting, at first, to fly all over the world, but do you know what we really are? Glorified waiters and waitresses, nothing more!"

"It seems that way sometimes." Mary Lou shrugged.

"Of course," Fourrier continued—and she knew he was sneaking up on her from a different direction—"one must 'ave employment, eh? Do you know that I once dreamed of the diplomatic service? Because of my languages. I spent my childhood in Algeria, you see, where we spoke both French and English at 'ome, and where the servants taught me Arabic. When you 'ave three languages as a child, the

71

rest come more easily. Spanish—I am studying Russian now. I can tell a woman 'ow beautiful she is in all of them."

Mary Lou had to smile. "I suppose that's one good reason to become a linguist."

"I am telling you all of this," said Fourrier, "so you will know me better. As I would like to know you. And what better way is there for both of us to know each other than to spend an evening together?"

"You don't give up easily, do you?"

"Not when there is a lovely woman at stake!" He lidded his eyes and moved toward her.

Still smiling, she regarded him coolly. "You're invading my territory, Bernard. The way some of those Arab nations are always doing to each other."

"Sometimes it is necessary. But let us not get into politics."

"Let's not get into much of anything."

"You see? You close your mind. Like those who oppose Arab unity. The Arabs are a great people—I 'ave much sympathy for them. I 'ave marched at the side of those who would restore them to their former glory. They were the center of learning and civilization when Europe was in the Dark Ages. Now, perhaps, they are coming into their own again. Though we still 'ave too many like Prince Ibrahim, who wish to make themselves puppets of the Western world."

"I thought we weren't going to discuss politics."

"Forgive me! It is only when I look at you—so refreshingly lovely as you are—I lose my mind!"

Having established the excuse for it—losing his mind—perhaps as much for himself as Mary Lou, Fourrier now came forward and put his hands on her waist.

She stood stock-still and stared back at him.

"If raping a marble statue turns you on, go right ahead," she said calmly.

He sighed and shook his head and stepped back again. "It is a long flight. You will 'ave time to change your mind."

When he had left the galley, Mary Lou smiled to herself, shook her head several times, and continued to put the snack items on the trays. They'd be late in rolling them down the aisles on the carts—most of the flight attendants were busy on the patrols Mike Corby had set up. Kind of a boondoggle, she thought, but at least the idea seemed to calm the passengers down a little. Terrible thing, that murder. Rita Schmidt had more or less taken it in stride, saying she'd had people die on her during a flight before. She was experienced. But that was one experience Mary Lou would rather do without, thank you.

When Mary Lou had stacked all the trays into the carts, she, for a moment, considered rolling them out to start serving the passengers. Then she remembered that Rita had given her strict orders to stay in the galley. She frowned, wondering if the time she'd spilled food all over a U.S. senator would ever be forgotten. The senator himself hadn't seemed to mind all that much.

Her eye fell on some leftover dishes with food still on them and she began to scrape them into the binlike disposal unit.

"I see you've got the garbage detail," somebody said.

Mary Lou looked up and saw Ted O'Malley standing at the galley entrance, grinning at her. His snub nose and his freckles were infinitely more appealing to her than Fourrier's finely cut features. She didn't know why, and knew it would spoil everything if she tried to look into herself to find out.

"Somebody has to do it," she said, grinning back at him.

"Like Cinderella," he said. "While the other girls go out and dance all night."

"I really don't mind."

"You ought to. If I were you, I'd foment an uprising. Give 'em hell with a machine gun from the back of a bakery truck."

"Haven't we had enough excitement on this airplane?"

"Yeah, but not of the right kind. A good rebellion of the oppressed, that's what we need. Off with their heads. You take Rita Schmidt, and I'll take Captain Fowler."

"I've heard he runs a tight ship. What's the matter? Did he have you flogged before the mast or something?"

"I think he's getting ready for it. A negative performance report'll be just as bad. With all the forms they've got on this airline now I wonder where anybody finds time to fly the planes. Usually the first officer just checks it off routinely—performance okay—and lets it go at that. But I'm afraid I'm gonna lose my temper and tell Fowler where to get off and that'll be it. At a very bad time. I've got pilot certification coming up, and a negative P.R. could put it off again. In fact, it's why I'm here. I had to get away from the flight deck and cool off."

"Well, everybody's got their troubles, I suppose," said Mary Lou. She said it sympathetically, and not as a rebuke.

"Especially in this chicken outfit," he said.

Mary Lou laughed. "Oh, come on now."

"I mean it. It's not just me—he's coming down hard on Jake Larkin, too. That's the copilot. Jake's damn good—flew fighters in the Air Force. Fowler won't even let him go back to see the prince."

"The prince? What's he got to do with it?"

"Larkin was his instructor at Davis-Monathan in Tucson when he learned to fly jets. You know, the military exchange program. The way I understand it, they got to be real buddies. Well, all Jake wanted to do was go back and look in on his highness, but Fowler had received instructions the prince wasn't to be bothered by anybody. When Fowler receives instructions the case is closed."

"You'd better forget Fowler. You pilots are supposed to keep your blood pressure down, aren't you?"

"I guess we are. Though I'm not a pilot. Theodore Kevin O'Malley, boy flight engineer. Till the end of his days." He sighed, then lifted his head, as though shifting gears. "But here I am, doing all the talking as usual. I don't know anything about you yet."

"Not much to know," said Mary Lou. "I was an Army brat. Grew up in Germany and learned the language right down to all the dative cases. Flight attendants on international runs have to speak another language, so I applied for the job. The only thing is, they keep putting me on runs

74

where hardly anybody speaks German. That's WIA for you. If it follows regulations it doesn't have to make sense."

"Get to the important part," said O'Malley. "What do you do with all your lonely nights?"

"They're not that lonely. I've got a suspicion yours aren't, either."

"Maybe not. But they could be improved when we get to L.A. I take it you like discos? I take it you like pizza joints late at night?"

"How cultural," said Mary Lou.

"Okay, some art museum, if you'd rather. You're worth yawning for."

"What am I getting into?" Mary Lou was laughing again.

"This," said O'Malley. He stepped forward, slipped his arms around her, then bent down and kissed her, pressing tight, holding it long.

She broke away with a smile. "Get out of here now," she said, "before the housemother discovers us."

He saluted with one finger and, grinning broadly, left the galley.

Mary Lou primped herself when O'Malley had gone. She didn't need to—it was instinct. She continued to stack the trays in the carts and straighten up the galley, liking it for a change. It was traditional for airline stews to get romantically involved with pilots, and that was a cliché she could live with. He'd been right about her nights. Some of them had been lonely lately. Of course, everything he'd said could still be so much blarney, and he might be after no more than a quickie or two—which was how she sized up Fourrier—but that was a risk that had to be taken. At least with O'Malley, the quickie itself would afford a certain amount of passing pleasure.

Rita Schmidt came in. She looked at the readied carts and the now-shipshape galley and nodded with reluctant approval. "You can take a break," she said.

"It's all right," said Mary Lou. "I don't mind serving."

"I'd rather you didn't. We have enough experienced attendants to cover, so you'll be more useful doing backup.

If you'd really like to help, you could go out there and do a patrol."

Mary Lou thought that over for a moment, then nodded. "Well, I've been a waitress and a chambermaid and a kitchen worker, so I guess I might as well be a night watchman, too. When do I get to be a stewardess?"

"When you learn a lot more," Rita said smugly.

Wandering aft, down the aisle, Mary Lou thought about Rita. Although she'd outgrown her youth the way her hips had outgrown her skirt, she was not an unattractive woman. It was just that she no longer fitted the image of a nubile stewardess that the passenger public seemed to have created. It was the youth cult: they had to have maidens dancing in attendance upon them. Air travel was an adventure, whisking one away from home, to somewhere where the usual rules of behavior didn't apply. Every man aboard an airplane, any airplane, nurtured the secret fantasy of a romance with some willing stewardess. Maybe women travelers had their counterpart of this, and that was why the airline threw in slinky creeps like Fourrier once in a while.

What the hell; it was a living.

She passed one of the staterooms just as Candy Vandermeer came out of it into the corridor. They exchanged smiles. Mary Lou enjoyed seeing someone so naturally lovely—so exquisitely lovely—for a change. More than just surface loveliness, thought Mary Lou; it came from inside. Candy wore blue jeans, a checkered shirt, and a freshly scrubbed look.

"I'm bunking in here with Blossom," said Candy, "and we can't find any towels."

"Coming right up," said Mary Lou, glad to be of service. There was a linen locker in one of the islands a few steps away, where she promptly found the towels. "Sorry you didn't have them. We put the staterooms together in an awful hurry."

"Of course," said Candy. "It's my fault anyway. I should have told the steward a few minutes ago."

"I don't think I understand."

Candy laughed lightly. "It's not important. He knocked

and asked if there was anything he could do for us. I was in the midst of changing and"—her smile broadened—"he seemed to be staring a bit, so I forgot about the towels. He had quite a charming French accent."

"M'sieur Fourrier," said Mary Lou, nodding. "He must have known you were in the midst of changing. He's got radar for that sort of thing."

"It's quite all right," Candy said, keeping her smile. "I'm sure he was only trying to help. Anyway, thank you for the towels."

When the stately young movie star had closed the stateroom door again, Mary Lou stopped for a moment, frowning to herself. She doubted Rita had sent Fourrier to look in on the two young and lovely actresses; it must have been his own idea. Not that she'd report him for it, or anything like that, but she herself would be even warier of M'sieur Bernard Fourrier from now on. Chasing after women had apparently reached the proportions of a compulsion with Fourrier, and astronomical odds against scoring evidently didn't discourage him at all. Probably one of those deep-rooted psychological things. Too bad there wasn't an organization called Wolves Anonymous he could join and get some help.

She shrugged and moved on.

This patrol business was ridiculous. What was she supposed to look for? A killer lurking in the shadows somewhere? Rita had called all the flight attendants together in the executive office and Mike Corby, who had been a celebrated policeman, had given them instructions. "Anything offbeat; anything out of place," he had said. "Make a note of it and report it." That was too vague. Like some of WIA's regulations, it could mean anything. Or nothing. It was probably just to keep the passengers happy—the prime directive, as William Shatner used to tell his crew on the *Enterprise*. She forgot what the prime directive for the *Enterprise* was, but hers was clear enough—keep 'em happy. She hadn't known that at times it would get to be a drag. But then, she supposed, any way of life might have its wearisome moments after a while—even slaving over a hot stove in a cute little cottage somewhere for the likes of Theodore Kevin O'Malley. And what on earth had prompted that thought? She'd been spending too much time by herself lately. She wished Rita, the old battle-ax, would relent and let her get out and serve the passengers.

There was an unused galley behind the bank of state-rooms. A curtain blocked it off, and at first she almost went past it. Then, just to be thorough, she halted, pulled the curtain aside, and looked into it.

Crumpled on the floor of the narrow space was the body of a small, neat Arab gentleman. She immediately recognized Mr. Ahmed Kebir, one of Prince Ibrahim's government officials. He had a powder-burnt hòle at the base of his skull.

CHAPTER SIX

Mike and I plopped ourselves down at one of the tables in the lounge area on the forward main deck. This was the bar near which Rod Larrabee had wanted to be seated. There was, indeed, a small bar, much like one in a family recreation room. Behind it was a white-coated man with a nose Jamie Farr or Danny Thomas would have been proud of. He had bright, alert little eyes and a friendly smile. I knew he was not one of the crew WIA had supplied, but was employed directly by the prince. His nameplate identified him as Abdul. The prince felt that proper hospitality toward his foreign guests required professional attention to the matter of alcoholic refreshment. It was also possible that some of the more westernized Arabs—maybe the prince himself—sneaked themselves a drink once in a while.

"What will it be, gentlemen?" Abdul said, bringing his smile to our table.

Mike looked at the early-morning darkness outside the ports, for it was still with us, and then at me, as though he wished my permission for a drink at this crazy hour. "I don't know," he said. "What goes good with a bucket of worms?"

"I'm going to have a nice tall glass of orange juice if you have it," I said.

"Of course, sir," said Abdul.

"A stinger," said Mike, coming to a decision. "You know how to make a stinger?"

"I can make anything," Abdul said, nodding with pride.

"I was once chief bartender at the St. George in Beirut."
He sighed. "That was before all the trouble."

Okay, I thought, that explained an Arab bartender. He was probably Lebanese, and a Christian instead of a Muslim. When people said Prince Ibrahim was enlightened it meant he didn't mind hiring an infidel here and there if it would get the job done.

"A stinger, then," said Mike, and Abdul pirouetted smartly and went back to the bar to mix.

I said to Mike, "Kind of early to be refueling, isn't it?"

"I don't know whether it's early or late or what," Mike said. "I never do on these airplanes. It's also a hell of a place for a murder investigation."

"I'd think it would make it easier. The murderer can't get away, after all. He's got to be somewhere aboard."

"Yeah, but so am I. Locked in, just like he is. I haven't got what it takes to make a proper investigation. No files, no snitches. Not even a crime lab, though all this science jazz solved fewer murders than you think. We could, for example, analyze everybody's hands for powder traces, which you get when you fire a gun. Providing our pigeon didn't wear gloves, which he probably did. I'm certain he knows how to cover his tracks. These two murders are sophisticated, you know what I mean? Just the right weapon, no doubt well-thought-out beforehand. Enough to kill if you find exactly the right place in the head—more evidence of special knowledge and careful planning—but not enough to make an exit wound and puncture the airplane. Now, anybody who's intelligent could cook up something like that; and we've got a lot of intelligent people aboard, but who among them would go to all this trouble to do it? And why? What's Rod Larrabee got to do with Ahmed Kebir? Is the killer taking potshots at random? That would make him a nut, and nuts don't usually go about it this coolly and, if I'm right, with this lack of emotion."

"Go ahead and ask me all this," I said. "But don't expect any answers."

"I don't. But you're a good sounding board, George."

"What we call in show business a straight man. Okay, I'll be Abbott and you be Costello. Who's on first?"

"Beats me," said Mike. "For the moment."

Abdul brought the drinks and slithered away again. I didn't really want to be in the bar, but Mike had insisted. We hadn't been assigned staterooms; apparently the criterion was women, children, and married couples first. Jimmy and Gloria Stewart had one, as did Bobby Troup and Julie London. The sleeper seats Mike and I had weren't conducive, in Mike's estimation, to the conference he wanted to hold.

"Not the least of it," said Mike, still running down the list of all his complaints, "is that all the passengers know about it. And are all flipped on account of it. They're starting to look at me as though to ask, well, why in hell don't I find this killer roaming around in everybody's midst? And everyone of 'em wants me to stop and hold his hand and tell him everything about it. I could spend the rest of the flight reassuring 'em all, one by one, and then I *wouldn't* have any time to figure this thing out. Which I kind of doubt I'll be able to do, anyway. You could tell the difference between me and Sherlock Holmes if you were a grade school kid."

"Elementary," I said wearily. It was a dumb enough play on words, but Mike didn't hear it anyway.

He tasted his mixture of chilled brandy and white crème de menthe. From the face he made I wondered why he'd ordered it. Maybe he was trying to cut down on cigarettes and wanted to give his hands something to do.

As we sat there, getting nowhere, a fourth person came into the lounge compartment, hesitated a moment while he looked at us, and then approached our table. I looked up, and I was surprised for a moment to see who it was, but then remembered that I'd glimpsed him among the other passengers when we'd boarded. It was the lanky professor with the neatly trimmed ginger-colored beard who had introduced himself to Rod Larrabee in the hotel bar. What had his name been? Hibner—Lowell Hibner; that was it. He was still in his bush jacket and looked as though he

81

ought to be riding a jeep across the veldt looking for rogue elephants.

"I hope I'm not intruding," he said.

Mike looked up at him. "Not at all." Even Mike could bring himself to lie politely once in a while.

"I'm Lowell Hibner," he said. "I know who you gentlemen are, of course."

"I saw you in the hotel talking to Larrabee," I said. "You've been teaching at Qram University, right?"

"Well, helping them set up their poli-sci department. But that job's done now, and I'm getting a ride home. What I want to talk to you about is these murders."

"So does everybody," said Mike. "Before you ask, I don't know anything. All I can say is what I've asked Captain Fowler to tell all the passengers. Don't go anywhere alone and report anything unusual. If there's any danger, that will minimize it."

"I quite understand all that," said Hibner. "But I think you'll be interested in hearing what I have to say.

Mike's head came up. "You know something?"

"May I sit down?"

Mike gestured to a chair. "Have a drink, if you want."

"I'll pass, thanks." Hibner lowered himself. It was a little like a gawky giraffe unwinding its legs. He took out a pipe and began to fill it from a fabric pouch with regimental stripes. "I am rather reluctant to tell you the following, and I haven't come to this decision easily. But these are very special circumstances, and I think I have no choice but to take a chance."

"On what?" asked Mike.

Hibner glanced at Abdul, who was busy behind the bar, and with the low hum of the airplane in the background, it was evident that, as long as we kept our voices reasonably low, he couldn't overhear what we were saying. Hibner reached into a pleated pocket of his bush jacket and took out a leatherlike folder. He flashed it open; we both glanced at the I.D. card it contained, and our eyebrows rose.

"I'd say you gotta be kidding," said Mike, "but I don't think you are."

"Just don't say aloud what you saw," said Hibner. "Super hush-hush and all that."

"I thought you guys never told anybody who you were," said Mike.

"We don't. Ordinarily. But if circumstances require breaking cover, we're authorized to use our judgment. And that's what I think we have now. Extraordinary circumstances."

"I know that much," said Mike. "What else is new?"

"What's new is that my interests now lie where yours do. A job of protection has to be done—and part of it may be finding out who's just committed a couple of murders. The intelligent thing, now, is for us to join forces. You can be assured I have some experience in matters of this sort."

"Probably you have," Mike said. "But you're into cloaks-and-daggers, or so I assume. Are a couple of homicides really your bag?"

"I'm afraid they are. In this case, anyway. Let me explain further. It doesn't hurt to tell you that my job at the university was a cover. Fact is, I do have a doctorate in political science, so it was easy enough for the Company to arrange it. It wasn't exactly to spy on Prince Ibrahim, who is a good friend of ours, but to gather routine information mostly about the opposition. It's managed to plant some of its own people at fairly high levels in his government—especially in the university. Somebody assigned to the embassy usually does this sort of work, but the opposition expects it there, so putting me into the university was better. That phase is finished, so there's no longer a great deal of risk in telling you what the setup was. I must, of course, ask you to keep it strictly confidential, but it won't blow the whole United States of America apart if you don't. In other words, by letting you know what's going on I'm taking a calculated risk, with the odds favorable enough to make it worthwhile."

"The only organization I ever joined dedicated to the overthrow of the United States government," said Mike, "was the Democratic Party. And they're only dedicated to that when the Republicans are in. I still don't know why

83

you want to help us find the murderer—if that's what you're saying."

"That's what I'm saying. You see, my assignment right now—and it was pretty much spur-of-the-moment—is to keep an eye on the prince. Another assassination attempt is always possible, even aboard his own plane, especially when he invites so many passengers. He's got his own body-guards, of course—one, at least—but we like to feel we're exercising our own control. I probably don't have to tell you how important it is to the United States—to the free world, for that matter—to keep his highness alive. Well, somebody on this airplane is knocking people off. Is he after the prince, too? I don't know—and maybe you don't, either. But it's obvious that if the killer could be identified and restrained, whatever danger there is might be eliminated. So I'm offering my services. For what they're worth."

Mike nodded thoughtfully. "You might be able to help at that," he said. "But—and no offense, Dr. Hibner—"

"Lowell. Even my cat calls me Lowell. Thank God, I've got somebody to take care of him while I'm away. He's a Siamese, bred from his dam and one of her offspring. You can do that with Siamese. Know what I call him? Eddie Puss. Get it?"

It took me a moment to get it and when I did, I groaned.

"Are you always this irrelevant?" Mike asked Hibner.

He smiled through a cloud of pipe smoke that smelled like malted milk. "Forgive me. I go off on sidetracks sometimes. Help me think. Must be the professor in me."

"Well, as I said, no offense," said Mike, picking it up again, "but I've worked on these interagency cooperation deals before, like when the FBI came around and muscled in on the NYPD. Sometimes, in the squabble over juris-diction, the cooperation gets lost. The only way to shortstop that is to have it agreed, from the beginning, who's in charge. I figure this is my squeal, and I'm in charge. Okay with you?"

"If you insist," said Hibner. But he frowned a little.

"Fine. We understand each other. I hope. And if we do, I've got a job for you right away."

"Fire away," said Hibner.

"As I've told George here many times," said Mike, "murder cases aren't closed by the inspector puttering around in the petunias. It almost always boils down to painstakingly sorting through information concerning all the suspects and witnesses. This time, just about everybody aboard this plane is a potential suspect or witness. That goes for our celebrity movie stars, too, though I doubt they'd like to hear me say it. If I were back in the department, the first thing I'd do is dig up a yellow sheet on everybody involved. And that's what I'm going to do here. With all those computer terminals in the executive office we can get a complete make on everybody. We can tie in to the NCIC—that's the National Crime Information Center, maintained by the Federal Bureau of Investigation—and get the criminal record of anybody aboard this plane who has one. Federal, state, even most major municipalities. Any arrest for something more than a parking ticket. You'd be surprised, sometimes, to find out who has a yellow sheet."

"I wouldn't be surprised at all, and I think it's an excellent idea." Hibner's pipe had gone out and he was fishing for another kitchen match. I had the feeling that, to him, getting that pipe lit again was more important, at least for the moment, than putting the collar on a murderer.

"So what I want you to do," continued Mike, "is to run interference for me with the CIA, so I can get a look at their files, too."

Hibner smiled. "First," he said, "don't say it out loud like that. If you have to refer to us, say 'the Company.' Second, the guys at Langley, whom I know oh so well, won't even give each other the time of day in the hallways. If you think you can get anything out of them, forget it. They even clam up on the President. And if they find out I blew my cover to you—even though it's authorized in this case—I'll be answering questions about it till I retire, which might even turn out to be next week."

"Okay, scratch that one," said Mike. "But all we're going to get from the FBI is data on American citizens. There are several other nationalities on this airplane."

"Right. So may I suggest Interpol in Paris? I can help you there; I know their code address and how to make the request. That's what they do mainly—keep records. They're not an operational espionage organization as so many people think."

"Now we're cooking," said Mike, nodding with satisfaction. His stinger sat half-finished on the table before him, already forgotten. "There's one more thing. We're going to have to let Florence Haverman in on this one."

"The gal from the embassy?" Hibner's frown was definite this time. "Well, I'm not so sure about that. She'd be cleared for top secret in her position, of course, but there's always the principle of containment. The fewer people who know a given item, the better."

"But I need Florence. To light a fire under the FBI, for one thing. The State Department has more clout with them than I do. And to handle some of these communications and whatever paperwork we run into. You know, like a secretary. She used to be one."

"You seem to know a great deal about her," Hibner said with a dry smile.

"Not as much as I'd like to," Mike said.

Our project wasn't off the ground yet, metaphorically speaking, that is. What I mean is that certain preparations had to be made before we could so much as open a conversation with the computers of the FBI's National Crime Information Center.

First, Florence had to be taken into our confidence and then briefed. Hibner left most of that to Mike and me while he went off to be sure that no one with assassination in mind was getting near the prince, or maybe just to find some wallpaper he could fade into, which, I presume, is what CIA agents are supposed to do when they're not rolling in the hay with beautiful, blonde Russian female spies. You can see that all I know about CIA agents is what I've gathered from movies on the subject, so maybe I'm wrong about that, though I've seen real life imitate movies often enough.

Mike brought Florence up to the executive office to fill her in. She listened quietly, nodding now and then. I liked the way she sat there, composed and well-groomed, alert but not unduly excited. It seemed to me she'd be a marvelous partner for Mike, but then I still thought that about Meredy, who was painting her heart out somewhere in Mexico. Point is, I could understand Mike's ambivalence a little better. It apparently *was* possible for a man to love two women.

"I'm not too surprised to learn about Hibner," said Florence.

"Oh? How come?" asked Mike.

"Well, we feel certain vibrations about these things in the embassy. One or two of the people there are CIA, though nobody's supposed to know about it. And it would be par for the course for them to have someone out on the economy, as we call it. As a visiting professor, Hibner had a perfect cover, and it just naturally occurred to some of us that he might be a spook. Probably this occurred to the opposition, too, so what it amounts to is that even a perfect cover can be conspicuous, precisely because it's perfect. Or is all this too much reverse-English for you?"

"It is," said Mike. "I like it when you can tell the good guys from the bad guys by the color of their hats, which you could in all the old westerns. Them were the days. Anyway, do you think you can work this computer?"

"It shouldn't be a problem," said Florence, looking at the screen, keyboard, and other units on a shelf along the bulkhead. "I did word-processing at the embassy on a smaller unit, and there's an instruction manual right here. I might need a little time to get used to it, though."

"Try not to take too much. I presume there's someone at the State Department you can get to intercede so that the FBI will cooperate, and that you can get in touch by radio."

"All locked in," said Florence. "Not to worry."

"Good," Mike said. "Now all we need is the passenger manifest so we know what names to send in. The purser, Rita Schmidt, ought to have it. George?"

"I'm on my way," I said.

An atmosphere of shadowy conspiracy had settled down on all of us, and Mike didn't have to tell me that it was best to find Rita Schmidt and contact her personally rather than try to locate her by the airplane's interphone system. Most likely, she was somewhere down on the main deck, but, just to be thorough, I checked the flight deck first. I opened the door, went in, saw Captain Fowler in the left-hand seat and Ted O'Malley in the copilot's chair. The airplane was on auto-pilot.

Silver-haired Captain Fowler turned his head and showed me his usual look of annoyance. "Oh," he said, seeing me. "I thought you were Larkin coming back. You didn't see him out there, did you?"

"No. I was looking for Rita Schmidt."

"Well, she's not here. And neither is my copilot. He said he was going out for a smoke. What's he smoking, anyway? A foot-long cigar?"

"You don't need him all that much, do you?" I nodded at the auto-pilot in the center pedestal.

"That's what I've been telling the good captain," said O'Malley, grinning. "He's got me."

"I'm aware you're a pilot, O'Malley," snapped Fowler, gesturing as he spoke. "When I'm flying I want everybody in their proper place. These wild-blue-yonder types they've saddled me with seem to think that's overdoing it. Fine. Fly with somebody else tomorrow. Today we do it my way."

I shrugged. "I can appreciate that, captain. I'm a safety nut myself when I fly." What I didn't add was that I also try to get along with whomever I'm flying with. I did, however, trade a glance and a quick smile with O'Malley to show him that if I were in this dogfight, which I wasn't, I'd be on his side.

Rita wasn't in the bar and lounge, or in the "A" section, forward on the main deck. I stuck my head into the main galley and saw Bernard Fourrier opening champagne bottles. I didn't think they'd have many takers for champagne out there at this hour, but that was his business. He was pretty deft with the champagne corks and looked more like a handsome headwaiter than a flight attendant.

"Have you seen Rita Schmidt around anywhere?"

Fourrier smirked. "I most certainly 'ave."

"Well, where is she?"

"I do not think she will wish to be interrupted."

"I'm afraid she has to be. Mr. Corby needs her in connection with the security plan."

"It is up to you, M'sieur Kennedy," he said, shrugging. "Don't say I did not warn you."

"What in hell are you talking about?"

"Rita is a woman, after all. With all the desire of any woman. She 'as looked at me in a certain way, on occasion, but I am a little more discriminating in the women I choose. Do not misunderstand me—I do not blame 'er in the slightest for trying to fulfill 'er appetite. It is only natural, *ne c'est pas?* But if she is to act this way, also, she should not be so 'ard-nosed about it with the rest of us."

"How come," I said, "that every time I ask a simple question I get a rundown on everybody's troubles?"

"Forgive me, m'sieur. You always look as though you might understand."

"Well, I don't. So where *is* Rita?"

"Most probably in the crew lounge. That is, if she succeeded."

"Succeeded in what?"

"When Second Officer Larkin went by 'er eyelids fluttered and I could 'ear the bells ringing in 'er 'ead. 'E is a very good-looking man, I must admit. She dropped everything and followed 'im. I've no doubt 'e was 'eaded for the crew lounge where 'e could smoke. Captain Fowler does not like it in the cockpit. So they will both be in there, I'm sure, indulging in more pleasure than smoking. Be sure to knock before you enter."

"Fourrier," I said, "you've got an X-rated mind."

He shrugged deeply, and I went out of the galley again.

And again, as I lumbered aft, people wanted to stop me and hear whether or not Mike had, somehow brilliantly, caught the murderer yet. They knew I was working with Mike as his unofficial assistant, and they were, of course, most uneasy over what had happened. Stubby Dawson looked up at me quizzically and said, "George, this isn't some kind of gag, is it? A publicity stunt?"

"It's real enough, Stub. Two people have been killed."

"You mean this airplane's a flying hearse? Why don't they land and get rid of the bodies?"

"They can't land. The prince has to get to L.A. non-stop."

Dawson sighed. "Well, at least that'll get us all home a little quicker. As far as I'm concerned, flying's for the birds. This kind, anyway. See the world from a window seat. I almost wish we'd get hijacked. Havana's very nice this time of year."

"Even their jails?" I said.

He grinned and I grinned, and then I swung away and moved on.

The crew lounge was aft of the staterooms, tucked away near the prayer room, which had now been firmly locked. It was a kind of small stateroom in itself, with comfortable seats, a little table, a magazine rack, and a small fridge for cold drinks. Just in case Fourrier's gossipy suspicions were well-founded after all, I knocked on the door.

No answer.

I knocked again.

Same thing—silence.

I pushed, and the door opened.

Second Officer Jake Larkin was on the floor, quite dead. So was Rita Schmidt. The airplane was more than a flying hearse now. It was a flying morgue.

CHAPTER SEVEN

Next in seniority to Rita Schmidt, Bernard Fourrier was now the purser and chief flight attendant, and he was rattling around in the job. I winced as he stood at the crew lounge trying to assign tasks concerning the removal of the bodies and the necessary cleanup, unable to make firm decisions and changing his mind every few seconds about just who was to do what, and how they were supposed to do it.

Dr. Fayez had been summoned again. He told us what we already knew—that Jake Larkin and Rita Schmidt were indeed dead. In Larkin's case, he went into his usual song and dance about a small-caliber bullet in the medulla oblongata. Rita Schmidt's death had been brought about by other means, however. Dr. Fayez confirmed what I'd already guessed when I'd seen her bluish, speckled face with its eyes popping, tongue hanging out—a sight that made me gag, I have to confess. She, Dr. Fayez said sagely, had been strangled.

In *Alice in Wonderland,* when there's a big hassle among the people, Lewis Carroll describes it as "alarums and excursions." I'm not sure what alarums and excursions are, but I think they're what went on all over the airplane after the discovery of these two additional bodies. The gamut of reactions ran from stunned to hysterical. Even the usually unflappable Jimmy Stewart came out of his stateroom, grabbed my arm, and said, "Uh, sorry to—uh—bother you,

George, but—uh—just what in the heck is going on, anyway?" I told him I wished I knew.

Captain Fowler made another announcement over the loudspeaker system, explaining honestly and briefly what had happened and urging everybody to be calm. It was like saying a cobra was loose in the plane somewhere, only don't worry. Roly-poly Minister Jabala twirled his eyes and fussed at Mike, demanding that security measures be tightened and blubbering that the prince had to be protected at all costs.

"If that's what you want," said Mike, "let 'em land this thing at the nearest airport and take *everybody* off!"

"No, no, no!" said Jabala. "That is quite impossible!"

"Then stop bugging me, and let me see what I can do, okay?"

Jabala retreated, quivering and sighing.

I found Florence sitting with Lisa Garcia, and I doubted they'd been talking about women's fashions, but they were apparently getting along quite well; I gathered they'd known each other back in Qram. I apologized for interrupting and told Florence Mike had called a council of war in the executive office, and she was needed there.

Ken Dilworth was in the office when we arrived. He was on the horn with his old man again.

Carter Dilworth's voice seemed to make the speaker jump. "This is too much!" he was saying. "Four murders, for God's sake! And that's not all. Somebody in our P.R. section didn't get the word and leaked the whole story to the press. They're making it sound like it's all our fault!"

"I'm sorry about that, Dad," said Ken, "but we're doing the best we can."

"Look," said Dilworth, "I got a call from the Secretary of State himself. He said he didn't want to *order* me to let that airplane come in without stopping, bodies or no bodies, but he'd sure appreciate it if I would. So I'm going to go along with that, but it makes it doubly important that you zero in on the assassin and restore a little passenger comfort, security, and peace of mind."

"If you'll stop bending my ear I'll get to work on it," said Ken.

92

"You just better get some results, that's all I've got to say," grumbled Dilworth.

Ken signed off and looked at the rest of us helplessly.

"Ken," said Mike, "don't take this the wrong way, but I want to kick this around a little with George and Florence on a confidential basis. Maybe some State Department secrets will be involved, and the fewer who know about them, the better. Can we have the office to ourselves for a while?"

Ken hesitated and frowned a little, but then said, "Okay. It's your job. Go ahead and do it your way."

After Ken had left, Mike said, "The kid's all right. He'll make a good executive. Maybe better than his old man, who doesn't seem to want to delegate responsibility."

"Well," I said, "now that you've got the responsibility, what are you going to do with it?"

"Patience," said Mike. "As much as we have time for, anyway. Where the hell's Hibner? I want him in on this."

"In his seat, maintaining a low profile," said Florence. "Shall I fetch him?"

"If you don't mind. And thanks."

When Florence had disappeared down the stairwell, Mike leaned back in his seat, his hands clasped behind his neck, his elbows winged out, and said, "I can't go over the background information until the FBI sends it. Which ought to be any minute, but let's not depend on it. What I'd like to do, meanwhile, is interview as many people as I can who saw Rita Schmidt and Jake Larkin go aft. We can assume Rita was following Jake. Maybe somebody was following them. Maybe somebody noticed. You can learn a lot, sometimes, canvassing bystanders."

"Okay. How do you pick them out?"

"Let's do it quietly. Let's get one of the stews to serve some pineapple juice or something and casually sound them out, one by one. If somebody says they saw Rita or Jake, she can ask them to report here. It means we'll have to trust somebody and assume *they're* not a suspect, but I think we can take that small risk. The strangling gives us an indication there. It would take somebody pretty strong and powerful — probably a man. So let's go to somebody pretty weak and unpowerful and female. The young lady who found Kebir's body. What's her name?"

"Mary Lou Carmichael. Though she doesn't look exactly weak."

"Well, you know what I mean. After we see if Hibner's got any ideas, we'll give her the assignment."

"Do you really think you're going to get anywhere with all this?" I asked. "Wouldn't it be better if we just went on in to L.A. and let them quarantine everybody, or whatever they want to do, and then conduct a proper investigation?"

"It may go that way if I can't come up with something," he said sadly. "All that fuss and delay for everybody, and a bunch of lawsuits afterward, maybe? And every cop in the country laughing up his sleeve at how Mike Corby, who was supposed to be a hot-dog detective, let a bunch of murders get committed right under his nose? They're all jealous because I got to be an actor. They shouldn't be though. Being an actor's not all that great. Not for me, anyway. Besides, I happen to be working for the airline now—the same as under contract. When I work for somebody I like to do a good job."

"All right," I said. "You've made your point. Don't hammer it into the ground."

By this time, Florence came up the stairs again with Lowell Hibner in tow. He smiled at us, took a seat on the corner of the desk, and began to fill his pipe again. It would be nice, I was thinking, if he never did manage to get it lit.

"We seem to have a massacre on our hands now, gentlemen," he said. "Do you know, I was almost afraid of it."

"Why?" asked Mike. "Do you suspect a motive or something?"

"Only a wild theory," said Hibner, "which could, of course, be wrong. But try this for size. The assassin is a terrorist, maybe with one of these Arab splinter groups that seem to proliferate in the Middle East. He can't get to the prince—if, indeed, that's his primary objective—so he does what terrorists always do. He spreads terror. It serves as a kind of warning. He knocks off people at random, and, while that seems senseless, it's no more bizarre than fanatics

94

shooting up a bunch of Israeli athletes at the Olympic Games or killing assorted diplomats in various world capitals. It's practically become an international sport. Kill and let 'em know you were there. Like a tomcat peeing on a door."

"If that's it," said Mike thoughtfully, "it narrows the field. We're looking for an Arab."

Hibner shook his head. "Not necessarily. They're not the only ethnic or political group that breeds terrorist organizations. The Germans, the Irish, the Japanese, American antiestablishment types, even the KGB. Those bastards'll do anything."

"Like the CIA?" Mike smiled.

"Yeah, we can get pretty raw, too." Hibner admitted blandly. "Or could, in the old days. But remember, the prince is on our side. There would be no advantage to us, whatsoever, to give him a hard time. Quite the opposite."

"Well, maybe you've got something," said Mike, "but before we do too much theorizing let's lay out a few more facts. Right now I'm wondering about this sudden departure from the M.O. The first three shot in back of the head. Not Rita Schmidt."

"That is disturbing," said Hibner, nodding with agreement. "Why would the killer strangle her—which is difficult and messy—when he had a very efficient *modus operandi* all worked out and even field-tested?"

"At first glance that would imply a second killer," said Mike. "But the bodies were found together, and we know that both were murdered at about the same time. There could be a much simpler explanation for that than two killers. It would also tell us more about the weapon that was used."

"I'm listening." Some people get a reputation for being wise by merely looking wise—as though they're way ahead of you—and I wondered if that was what Hibner was doing now.

"We can be sure the gun had a silencer, and a very effective one. No one heard shots or even a sharp pop! like a silencer makes. The best silenced weapon would be a single-shot firearm. No cylinder, no apertures for the gas to escape and make noise. Probably specially made for the purpose of assassination. If so, the killer couldn't use it on Rita Schmidt because he'd already used it on Jake Larkin and didn't have time to reload. And that suggests that Rita Schmidt walked in on him, saw what he'd done, and had to be eliminated quickly."

"I like it," said Hibner, nodding. "It also begins to characterize the killer. Possibly a professional assassin. At the very least, someone who's had some training in the darker arts. There are all kinds of places where that's available for terrorists. Cuba, Libya, Rumania, Moscow itself— you name it. How to do it yourself and where to get the tools for it."

"Which, more than ever, makes it political," said Mike. "And, to me, somehow connected with Prince Ibrahim. We know somebody tried to blow him up at the airport. Here, on the plane, he'd be very vulnerable for a second attempt."

"Then why has the killer gone after these other people instead of the prince himself?"

"For practice? Like taking a few swings with your club before you hit the golf ball?" Mike smiled to show that he knew what he was saying was absurd.

"That one I don't like too much," said Hibner, matching his smile.

Mike looked at Florence. "You're the expert on Qram politics. Is there anything we don't know that might explain some of this?"

"No. If the victims, like Kebir, had all been associated with the government, we might suspect that the prince himself wanted them out of the way for one reason or another. If not the prince, Jabala. He doesn't run things altogether, but he does take care of all the nuts and bolts. And he and the prince don't always see eye to eye. Jabala tends to be somewhat isolationist, in spite of his affability to foreigners. Ibrahim accepts all the gift horses gladly, Jabala looks them in the mouth. He's far from being a Marxist, but he wouldn't mind making alliances with some of the other Arab countries that have drifted to the left. The prince won't allow it; he's in love with the free world and its airplanes. To say nothing of its women."

"His wife is Arab, isn't she?"

"Yes. One of these arranged marriages when they were both in their early teens. He lost interest in her when she produced a couple of daughters instead of sons. As a matter of fact, she seems to have lost interest in herself. She's gone to fat and doesn't care about anything anymore. You never see her at official functions. She's home, watching TV and stuffing herself with chocolates. That's her way of life, and she prefers it."

"Maybe I'd better have a talk with Jabala," said Mike, frowning.

"I doubt he'll tell you anything," said Florence.

"Maybe not. But I can watch the way he twitches. I've got a built-in lie detector."

Mike phoned Jabala in the master stateroom he and the doctor shared with the prince. With some reluctance, he agreed to meet Mike briefly in the bar-and-lounge area. There were no drinks this time; Abdul, the bartender, was told to take the scimitar nose somewhere and powder it. Mike invited Hibner to take part in the interview, but Hibner reminded Mike he was undercover, even from Jabala. I don't know why Mike invited me. He was used to having me around by now, I guess. My role was that of some St. Bernard dog who is supposed to just stand there wagging its tail. It was okay, I told myself, but I didn't really like it.

Yakub Seif al-Jabala, looking a little like the Michelin Tire man, lowered himself into a comfortable chair and showed that rubbery smile that didn't match his tungsten eyes.

"We're not sure of anything yet, your excellency," said Mike, "but we feel that the murderer aboard this airplane is most likely someone from Qram, or at least from some other country in the Middle East."

"Are you stereotyping again, Mr. Corby? If there's been violence an Arab is responsible for it? I might point to your

97

own crime rate in the United States. In Qram City, you know, it's safe to walk the streets at night."

"For tourists, maybe." And then, almost to himself, "As long as they don't end up in hotel rooms with whump-whump fans. As for his highness, even this private airplane of his isn't entirely safe. Someone aboard may be politically motivated either to spread terror or to go after the prince himself. Because of Rod Larrabee, I can't even rule out those in the movie company. But you invited some others along for the ride—Kebir, for example. I understand the prince fired him, and that might have given him a motive to make trouble for the prince."

Jabala shook his head. "Two businessmen—Tawfik and Masudi. Their prosperity depends on the prince's policies. A cook from the palace, one Gaddoumi, who's going to see his son in the States, where he's studying to be a geologist. His highness has always been very kind to the household help. Khaled, who is one of the ulama, is a scholar, an interpreter of Islamic law. We don't have priests, per se, as you do, but you can think of him as a kind of chaplain. I, personally, can vouch for the complete loyalty of all these people. It would be absurd to think of them as terrorists or assassins."

"In a murder investigation," said Mike, "you don't dismiss anybody as a possible suspect. At least, not in the beginning."

"I am quite familiar with police procedure, Mr. Corby," said Jabala. "But I'm not so sure now that you're the one to be investigating this matter, in spite of your reputation. This is not meant as a criticism of your professional abilities, but one of our own secret police—who understands our culture—would be better. Unfortunately, we didn't think to take any of them aboard. It was all done in such haste, as you know."

"I've met your secret police," Mike said, "back at the hospital."

"That was unfortunate. You must understand, they had their orders."

98

"Yeah. Like the one who tossed my room at the hotel, maybe."

"I beg your pardon?"

There's a funny take good comedians use. A character is trying to pretend he's innocent in a situation where obviously he is not. Jabala now looked like Dom DeLuise doing just that. And I could see now what Mike meant by having a built-in lie detector.

"Somebody went through all my things. They didn't take anything valuable, but they seemed to be looking for the film in my camera. Now why would anybody want anything like that?"

"I assure you," said Jabala, "I haven't the faintest idea what you're talking about."

"Let it drop," said Mike. "The next problem I want to talk to you about is the weapon. Obviously special-purpose. Small-caliber, with a silencer, and possibly single-shot. No search to detect it when we came aboard. Now, it's possible that the killer has it in his possession, but it strikes me as even more probable he stashes it somewhere when he isn't using it. It would be hard to conceal, I think, in ordinary clothes, and he wouldn't want to risk being found with the thing on his person. That means it's on the airplane somewhere. I want to organize a search and see if we can't find it."

"Very well," said Jabala, "go ahead and do that."

"The master stateroom will have to be searched, too."

Jabala's frown filled his face with accordion folds. "I'm afraid, Mr. Corby, that will be out of the question. The prince is not to be disturbed in the slightest. This is Dr. Fayez's order, not mine."

"Then let me talk to Dr. Fayez about it."

Jabala shrugged. "If you wish."

"The prince is still okay, isn't he? There's nothing in that stateroom you're trying to hide, is there?"

"I believe I resent that, Mr. Corby," said Jabala, puffing with dignity. "The prince will be seen by a great many people after we land and it would be foolish for us to conceal anything about his condition. On the contrary, we will issue press releases from the hospital once we get him there."

"As long as you're ready to open up, then—just what is his condition?"

"Grave. There's a fragment from the bomb blast still in his skull. At the moment, according to Dr. Fayez, it is not doing serious damage, but it could migrate—even a centimeter or so—with what effect only Allah knows. This is why we cannot allow the delay of a landing en route."

"You could have made a shorter trip. There must be good neurosurgeons in Europe."

"We considered that. But the prince owns the Pilgrimage Hospital in Los Angeles, and the advantages of that far outweigh the slighter risk of a few more hours in the air. He will be much more comfortable, much more secure. We will be in complete control. There will even be a villa available—a place he owns on the coast of northern California—for his convalescence afterward. It may be rather an extended convalescence. There's some indication that he may also need some plastic surgery. That's the entire story, Mr. Corby, and I hope it satisfies your suspicious mind."

Mike shrugged. "I figure I rub you the wrong way, Mr. Jabala. Can't be helped. It goes with the territory."

"Are you finished with your interrogation now?"

"Back at NYPD," said Mike, with a slow smile, "we never called it interrogation. We just said interview. There's a difference."

"Let's not play word games," said Jabala. "To be quite frank, my only interest in allowing you to continue your investigation is the possibility that by identifying the murderer you may eliminate any danger to his highness. Otherwise, I would wait until we land and let the proper authorities take over."

"That's what might happen," said Mike. "But the very fact that I'm snooping around ought to make the murderer pull his horns in. So it doesn't hurt, and might do some good. Can I count on your cooperation?"

"It is in Allah's hands," said Jabala, wriggling to his feet.

After Jabala had left, Mike and I headed for the executive office on the upper deck again. As we made our way to the stairs, I said to Mike, "What do you think?"

"About Jabala? Hard to say. He'd rather have his own secret police handling this, I'm sure. Probably they'd round everybody up and beat hell out of 'em till somebody talked. I guess that's one way to do it."

"I noticed he wouldn't commit himself," I said. "When you asked him if he'd cooperate, he just ducked the question."

"That only proves he's a politician. Or do you call a politician a statesman at his level? There was only one time I felt he was lying, and that was when I mentioned the prowler in my hotel room. Now I could be wrong. The polygraph isn't considered one-hundred percent reliable, and that's why it's not admissible in court. The same goes for my hunches."

"Why would they want the pictures you took, anyway?"

Mike shrugged. "To study, I guess. For intelligence purposes. Like, if I'd caught some of the crowd and they could pick out the face of a known subversive."

"Then why wouldn't they just ask you for the pictures?"

"Could be they're so used to conspiracy they have to do everything the hard way. I've known thieves like that. They could afford to buy a pack of cigarettes but they'd rather steal it. And speaking of those pictures, I wonder what Florence did with them. I forgot to ask."

"Maybe they'll tell us something pretty soon," grumbled Mike. "Time's running out."

Florence was at the computer console as we emerged from the stairwell and turned into the office space. Part of the computer gear was a printer, much like a typewriter without keys, from which sheets of paper, stacked in folds, were emerging. She had ripped off several already printed and was holding them in her hand. "The FBI came through," she said.

"Good." Mike came forward. "Anything juicy?"

Florence frowned with discomfort. "I feel like a peeping tom. Most of the names we submitted aren't in their files, but there are one or two I wish I hadn't seen. A certain actor arrested on a drug charge before he became prominent. Your unit manager once found guilty of income-tax evasion. You'd better be sure the gossip press never lays eyes on this."

"We'll shred and burn after we study it," said Mike. "I don't like prying, either, but it's got to be done."

"There's one I wish you'd burn right away."

"Yeah?" Mike sat at the desk.

"This one." Florence put a sheet of paper down in front of him and pointed to one of the entries. I could see, without reading closely, that whenever one of the names had produced an arrest record several paragraphs had been appended to it, along with cabalistic file numbers and initials that had meaning only for professional law enforcement personnel.

Mike swiftly read the paragraph she'd indicated, then looked up and said, "What do you know!"

"Too much," said Florence. "I wish I didn't."

He looked at me, though there was a blankness in his eyes that showed he was really talking to himself. "Lisa Garcia. Convicted of prostitution. Sentence suspended, one year probation. Well, it could be worse. And it doesn't seem to have much to do with political assassination."

"Mike," said Florence earnestly, "I hope you'll make sure Ken Dilworth doesn't find out about this. You know how it is between him and Lisa."

"Don't worry. Unless, of course, it turns out Lisa's got some connection with the murders, which is pretty doubtful. I had no intention of showing anybody else this list, anyway."

"The hell of it is," said Florence, "that Ken might find out about it some other way—sometime in the future. I don't know how he'll react, but that old man of his is bound to hit the ceiling."

Mike shrugged. "That's their business."

"My business, too, I think," she said. "Lisa's my friend and that makes it my business."

"You want my advice? Stay out of it."

"I don't think I can. I'm going to talk to Lisa."

"Don't say I didn't warn you," said Mike. "Anyway, we've got more important things to worry about. And before I forget, whatever happened to those pictures of mine you were going to have developed?"

Florence laughed.

"What's so funny?" asked Mike.

"Every one a blank," said Florence. "You must have forgotten to set the film speed properly."

"Sonofabitch!"

"I thought that's what you'd say," said Florence.

CHAPTER EIGHT

We'd been flying for hours, but now the dawn was just catching up with us. We could begin to see the peach-colored flushing outside the starboard windows. With so many people indulging in international air travel these days, I guess just about everybody has an idea of elementary global navigation, but just in case you don't know, this might be a good place to explain it. Although our destination was west, we were heading, at first, in a more or less northerly direction, across Europe, then the North Atlantic, and after that the upper part of Canada, where, eventually, we'd curve back down into the States again. This is called a great circle route and, on a globe, it's the shortest distance between any two points. Put a rubber band around an orange at maximum stretch and you'll see what I mean.

So clock time didn't match sun time and it was throwing everybody out of kilter. Some of the passengers were accepting a meal and some were trying to sleep and some were reading or listening to music on the stereo system and some were just staring. *Everyone* was uneasy.

I was in the executive office with Mike, yawning, and trying to keep up with him. He'd been going over the FBI records, which didn't seem to tell us anything, and he'd also been quietly interviewing several passengers Mary Lou Carmichael had dug up after learning they'd noticed Jake Larkin going aft with Rita Schmidt following him. They all saw it in passing and were unable to add to what we already knew or assumed. It had been quite normal, as far as they were concerned, for two of the crew members to drift down the aisles and disappear somewhere in the rear.

Mike glanced at the computer. "Where the hell's that stuff from Interpol? They're dragging their asses."

"Maybe we should have had Florence ask the State Department to put pressure on them, too."

"I don't think it would have done much good. Bureaucrats are bureaucrats in any language. If there's a time-consuming way to do it, they'll find it. Where the hell *is* Florence, anyway?"

"On the main deck, talking to Lisa Garcia."

"Oh. Well, that's Florence for you, I guess. She really gets concerned about her friends. You'd never know she has troubles of her own."

"Has she?"

"She's at loose ends, the same as I am," said Mike. "Originally, she gave up her job with State to get married, and her husband wasn't too bad a guy, but his values were back in the last century. To him, a wife was somebody who stayed home, barefoot and pregnant. Well, she didn't get pregnant, and she wouldn't take her shoes off. One thing, as they say, led to another, and finally they agreed to call it quits. She got her old job back and made like a career woman, plunging into it deep. But now she's not sure that's what she really wants, either. We get along great and we really like each other, but she's been burnt once and is afraid to let it go too far. Meanwhile, I'm attracted to her—maybe more than just that—but I keep thinking about Meredy."

"Sounds like you're both a couple of mixed-up kids," I said.

"I know," sighed Mike. "It's what we've got in common."

Florence Haverman was indeed down on the main deck, talking to Lisa. And once more I've got to reconstruct, rather than give you an eyewitness account.

Lisa listened very quietly while Florence, with enough tact to have elevated her to ambassador status then and there, told her what she knew. Lisa, I had noticed, had a way of remaining cool whenever the heat was on—literally or figuratively—and that was part of her almost unreal beauty.

"I knew it would have to come out sometime," she said. "I really knew that all along."

"What happened, anyway? Did you get caught in something, like the bird who flew into a badminton game?"

"Thanks for giving me an out," said Lisa. "But the fact is, I was exactly what that record says. Shall we say prostitute? Somehow that sounds a little nicer than whore."

"I can't believe it!"

"Well, I didn't walk the streets in high boots and short pants, if that's the image you're getting. I was a call girl, Florence, and a pretty exclusive one, though I'm not saying that to excuse it. You know, sometimes one of the johns would ask how a nice girl like me ever got into it, but I'd never give him a decent answer because it was such a long story. And I can't point to any one day or moment when I said to myself, 'Enough of this rat race, I'm going to hit the pavement.' I'd grown up in what sociologists call a slum environment, but my parents pinched pennies to send me to this parochial school where some really good nuns took the rough edges off. Sister Veronica was especially good; she was crazy about the theater and she was into diction and how to dress and how to walk with books on your head, and that sort of thing. I thought I'd be an actress or maybe a model, but you've no idea how tough that is to break into."

"The way you look, Lisa," said Florence, "I would have thought somebody would have snapped you up right away."

"You need more than looks. You've got to be ready for the breaks, of course, but you need luck to get them. You decide on a given day to see one modeling agency instead of another, and, according to luck, you either get the key assignment that would start the ball rolling or you miss out on it. Take Candy Vandermeer. She's phenomenal. Absolutely exquisite beauty and a tremendous I.Q. to go along with it. But for every Vandermeer who makes it—

deservedly—there are nine other very smart and beautiful gals somewhere who didn't make it. Top model, and now a movie star. She played her cards right or someone played them for her. I'm not taking anything away from her and I'm not giving myself anything I'm not entitled to. I'm just explaining how it is."

"I know that," said Florence. "But I still wonder how it happened."

Lisa told her how it had happened, matter-of-factly, and without a trace of self-pity. For a while she'd worked at whatever job she could get: waitress, stacking fruit in a supermarket, selling dresses in a boutique. She'd kept trying to break into modeling or the theater on the side, getting a few jobs now and then, but nothing to lead to fame and fortune, let alone a living. Meanwhile, she had what to most people in this day and age is regarded as a normal sex life. There were boyfriends, and she enjoyed them. Some, she supposed, fell in love with her, and she got quite fond of a few, but none was the guy she wanted to spend the rest of her life with. And she told herself that if she ever did get married, that would be it. Rest of her life, till death did the partners part. That much of her remained old-fashioned.

"Then one time," she continued, "I went out on a double date with this importer who was a friend of a friend or something like that. Early thirties and on his way to his first million. Nice-looking, nice guy all around. He was lonely that night and so was I. I didn't usually let a first date go all the way, but this time I thought what the hell. We'd been together for hours anyway and I thought I knew him. It turned out he thought he knew me, too, only what he thought he knew was wrong. He ducked out of the hotel room early and when I woke up there was a big wad of cash and a note of thanks on the night table."

"You kept it, I hope," said Florence, smiling. "As you say—what the hell."

"Oddly enough, I tried to return it. And I thought of giving him a good swift kick you-know-where when I did. I was furious. But I couldn't track him down right away, and, as it happened, my father had just lost his job at the

107

parking lot and really needed some extra money. Time passed and I managed to forget the whole thing. Things got worse at home—the unemployment compensation ran out. Things weren't too good with me, either; it's expensive keeping yourself looking like a model. Suddenly somebody called me, said he was a friend of the importer, in town, lonely, and all that, and that his friend had said I could take care of that sort of thing. I was down to my last dollar and fifty cents, which, in the places I was going to in order to be seen, is what a cup of coffee costs. Okay, just this once, I told myself. I met the guy, saw he was quite decent, and decided just this once."

"You don't have to tell me the rest," said Florence. "Just this once turned into a lot of times."

"Right," said Lisa. "It got easier and easier. And it paid one hell of a lot more than putting bananas on the shelves."

"But how on earth did you ever run afoul of the law?"

"That was one of the really rotten breaks. I was seeing this john I thought was in the shipping business. I guess he was, at that—for a front. It turned out he was mob-connected and there was a warrant out on him. They busted in on us at a most embarrassing time. The way they were grinning I thought at first they were going to ask us not to mind them and go on with the show. Well, there was a big vice crackdown on at the time and I guess they felt they had to slap me with something, too. That turned out to be what you saw: one year, sentence suspended."

Florence sighed. "It could be worse, I suppose. And you're not the only one who has a criminal record. You'd be surprised at some of the people on that list we got."

"It wouldn't mean a thing ordinarily. But now I've met Ken."

"He's the one you've been looking for all along?"

"Don't ask me how these things happen. Chemical, electrical, some kind of magic—who knows? He's not suave or sophisticated or even remarkably handsome, but he's the one. I'm in love with him—whatever the hell love is. It surprises me, too."

"I'd say he's a pretty good catch."

"He is—but that's not it. I'd feel the same about him if he were still a baggage handler with not much prospect of ever being anything else."

"I believe you. The man *I'm* thinking about right now is no Robert Redford. But he has other virtues. As I'm sure Ken has. Among them, I imagine, tolerance and the capacity to forgive. What you've been through really calls for forgiveness."

"I wish it were that simple," said Lisa.

"Isn't it?"

Lisa turned her head and looked directly into Florence's eyes. Lisa's lovely eyes, almost purple, didn't blink. "What do you think I was doing in the palace?" she asked.

"Oh," said Florence.

And now, as Lisa continued, Florence kept telling herself, Of course, of course—should have known it all the time. Somebody had procured Lisa Garcia for his highness, Prince Ibrahim, Lion of the Desert, etcetera, etcetera, when he'd been in New York, and there had been a lot of secrecy about that, too, right from the start. The prince had become more or less smitten with Lisa, which made him not much different from ninety percent of the male population of the rest of the world. It was as though he'd come across a custom-made Rolls Royce that was just a little different and in most respects a lot better than any he'd ever seen before. He had to have it for his own.

The elaborate cover story was created: Lisa was to pose as a kind of governess for the prince's daughters, to teach them to walk with books on their heads and use makeup and sit with their pretty legs crossed properly. To strengthen the illusion, she actually worked at that; only a handful of Ibrahim's chief advisors knew why she was really there. His fat wife wasn't told about it, but she probably guessed. The palace was a pretty big city, you could carry on all sorts of clandestine activities. It had to be kept secret from the good citizens of Qram, of course; if they knew what was going on they'd stop thinking of their beloved ruler worshipfully.

"I had everything I'd ever wanted," Lisa reminisced,

her eyes getting dreamy. "Clothes, jewels, servants, fabulous surroundings. It was even fun teaching the young princesses. When the prince wanted me to sneak into his quarters for the night it wasn't all that bad. He was a nice guy, and even an adequate lover. But for all this, I was a prisoner."

"Couldn't you guess beforehand it would be that way?" asked Florence.

"Oh, I think I had an idea it might," said Lisa. "But for a long time I'd been thinking about getting out of the business I was in. You don't stay young forever, you know. A few wrinkles only I know about are starting to show. I'm not sure what I wanted to do instead—open up a string of boutiques, maybe. Whatever it was, it would require a stake. If I were underfinanced, I'd be on the phone making dates with johns again. I figured I'd make this one my last big trick, and come out of it with enough to start a new life. That was my original intention, anyway."

"And what happened?"

"The days and weeks went by and after a while I knew it wasn't working out the way I'd thought it would. When you're a prisoner you want to climb the walls, no matter how luxurious they are. I told Ibrahim honestly how I felt, and the funny thing was he seemed to understand. Maybe he was getting a little tired of his Rolls Royce now that he'd played with it enough—I don't know. Anyway, he said go in good health, maybe we'll meet again sometime."

He had set her up in a luxurious apartment in the city until such time as she could decide firmly on her future plans. She'd been in no hurry; she had agents in the States looking for a suitable business she might buy, and she wasn't sure where it would take her if they found one, so she stayed in place, putting her affairs in order and getting her emotional act together.

Then she met Ken Dilworth.

Stars began to explode unexpectedly.

Florence knew the rest...

"You can't think right when you're in love," said Lisa. "Common sense just becomes a rosy mist. There was a part of me that knew all along Ken had to find out about me someday, but I just shoved that aside. Sometimes I shuddered about meeting his father. Would it turn out I'd met him before? He must have come to New York on occasion. Would I recognize him with his clothes on?"

"That's a long shot," said Florence.

"I've been hit with long shots before," Lisa said. "Anyway, it's one of those secrets that just can't be kept forever. So, in a way, I'm almost glad you saw that arrest record. I know what I have to do now. The rosy mist is gone."

"You're going to tell Ken everything, is that it?"

"Wish me luck," said Lisa.

Jennings Lang, our producer, put his hand on my arm as I headed down the aisle toward a rest room. "George, I've got to talk to you."

"Okay," I said, sitting down beside him.

One of the things about the modern world is that producers don't look like producers anymore. I mean they don't wear hibiscus sports shirts and dark glasses and keep long cigars in the corners of their mouths and talk in a Lower-East-Side accent. That went out with puttees for directors. Jennings could have been the vice president of some oil company on his way back from making a profitable deal with the prince.

"You've been with the *Airport* pictures from the beginning," he said, "so I feel you've got more than just a dollars-and-cents stake in them. I have, too, though I'm certainly not going to turn down any dollars and cents."

"I know," I said. "You don't have to explain it. What's on your mind?"

"The prince—how is he?"

"Still alive, last I heard. Actually, I don't know any more about it than you do."

"But you're working with Mike on this investigation. How much danger do you think he's in?"

"We don't know. These crazy murders may have no connection with the prince. On the other hand, as long as the killer's roaming around, uncaught, everybody on this airplane is in a certain amount of danger."

"If Prince Ibrahim should die," he said, frowning, "we

111

might be stuck with nothing but a lot of exposed film. You see, the arrangement he made was to meet expenses as they came along with countersigned checks from a special account. Which is only prudent from a business standpoint. His own signature, personally. And the trouble is, we've still got a lot of expenses to come. I don't have to tell you about post-production costs and advertising—publicity alone can be fifty percent of the cost, and the film has to gross two-point-four times the cost just to break even. If the prince's well dries up, we'll have to go to the banks, and their interest rates will kill us. Besides, there's no guarantee they'll agree to a loan. It's the same old story. We can point out that no *Airport* picture ever lost money, but all they'll say is, 'Yeah— but how about lately?'"

"What about Universal? They did the other *Airport* pictures."

"A slim possibility. There are some people there who think the *Airport* series has run its course. It's why I had to go to the prince for this one. The bottom line, George, is that everybody's pretty cautious when it comes to handing out millions, and, frankly, I don't blame them."

"You're being reasonable," I said, smiling. "Reasonable guys get caught in the middle where both sides take potshots at them."

"I know," he said with a sigh. "You and Mike take care of the prince, will you?"

"We're trying to take care of everybody. Including you, old pal," I said with an affectionate smile as I left.

When I got back to the executive office, Mike had an arrangement plan of the airplane spread out on the desk in front of him. Probably Ken Dilworth, who kept all sorts of data in his briefcase, had supplied it.

"What we'll do," said Mike, his finger on the plan, "is get somebody to give up their stateroom temporarily and conduct the searches in there, privately. Maybe Jimmy and Gloria Stewart. Hate to do it to them, but they're always so agreeable about everything."

"What search?" I asked.

"A search. Like they do in a jail. I'll frisk the men

112

myself and we can get one of the stewardesses to search the women. Maybe we'd better have two staterooms. That'll make it a lot quicker."

"Mike!" I said. "You can't do that!"

"Got to. This weapon—this single-shot pistol, if that's what it is—is aboard the airplane somewhere. We'd be overlooking one of our best bets if we didn't try to find it."

"But if he knows he's going to be searched, the murderer's going to be damned sure not to have it on him!"

"Right," said Mike calmly. "So this forces his hand to stash it somewhere, if he hasn't done so already. And gives us a better chance of finding it when we toss the rest of the airplane."

"Do you know how many places there are on this airplane to hide something like that? Mike," I said, "why can't you make like Peter Ustinov as Hercule Poirot and just let your little gray cells do all the work?"

"From him, I'll take acting lessons," said Mike. "But not instructions on how to be a detective."

Acting Purser Bernard Fourrier, popping up from the top of the stairs, now came into the executive office. I'd noticed before that he was on the swarthy side, but the color of his cheeks was now like the belly of a fresh-caught shark. It made his eyes look larger.

"M'sieurs!"

Mike looked up. "Yeah, what is it?"

"It is better that you come with me and see for yourself."

"No it isn't. It's better you speak up."

"I insist, m'sieurs."

"Oh, for Christ's sake," said Mike, rising.

From the way we bustled aft on the main deck, with Fourrier leading the way, those passengers who weren't sleeping must have sensed that something was wrong. I certainly knew something was wrong, and I was trying to tell myself it didn't have to be what I thought. Like hoping the ax will turn out to be rubber, even as it's falling—

He took us to one of the lavatories in the rear, which, because it was in an island side by side with two others, wasn't visible from the seats. He opened its door and stood aside. We looked.

The lavatory was pretty small. Muhanna, the prince's bodyguard, was pretty big, and was folded there within the narrow space, more or less in the fetal position. The usual blood-ringed, powder-blackened hole was between his shaven skull and his thick neck in back. I say that as though I was getting used to it. Believe me, I wasn't . . .

CHAPTER NINE

Before she died, Rita Schmidt had made much of having an experienced crew of flight attendants under her. The crew of Prince Ibrahim's airplane, *The Star of Qram,* as he called it, was getting the kind of experience now that wasn't in the manuals of WIA or any other airline. They were learning exactly what to do when a murdered corpse was found aboard. They were almost getting efficient at it.

Once more, Dr. Fayez was summoned to put his medical stamp of approval on the obvious. I had no idea what the procedure concerning a death certificate was supposed to be; I didn't care, and I don't think Dr. Fayez did, either. Ultimate responsibility for handling the mess rested at least temporarily with Captain Fowler as the airplane commander. He accepted his responsibility with the deepest of frowns, clearly wishing to get back to flying the airplane without interruption or distraction. Both young Ken Dilworth and Mike were on hand to carry the bucket of worms—which was getting heavier all the time.

Muhanna, as heavy as a beached whale, was carried back into the cargo space and laid out there, wrapped in a blanket, with the other corpses. It was a shadowy space back there, with crates on pallets secured to the floor; presumably they contained the personal effects the prince always took along whenever he traveled. In his opulent way, what he regarded as personal effects were what anybody else would have seen as a full set of household goods. The

115

crates were dogged down with ropes tied to rings on the floor, and now so were the corpses. One could go back among the crates, if one wished, but now, with all the bodies in place, the cargo compartment had turned into an eerie tomb, like those I'd seen in Egypt when we shot *Death on the Nile*, and I had no desire to explore it, not even with a guide holding a flickering torch leading the way.

"Ladies and gentlemen," Fowler said on the loud-speaker system, "there has been another unfortunate incident, but let me assure you immediately that it does not affect the operational safety of the airplane, and that we are still on course and will land quite safely at our destination. For the time being, however, I must ask you to remain in your seats or in your staterooms. This is only a routine precaution to enable us to continue our investigation."

He identified the victim and told where the body had been found, and was—wisely, I thought—generally open and aboveboard about it, delivering this information calmly and casually so the passengers would feel that everything was under control. Of course, it wasn't.

In the executive office I stared at Mike with what was probably a stupid expression and said, "Now what?"

"No change in plan," he said. "All Muhanna's death tells us is that our pigeon is still doing business at the same old stand. It doesn't tell us why, who he is, or how long he intends to keep this up. I wish to hell it did."

"What are we supposed to do—just get used to it?"

"Well, we shouldn't panic. Though I can see where some of the passengers must be on the verge of it. The antidote to that is to give everybody something to do. I've got the flight attendants lining everybody up to be body searched right now."

"I don't think they're gonna like it," I said.

"So I make a few more enemies," said Mike. "At least they won't be the kind who'll want to kill me for it."

"Don't even be too sure of that," I said.

Which was another dumb remark on my part, I suppose, but somehow I always feel better if I get the tag line.

All the male passengers, as Mike directed, came into

116

the executive office one by one, where he had them strip to their skivvies while he searched their clothes. The reactions ranged from flaming resentment to grinning good humor. Stubby Dawson, after stripping, struck a couple of body-building poses and said, to no one in particular, "Any girls on the beach?...No?...Okay." Then somehow, his whole physique seemed to collapse, his belly popped out, and he stood in front of us like a total schlemiel.

While this was going on, several of the stewardesses checked all the carry-on baggage, making the necessary apologies, but nevertheless being firm. They also managed to explore the overhead storage compartments and some of the other nooks and crannies throughout the seating section on the main deck. The rest of the airplane would be searched later, but, meanwhile, they were getting this much of it out of the way.

As Mike had anticipated, Jimmy and Gloria Stewart graciously vacated their stateroom for a while, so the women could be searched in there. Gloria, seeing the necessity of this decided inconvenience, insisted on being first. Florence and Mary Lou Carmichael frisked the females and, at Mike's embarrassed suggestion, even searched each other. Bernard Fourrier, after he had been searched, hung around outside the Stewart stateroom, looking fussy and distressed, and when Blossom Foster and Candy Vandermeer went in for their turn he almost went up into a flying spiral like the coyote in those Road Runner cartoons. I could hardly believe that he hoped for a glimpse of one of these magnificent beauties in their undies, or less, but that was how it seemed. Let's give him the benefit of the doubt. Let's say he was just as flipped as the rest of us by all that had happened and unable to keep his cool—of which he had never had very much.

The search, as Mike had predicted, produced neither the weapon we were looking for nor anything else of significance. We did dig up one small bag of marijuana and a tiny envelope of cocaine, but if you think I'm going to tell you who they belonged to you've got rocks in your head. None of the big stars, anyway.

The search ate up time as we flew along and, to a degree, achieved its purpose of getting the passengers' minds off the danger of having a mad assassin aboard. When we'd checked off the last name on the list, Mike said to me, "Two more, and that'll be it."

"Two more?"

"Captain Fowler and Flight Engineer O'Malley."

"Now, wait a minute," I said.

"*Everybody*, George. You already searched me and I already searched you. There can't be any exceptions."

"They won't like it."

"Do you think I liked you caressing my fair skin? Or vice versa?"

"No, neither one of us likes our vice versa, but that's not the point."

"Do it my way, George. Please. If even Minister Jabala agreed to a search, so can Fowler and O'Malley."

I recalled how Jabala had glowered and trembled when he'd stripped in the executive office. "I thought he'd explode," I said.

"He did—inside. Go get the pilots, George. Then we'll be finished."

"Look," I said, "if you're being so damned thorough about it, what about the prince himself?"

"I haven't forgotten him. We'll take a good look at his bunk when we search the master stateroom later. Dr. Fayez'll scream, but the least he can do is search the prince with me looking on. Come on, George. The pilots."

"Why don't *you* get them?"

"You're another pilot, George—they'll take it better from you."

"Like hell they will," I said. "If I come back here with my head bitten off you'd better be ready to sew it back on again."

This was a little like testing a Cuisinart with your bare hand, I thought as I went forward into the flight deck and told Fowler what Mike was insisting on. O'Malley just laughed, but Fowler glared at me in furious disbelief, and

118

I kept watching for signs that he was about to attack. He had a look I was familiar with.

"You can tell Corby to go and get lost," Fowler said coldly. "I have to stay here and fly this airplane."

"You left it to go back and look at the bodies," I said. "You've got the auto-pilot and O'Malley."

"Yeah, but that was before we ran into this goddamn jet stream," said Fowler.

"What jet stream?" I asked.

"The one out there," he said, angling his head toward the windshield. "Flight control gave me another altitude, but it doesn't seem to make much difference. And we can't make a major change in course on account of our fuel reserve. I don't have a copilot now, so I have to work it all out myself, the exact trim and throttle setting to keep us from landing on the fumes when we get there. Or gliding in, which this baby won't do."

"I'll work it out for you," said O'Malley.

"Like hell you will," said Fowler. "Like hell anybody will. This calls for more experience than you have. Some of it's not even in all those books you've been studying."

"Captain," I said, "I have every confidence in your ability to put this thing down on its wheels when the time comes. And I know very well how much calculation and pure instinct it's going to take. I can't think of anybody I'd rather have in the left-hand seat under these circumstances. But the search is important, too, and, if it's to have any meaning at all, it has to include everybody. Mike and I have already submitted to it ourselves. It has to do with the passengers' peace of mind—which is certainly your concern. We have to be able to tell them that everybody was searched, including the pilots. Knowing that you both agreed to it will show them that you're perfectly calm and taking these unfortunate murders in stride, like they should be doing. What's more, it's not going to take you away from the flight deck for more than a few minutes. So what do you say, John? How about going along with it?"

* * *

The body frisk we gave Captain Fowler and O'Malley in turn revealed absolutely nothing, except a small tattoo on Fowler's upper arm, about which he seemed embarrassed. Maybe that was why he hadn't wanted to strip in front of us. It was, curiously enough, the Orion insignia of the Fifth Air Force, which had fought both in World War II and in Korea. Fowler wasn't old enough to have been in World War II so I presumed he'd seen action in Korea. I asked him about it.

"Yeah, I was there," he said, scowling. "Young and dumb—that's why I got this tattoo one time on R and R in Tokyo. It was a boring goddamned war as far as I was concerned!"

"Boring?"

"I flew gooney birds on the Itazuke-Pusan run, and sometimes a few flare-dropping missions up around Wonsan to light things up for the Marines when they did the strafing. The old C-47 was a great airplane, but not very exciting. I guess I shouldn't complain, though. Flying transports led to airline work, which calls for a lot more than all this wild-blue-yonder jazz. It was what I couldn't seem to get across to Jake Larkin. Though he's dead now, and I don't want to say anything bad about him. He may have been a fighter ace at heart, but he *was* a helluva good copilot. And I need him in that seat, goddamnit!"

When Fowler had gone back to the flight deck I said to Mike, "I think I know what makes him tick now."

"What?" asked Mike, not terribly interested.

"There he sat, flying twin-engined gooney birds straight and level while all the other guys were out there knocking down MIGs and getting medals. It gave him an inferiority complex which he compensates for by trying to be the best air-going bus driver who ever came down the pike."

"Now you're a shrink," said Mike.

"Every actor is, to a degree," I said. "You've got to know what motivates people."

"Figure out what's motivating our murderer," said Mike. "Do something useful for a change."

"I thought that was your department," I said.

"It is," said Mike. "And I'm working on it. You've heard me sneer at the little-gray-cells approach, but you've got to crank some of that in, too, once in a while. The only trouble is that, right now, all the little gray cells are making nothing more than a bowl of oatmeal. I keep stirring them and stirring them—I know something's there—but I just can't put my finger on it."

I nodded. "More psychology. It's your subconscious trying to tell you something. Why the subconscious never comes up and says what it means, I don't know—but that's the way it is."

"It's something we already heard or saw," said Mike, wrinkling his brow. "Something that went by, and we didn't notice. A pattern, you know what I mean? Something that pulls all the murders together so they make sense. Like Hibner's theory that they were all acts of terrorism. And that may be it, but somehow I don't buy it."

"Think about something else," I said. "Pretend to your subconscious you don't notice what it's doing. That works, sometimes."

"It might work if I had the time. Like when you sleep on a problem and, in the morning, there's the answer. But we've got to come up with something damn soon, or risk never getting these murders solved. That could happen, you know. We land, and they question everybody—for hours, days, weeks, who knows?—and the murderer, with his tracks covered perfectly, gets away with it. The way he's apparently planned, so far, you can be sure he's given some attention to his getaway."

I stared out one of the ports. It was getting light now, and there was woolly cloud cover over the earth far below, as far as the eye could see. We were probably over the North Atlantic, or maybe by now we'd already crossed Greenland. On this flight, the pilot hadn't made cheery little announcements as to where we were and what might be seen below if one had the eyes of an eagle and a window seat.

"I've had another revolting thought," I said.

"Yeah? What?"

"Let's say we land and never do uncover the murderer. Everybody aboard is investigated by the FBI—which probably has jurisdiction—and they have to let them go eventually, but they keep poking. Put a task force on it and keep tabs on everybody who *was* aboard. Tail them, look into their bank accounts, call on their relatives—whatever it is they do. This goes on, maybe for years. Everybody gets more than irritated and blames the airline or the movie company or both. But that's not the worst of it. The parrot cage press picks it up and every week there's a new headline insinuating that this star or that has been newly implicated in the still-unsolved murders. It's likely to drive Jackie Onassis and Liz Taylor right off the front pages of these crummy scandal sheets."

"Wouldn't that be good publicity for the picture?"

"I don't think so. Ira Yoder, our P.R. man for *The Godless,* when we shot it down in Mexico, used to say that the only bad publicity is no publicity at all. But that's a crock, and I don't think Ira believes it himself. This is the kind that could backfire."

"What other sparkling ideas do you have to brighten this lovely morning?"

"That's right," I said, looking outside again. "It is kind of morning, isn't it? I wonder when the hell they're gonna serve breakfast."

"Let's find out," said Mike. "We're not doing any good sitting here."

It was, as I had said, sort of like morning, and the meal they passed out presently was sort of like breakfast. If you like quiche for breakfast. And you know something, folks? Before it was fashionable for real men not to like quiche, I didn't like quiche for breakfast, lunch, or dinner. I didn't enjoy any of it too much, though it filled a hollow place in my stomach that wasn't there only because of hunger.

Mike and I ate in the bar area, where we could continue to talk, and where Mike could get a drink if he wanted one. It turned out he didn't want one, and by that I knew he was still trying to think. From the stewardess who served us we learned that the search of the plane was in full swing. Only a few flight attendants were needed to pass out the quiche which left the rest of them free to poke around. When we were almost finished, Mary Lou Carmichael trotted pertly up to our table and showed us her wide, blue eyes.

"Mr. Jabala wants to see both of you."

Mike's eyebrows rose. "Yeah? Did he say what for?"

"It's so you can search his stateroom. I went there, but they wouldn't let me in. At first he said nobody was going to bother the prince, and I tried to tell him how important it was, and then he made a great big sigh and said okay— only not me. Nobody but Mr. Corby and Mr. Kennedy personally."

"Come on, George," said Mike, rising. "This breakfast is for the dogs, anyway." I couldn't have said it better.

Jabala, looking harried and blubbery, answered our knock in a moment. We stepped into the master stateroom about two-thirds of the way aft in the airplane. It was done up luxuriously, like the bedroom in a particularly expensive mobile home. It had its own washroom and toilet, off to one side, and there was a double-tiered bunk bed against one wall, presumably for Jabala and Dr. Fayez, while Prince Ibrahim himself lay in a queen-size job with its headboard to the outer bulkhead. They had curtained the ports and dimmed the lights, and I had to blink a few times before my eyes became adjusted to the partial gloom.

The prince, with a sheet and blanket up to his chest, was on his back and very, very still, though I thought I could detect a slight rise and fall as he breathed. His head was bandaged and the bandages came halfway down over his face, so that only his chin and finely chiseled lips and hairline mustache were visible. There were eye apertures in the bandage wrapping, and I had the impression that his eyes were closed. On either side of the bed were two metal pole stands, each with an upended bottle and a plastic hose going down to the crook of the prince's arms where, in each arm, an inserted needle was taped in place.

Dr. Fayez, looking like a modern version of Joseph and his coat of many colors, stood near the bed and glowered at us as though *we* were the assassins. Jabala bounced about nervously, apparently ready to change his mind and toss us out on our ears at any moment.

"Is he conscious?" Mike spoke in a near-whisper. Somehow, the occasion called for it.

"He is not sedated, if that is what you mean," said Dr. Fayez, with his supercilious air of special knowledge. "With intracranial injury, you do not sedate. He is sleeping. Which he very much needs. Vitamins and glucose I.V. in one arm, plasma in the other. If we keep him absolutely quiet and move him only when absolutely necessary—which it will be when we transfer him from the airplane—we can hope for a favorable prognosis."

Mike nodded. "Okay, doctor—I get the picture. Now, what I want you to do is get the lousy part of this over with first. I've got to search this stateroom, the way the rest of the plane is being searched. It means looking at everything. Even the prince's person, and under the covers."

"That is ridiculous!" said Jabala, puffing himself up. "Mr. Corby—you are going too far! His highness is the one under attack! What could he possibly be concealing?"

"I'm not saying he is," Mike answered stubbornly. "But this whole thing is so wild I'm not dismissing any possibilities. Unless the search includes everybody and everything it's not a search, and we might as well have never made it."

Dr. Fayez shuffled closer to the prince, as though to protect him. "Mr. Corby, I don't care what you imagine your responsibilities to be, I cannot allow you to touch his highness or come any nearer to him!"

"I know that," said Mike. "That's why you're going to do the frisking. With me watching."

"Frisking? You mean I'm to go over him as though he were some common criminal? Absolutely not! I put him into that bed, Mr. Corby, and I can vouch that nothing is concealed!"

"What you're looking for," said Mike, as though he hadn't heard, "is a small-caliber pistol with a silencer. The way this thing has been going, the killer could have stashed that weapon anywhere. If he's as clever as I think he is, putting it near the prince would be a smart move, precisely because nobody would dare to look for it there."

"No one could have gotten in here," said Jabala, shaking his jowls. "There was someone with the prince at all times. Until Muhanna was killed, he was on guard at the door."

"Are you quite sure of that? The doctor left the room several times to look at the bodies. That left you alone with the prince. You could have ducked into the washroom for a couple of minutes, or something. All he'd need is a few seconds to slip in and tuck the thing away. Try to remember now. Was the door locked when Dr. Fayez was out? *Did* you go to the washroom?"

"Well . . ." Jabala's frown made Michelin Tire rings all over his fat brow.

"So you see, Mr. Jabala," said Mike, "clearing this point up once and for all is as much to your advantage as ours."

Jabala trembled with the agony of coming to his decision. He finally pouted at Fayez and said, "Very well. Do as he asks, doctor."

Dr. Fayez, pale, as though he were committing desecration, gently removed the covers so that we could see Prince Ibrahim's small but trim form stretched out in pajamas. The prince stirred a little and murmured; Jabala said something in Arabic that evidently was meant to be soothing. He slid his hand under the pillows and under the prince's body. He exposed the entire bed, and then, glaring at us angrily, pulled the covers back into place again.

"Thank you," said Mike.

"You haven't heard the last of this, Mr. Corby," said Jabala. "It will be reported to his highness when he's able to listen. I think he will be displeased. I might as well tell you that I was against his going into this motion-picture venture in the first place. It has meant nothing but dealing with a great many troublesome individuals."

"Yeah. Let's toss the rest of the room now," Mike said.

Mike and I sauntered back toward the executive office after we'd searched the entire master stateroom, including the toilet cubicle, and found nothing. I felt that Jabala's glare, as he showed us out of the door again, had given us both a touch of sunburn.

The passengers were eating, sleeping, staring from the windows, or stirring restlessly in their seats. A few looked up at Mike as he passed, as though to ask if there had been any new developments, but he either scowled at them or shook his head, and continued on his way.

He paused at the space at the bottom of the stairs, where we were out of earshot of anyone who might be trying to listen, and said, "George, there's a sour note in all of this somewhere."

"What do you mean?"

"If Jabala was so damned sure nothing was in the state-room, why did he object so strenuously to the search at first?"

"I can understand why he did. Arab pride. You've got to remember about different cultures, Mike. Not everybody thinks the way we do. I started to learn that way back in the Army when they sent me overseas. They had these programs about learning about the host country and getting along with the people. You ran into some pretty strange ways sometimes, but you got to where you didn't bat an eye at them after a while. I'll never forget the candied grasshoppers."

"The *what?*" Mike stared at me.

"That was in Japan. They have these candied grass-hoppers that are considered a delicacy and you can buy them in little cans. I bought a few, forgot 'em, and then came across them again recently. I had a little get-together at the house and dropped the grasshoppers, instead of olives, into the third round of martinis. You should have seen my brother-in-law Frank's face when he stared at it. 'Who mixed this goddamn thing, your gardener?'"

"Okay," said Mike impatiently. "Different strokes for different folks, and maybe that explains Jabala's behavior. But I still wonder about the pajamas."

"Pajamas?" He'd lost me.

"You saw them. All silk, I imagine. Very nice. Per-

126

sonally tailored, to be sure. But don't they put hospital patients into green gowns or something instead of fancy pajamas?"

"Oh, come on, Mike," I said. "You're reaching."

"Maybe. But doesn't it suggest, somehow, that the prince isn't as sick as they say he is?"

"No, it doesn't suggest that at all to me. But, then, I don't have a suspicious mind like you do."

"If you want to be a cop, George, a suspicious mind is standard equipment."

"Who says I want to be a cop? I just got dragged into this."

"So did we all," sighed Mike.

When we mounted the stairs and came into the executive office again, Hibner was there, at the computer console. He was holding a printout that had evidently just come off the printer, and his unlit pipe was in his mouth. He removed it and turned to us. "Glad you got here. I was going to send for you. This just came in from Interpol. I had to go through the Company to make 'em respond to our query—you can look at the messages I sent to Langley, but after that we've got to burn 'em. I don't think they liked it, and my control officer's probably gonna chew my ass when I get back, so I want you to know how I'm sticking my neck out to give you an assist here."

"We appreciate it, Lowell," said Mike. "What's Interpol got?"

Hibner handed Mike the printout. "Nothing at all on the non-American passengers, but take a look at that rundown on our friend Bernard Fourrier."

Mike took a look. He nodded thoughtfully. Very thoughtfully. "Arrested in Casablanca for taking part in a demonstration for Arab unity. Resisting arrest, inciting to riot, blah, blah, blah. Well, I don't know. It says something about his political sympathies, but that doesn't make him an assassin."

"What happened to your suspicious mind?" I asked.

"It's still suspicious," snapped Mike. "And Fourrier will bear watching. But the fact is, assassins don't usually

127

go on protest marches. They lay low, and sometimes they don't even have political sympathies. Or am I wrong about that, Lowell?"

"No, you're quite right. On the other hand, fanatics have been known to flip their lids and try to do things on their own. I have a suggestion. Let's not confront Fourrier with this—which would warn him if he is up to any hanky-panky—but let's try to keep a close eye on him. I don't think you, personally, ought to put a tail on him, Mike, because he knows you're in charge of the investigation. He'd make you right away, I think."

"Yeah," said Mike, nodding. "And it's not easy to put a tail on somebody aboard this airplane. No place to make yourself inconspicuous."

"Maybe George here could try to watch him," said Hibner.

"Me?" I shook my head. "I'm hardly the inconspicuous type. And Fourrier knows I'm also assisting in the investigation."

"Then I'd better do it," said Hibner. "I'm still an absentminded professor, as far as Fourrier knows. You haven't spread it around who I really am, have you?"

"What do you take us for?" asked Mike, bristling just a little. "You're secure, Lowell, so relax. And maybe you'd better be the one to bird-dog Fourrier."

Hibner took his lanky frame over to one of the easy chairs, lowered himself into it, tamped his pipe with his thumb, and got out his kitchen matches. "Before I start," he said, "I want you two to know that I'd rather not be doing this. I will, though, because it may have a bearing on my own mission, which is to see that the prince is protected. But I'm going to have a hell of a time keeping an eye on the guy without tipping my hand as to what I'm doing, especially if he's surveillance conscious. There aren't any crowds on this airplane to mingle with, no shop windows to pretend to look into. If I follow him back to the john or something, he might think I'm gay and trying to make a pass at him."

"Not a bad cover," said Mike, grinning.

"It's been used before," said Hibner. "You'd be surprised."

"Right now nothing would surprise me," said Mike.

Hibner had his pipe going now. The odor of malted milk filled the executive office. He took a couple of puffs, then unwound himself from the chair. "'Once more unto the breach, dear friends!'"

He was gone.

Mike shook his head. "Shakespeare, already. Don't tell me he wants to be an actor, too."

"Everybody does," I said. "It's a secret vice . . ."

CHAPTER TEN

When you're an actor, you're working all the time. What I mean is that you're constantly working at your craft. Thinking about it. Thinking about people and how they, according to their individual chemistry, would react in a given situation. If you're a man you may even apply this to women. You never know when you might be called upon to depict a certain kind of behavior that springs from inside the character you're pretending to be. Laurence Olivier said that in his view everyone is composed of many aspects of the opposite sex, and on many occasions he has drawn from female attributes within his own makeup. Dustin Hoffman surely paid a lot of attention to what makes women tick, or he never would have been able to do the great job he did in *Tootsie*. All this explains why I now dare to imagine what Lisa Garcia must have said to Ken Dilworth when she renewed her makeup, squared her shoulders, and strode forward to find him in his seat.

"Ken?"

"Hi. Sit down."

"I suppose I have to. You can't really stand on airplanes the way you do on New York subways. Funny, I never thought I'd get tired of just sitting."

"The way things are, it's the safest thing to do right now. Cheer up. We'll be back at the old ranch by nightfall."

"I almost wish we wouldn't."

"Huh? How come?"

"I wish things could just go on forever the way they are."

"With us in an airplane, wondering who's going to get shot in the back of the head next?"

"Well . . . that part of it's not too good. What I mean is that I wish you and I could go on forever, the way we are now."

"But that's how it's going to be. We're going to live happily ever after, just like in some storybook. Barring a few little spats, of course. I still don't see why I have to wait around while you change clothes six times every time we decide to go somewhere. Maybe the answer to that is never to go anywhere and stay in bed all the time. That's where we really get along."

"You're making it hard for me, Ken."

"I am? I thought it was supposed to be the other way around."

"Stop grinning like that. This is serious."

"You're not going to start worrying about the old man again, are you? I told you—his bark is worse than his bite."

"It's not his acceptance I'm worried about. It's yours."

"Come on, now. You know me better than that."

"I know you, yes. I know you so very well. And we got to know each other in such a short time. The trouble is, neither one of us got to know *everything*."

"So what? We can learn the rest as we go along. It'll give us something to do when we're not in bed."

"You'd better think about it carefully, Ken. Are you sure the physical part of it isn't blinding you to everything else?"

"What are you talking about, anyway? Is *this* what we're going to have our first quarrel about? I love you in bed and out of bed. I love you when you step out of the shower. I love you when you cross a room. I love you when you laugh and when you speak and when you're just sitting somewhere staring out of a window. Name the time and place and that's when and where I love you."

"But you don't really know anything about my past, do you?"

"Don't know, and don't care. Are you going to tell me now you've had other boyfriends? I know that, for God's sake. You don't think *I've* been living like a monk all these years, do you?"

"I don't suppose it's ever occurred to you that I might just be looking for a meal ticket to a fancy restaurant. Where a gal from Spanish Harlem doesn't ordinarily belong."

"Cut it out, will you? That kind of attitude went out with corsets. Besides, the restaurant's not all that fancy. The Dilworth clan's pretty comfortable, but not exactly Social Register. The old man himself would have been from the wrong side of the tracks if they'd had anything as luxurious as tracks in the farm country where he was raised."

"Ken, you found me at loose ends in Qram City. I told you how I'd got there, and all about my job as a charm school teacher for the prince's daughters. Didn't it ever strike you as odd?"

"Of course not. After working with all those money-laden Arabs in Qram, nothing would strike me as odd."

"Think, Ken. There I was in the palace. Not exactly in see-through pantaloons and a spangled vest that didn't hide anything—but I might as well have been."

"Huh?"

"Are you beginning to get it? Is that what that sweet, dumb stare of yours means?"

"I can't believe it!"

"You had better believe it. And everything else I'm going to tell you right now. The whole story..."

You guessed it. Ken Dilworth heard her out, then sought me out.

I see myself in a lot of ways: a loving husband, an indulgent father, a considerate son, and someday soon I hope, an attentive grandpop. Do you see in there anything about a Dutch uncle? The funny thing is I usually *do* listen, and seldom offer spectacular advice. Maybe that's what keeps them coming back.

The bar again. Ken ordered a scotch and soda, and Abdul sliced the air with his nose as he nodded and looked disappointed that Ken hadn't called for something more exotic so that he could show off his skill in mixology.

What the hell. I ordered a King Alphonse. That'd keep Abdul's steady hand busy.

"George," Ken said earnestly, "I was stunned when she told me. I've always thought I wasn't old-fashioned, or anything like that, but, Jesus—a call girl! I mean, a real professional call girl, and probably a very high-class one, but—Jesus!"

"I know how you must feel," I said.

"I don't think you do," he said, "because *I'm* not sure how I feel. I mean, really mixed up. I keep telling myself that she's the same person I fell in love with, and that all this doesn't make a damn bit of difference, but common sense tells me it *will* make a difference."

"How?"

"Can't you see it? The first time I get a little irritated with her about something my tongue will slip and I'll say she's acting like a whore, or something like that. I'm human, after all. Goddamnit, I can't even buy her an expensive present without thinking it's for the great roll in the hay she just gave me!"

"Everybody's got some kind of marital problem. That'll be yours. You'll just have to learn to live with it."

"But what about her? How can I ever believe she really loves me now, the way she says she does? You know, I wondered about that from the beginning. It wasn't a comfortable idea and I shoved it aside. But here's this gorgeous woman who can have practically any man she wants— princes, for God's sake—and what does she see in a guy like me, anyway? You know what call girls do. They fake their orgasms."

"Do they? Damned if I know, and you don't either. Maybe some do and some don't, which I would guess makes them like a lot of wives for that matter. They must range all the way from the traditional hooker with a heart of gold to the sleazy broad with a cash register where her heart once was. All I'm saying is, they're people and do all the foolish things people do, including falling in love for reasons they can't explain."

"But how do I know how it really is with Lisa? She's already lied to me—or left out the important part, anyway—so how can I ever be sure she's really in love with me, the way she says?"

"Did she say so?"

"Not in so many words. She told me the way it was, and then said, in effect, 'your move.' And not the least of this is what the old man'll think when he finds out. Which he's bound to do sometime. You just don't keep a secret like this all the rest of your life. Actually, she's the one who pointed that out. She said if I had to go get a job somewhere instead of going up and up in the airline, it was still okay with her. But how can I believe even that? Besides, it's not okay with me. I *love* the airline. It's the other part of my life."

I nodded. I watched him drink deeply of his scotch and soda. I saw Abdul, at the bar, looking at us brightly, ready to jump if he wanted another. *I* certainly didn't. A King Alphonse is pretty to look at, but you're as well off drinking Aunt Jemima syrup. I wondered vaguely if Abdul had sharper ears than we thought and had caught the drift of our conversation. That would mean he'd heard more than he should have when Lowell Hibner had buttonholed Mike and me here in the bar. But that notion glided past me, like the shadow of a bird on a lawn.

"Ken," I said, "the only advice I can give you—if you're asking for advice—is don't make any decisions right now when you're all upset. Calm down a little first. We've got quite a few hours left before we arrive, so that ought to give you plenty of time."

"Yeah," he said, frowning, nodding. "Thanks, George."

And I wondered for what, then remembered that a whole lot of shrinks get a hundred an hour for not saying much of anything.

We had reached a point where nothing much was happening—no murders every hour on the hour to keep the new day from getting dull. I should have appreciated this respite, but somehow I kept thinking of it as a lull before the storm. One thing was certain, I couldn't sleep. There was an organized conspiracy somewhere to keep me from getting the sleep I badly needed now, in spite of my getting a second wind.

Restless, I dropped in on the flight deck again.

"Sonofabitch," said Captain Fowler.

"What now?" I asked.

"I've been on the horn with Mr. Dilworth, back in flight ops. I thought he was a pilot once. Navy—that might explain it. Anyway, he must have rocks in his head."

"Is that so?" There was no use taking sides, I thought, before I even knew what the sides were.

"With these headwinds we ought to land short of LAX. SFO would be great, but even if they'd let us land there we'd just barely have the required reserves. Those are FAA regulations, and I don't care what Dilworth says about not coming under FAA. Their minimums are for safety reasons, and I'm all for them. But Dilworth is begging me not to land at San Francisco or Edwards Air Force Base or anyplace but our original destination. Now, I'm the pilot of this airplane, and it's up to me. The only trouble is, Dilworth's got a point."

"He has?"

"You must must know the situation. The prince has to get where he's going without delay. That slinky doctor of his even says the jolt of a landing might dislodge that fragment in his head and kill him if I don't happen to grease the airplane in. I don't know whether to believe that or not, but it's a helluva thing to take a chance on. I've made a couple of detours already to avoid turbulence, and that's another reason we're short of fuel. All this wouldn't be a problem at all if the prince's death weren't likely to kick off Armageddon. To me, he'd be one life stacked up against all the passengers, and the fact that he's a prince wouldn't mean a thing. But if I don't bring him back alive we might be talking about the slaughter of millions—do you realize that?"

"I know that's what the State Department thinks. But they could be wrong."

"What if they're not? What if kids open their history books a hundred years from now and read that one Captain John Fowler, airline pilot, nearly got the human race wiped out?"

"You know what I think?" said O'Malley, bringing his freckled face around.

"No. And I don't give a goddamn. I want to hear what George thinks."

"I don't think anything," I said. "This is your decision, John."

"That's what I thought you'd say," he growled. "That's why I asked you."

"Well, what *are* you going to do?"

"I'll know better when we're over California. Hell, maybe the prince will expire by then. World War III, maybe, but it won't be *my* fault."

"Well," I said, and then there was a long pause. "I wonder why that doesn't make me feel any better."

And I didn't. My stomach was now hollower than ever, and I knew the biggest, juiciest steak in the world wouldn't do it any good, let alone the bite-size, overcooked, rubbery tenderloins they were serving on the plane.

I dropped in on Jimmy Stewart, to see how he was doing. I told him everything I knew, though he was already aware of most of it.

"Well...uh...George," he said, his drawling voice somehow having a calming effect upon me, "Remember the Super Cub I had?"

"The most highly polished airplane in the world?"

"That's the one," he said.

Gloria said, "That thing made more noise than Spike Jones."

"Gloria never cared for it," Jimmy went on in his deliberate way. "I wanted her to fly in it with me to Vegas, and she said she'd rather walk so she could get there faster."

Gloria chortled in remembrance.

"Kinda hurt my feelings," said Jimmy, "so, uh, I offered to race—her in the car and me in the Cub. Got us a couple of radios so we could talk back and forth, and, well, off we went. I told her I'd have the champagne chilled by the time she got to the hotel."

"I made him give me a handicap," said Gloria, wearing a very sly look. "I made him promise not to break the sound barrier."

"So she did . . . so she did," said Jimmy. "Anyway, we kept talking to one another over the radio. I fudged a little bit when I was just barely out of town and told her I was comin' up on Daggett, which is really pretty near halfway. A little later when she asked, I told her I'd hit some headwinds and was still comin' up on Daggett."

Gloria was laughing out loud, and my face was bathed in a smile of anticipation.

"Uh, well . . . I stayed off the radio a lot after that," said Jimmy. "I could hear her callin', but I didn't have much to report. It wasn't till she just faded out that I told her the winds were awful heavy and I was still comin' up on Daggett." A long pause. Jimmy would get to it when Jimmy got to it. "Couldn't hear her after that. Next time I heard her voice was when I phoned her at the Vegas hotel. She asked me where I was. I told her I took the plane back and, uh, I was in a cab and we were comin' up on Daggett."

Gloria and I laughed happily. Jimmy said, "I don't think we've got headwinds that bad on this flight, but, uh, do me a favor, will ya, George?"

"Sure," I said.

"If Captain Fowler should tell you we're comin' up on Daggett . . ."

"You'll be the first one I call," I said. "Thanks, both of you."

"Uh . . . ah . . . awrrr . . . anngh . . . anytime."

"George," Gloria called, and I hesitated at the door. The smile was still there but her tone was serious. "Please be careful."

As I barged forward again, through the seating section, I was trying to make my own decision about a certain course of action—or maybe it could be called inaction. More than

137

anything, I wanted to sleep. I was like a lush who wants a drink and hasn't had one for too many hours. Even a tiny shot of sleep, tossed down quickly, would have been fine. Booze means very little to me, but by analogy, I could now sympathize with those who have a problem with it, as poor Rod Larrabee had had. When you want it, you want it, and nothing else will do. Life hardly seems worth living without it. That was exactly how I felt about sleep.

But there seemed to be no way to grab a few winks safely. If I went off by myself somewhere, where I wouldn't be disturbed, I might well be a tempting target for whatever flaked-out killer was stalking through the airplane, and get the now-familiar hole in the back of my head. A tiny doze might be as fatal to me as that one little nip to an alcoholic. I could drop into my own seat and try to sneak it there, but Mike and Florence were in place now and I knew they'd keep me awake, if only to keep in practice. If I sat near anybody else, they'd want to know if Mike had made any brilliant deductions lately that might lead to the apprehension of the murderer.

Bernard Fourrier, trim in his steward's uniform, came down the aisle toward me and squeezed past me, saying, "Pardon, m'sieur." From the way he glared at me, I felt he must have disapproved of my jogging suit as a costume for airline travel. Which was okay with me; I'd wear the damn thing to a formal dinner if I could get away with it.

In Fourrier's wake came Lowell Hibner. I thought he'd push by me, too, but instead he watched Fourrier duck into the galley, where there were some other flight attendants. Then, blocking my way, he took his pipe out and began to fill it from his pouch. As far as I was concerned there was too much traffic in the aisles; I had thought Fowler's directive that everyone stay in his seat would keep them clear. But it was obvious that no one could stay in his seat all the time, and that the calls of nature had to be heeded and that legs had to be stretched before they became numb, so this directive had gradually become ignored by mutual consent, and some people were wandering again—though usually in pairs. Anyway, Hibner, as I knew, was on duty.

"I don't think he knows I'm following him yet," Hibner half-whispered.

"What's he been up to?" I asked.

"Nothing. Not so far, anyway. He's only a suspect, George, and we don't know that he's guilty of anything."

"You were the one who thought he ought to be watched on account of his background."

"Yes, but that was because nobody else had a background even remotely connected with political shenanigans. What I'm saying is that it's not much of a connection, but it's the only one we've got."

"Maybe it would be better if he did know you were keeping an eye on him," I said. "That way, if he *is* the murderer, he won't dare knock anybody off again."

Hibner applied a kitchen match to his pipe and sucked noisily. "There's something in what you say," he agreed, "though in that case we may never be able to pin it on him. Which reminds me. If nobody else has been killed by the time we land—and let's fervently hope that's how it is— you and Mike had better call the attention of any investigators to Fourrier's record. They can take it from there."

"That's your job," I said. "You dug up the record."

"Yes, but I'm undercover, remember? Personally, I don't give a damn if the FBI finds out the Company had an agent aboard the plane, but if they do every director and deputy director of every branch, section, and special group in Langley will blow his cork and I'll end up posted to some embassy in an emerging African nation with a name that sounds like Iguana. I think sometimes they have tighter security against the FBI than they do the KGB. It's because the FBI likes publicity. Tell them something, and you might as well publish it in Jack Anderson's column. I can't afford to goof now—I'm too close to retirement."

"You don't seem that old."

"I feel that old sometimes." He spoke through clouds of smoke as he tried to keep the tobacco lit by puffing vigorously. I knew it would go out again soon, as pipes always do, and that was what I was waiting for. "I started pretty young, actually. Special Forces in 'Nam, flying choppers and light planes. The Company did a lot of recruiting among those of us who managed to come out of it with our asses in one piece. And military time counts toward retirement, so it adds up." He laughed, half-embarrassed. "But you don't want to hear all this, do you? It's like a Wagnerian opera where some character comes out, sits on a rock, and sings his life story for forty minutes while everything stops."

I laughed with him. "Well, it gives me an insight into what an intelligence agent's really like. I never did believe all that jazz about hopping from bed to bed and running from bad guys in exotic automobiles. You know something? When Ian Fleming wrote the original James Bond stories he thought he was telling it like it was. Then Cubby Broccoli came along and produced all those pictures and they got wilder and wilder. I'll say this for them, though. They're cinematic as hell and they've made millions."

"Millions you can have," said Hibner, his eyes misting over a little. "I'll take retirement and that forty-foot motor sailer I'm gonna buy. Maybe go around the world in it. I'm lucky, you know. I've got a wife who knows how to sail and actually likes it. No man could ask for more."

"I didn't think of you as married," I said.

He shrugged. "It hasn't been the old comfortable suburban routine, the way I've had to travel all the time. We've got a lot of catching up to do. Scratch a Company agent and inside you'll find just another bureaucrat plugging for retirement."

"Well, best of luck," I said.

"Just be sure you and Mike don't blow my cover and I'll probably make it."

His pipe finally went out again, but by that time it didn't make any difference; he stepped aside to let me pass and I continued on up to the executive office.

Ken Dilworth was at the desk, frowning at papers. I guess that's what executives do a lot—frown at papers. It came to me that as long as he was here, and busy, and quiet, I could stretch out on one of the comfortable chairs and doze a little with someone standing watch over me.

It was not to be, and I should have known that in the first place.

"I'm glad you're here, George," Ken said earnestly.

"I am, too. Maybe I can catch a little sleep."

"Wait. Before you do, I've got to tell you what I've decided. I want to know what you think."

"My head isn't turned on. Try the computer. They say those damned things can talk to you now."

"Be serious, George. This is about Lisa."

I dropped into the chair, lidded my eyes, yawned, and said, "Okay. Go ahead."

"If I broke with her now I wouldn't be true to everything I believe in. I'm in love with her and I know she's in love with me—even though I started to doubt that when I heard what she'd been. She couldn't fake all the ways she's shown me she's in love—nobody could. All the rest is garbage. The old man, the airline, the promising career. What counts is that we *are* in love and that we're going to get married. What's more, I'm going to take her right up to the old man and say, 'Dad, this is Lisa. She used to be a call girl, and what are you going to do about it?'"

"What does Lisa think about all this?"

"I don't know. I haven't told her yet. Did you see her down on the lower deck?"

I frowned, trying to remember. "I'm not sure, but I think her seat was empty. She's probably somewhere powdering her nose."

"I'll go find her right now."

I sighed and jacked myself up out of the chair. "In that case, I might as well go with you and find someplace to sleep with a guardian angel watching over me. I wish I could think of someone in that bundle of geniuses down there who wasn't talkative."

"But what do you think of my idea?" Ken asked eagerly.

"All I can say is for you to do whatever seems right for you."

"I knew you'd approve," he said.

Had I approved? No matter. It wasn't so much what I'd said that counted as much as what he'd thought I'd said.

141

So endeth today's lesson in being a wise man and a counselor.

Lisa wasn't in her seat downstairs. A stewardess came by; Ken asked her if she'd seen Lisa and she said no, but didn't we think we ought to be back in our seats? Ken frowned at that and for a moment I thought he was going to remind her that as a senior executive aboard he was in charge of everything and didn't have to remain in his seat, but he let it go, and took my arm. "Maybe she's powdering her nose, like you say—or maybe just wandering around. She used to stalk back and forth in the hotel room when she was trying to think. If that's what she's doing, she shouldn't be. Come on, George, let's find her."

We went down the aisles and past the bank of staterooms. We looked in several alcoves and knocked on a few washroom doors. There were murmurs of protest, some in voices anybody who watches movies would recognize. But no Lisa.

By the time we arrived at the bulkhead that separated the cargo compartment from the passenger space, we had covered most of the lower deck with the exception of the locked staterooms and the miniature mosque Prince Ibrahim had had installed. Just so you understand the layout better, I want to explain here that cargo, on a passenger airplane, is usually placed below the deck in what they call the lower lobe. But, for some carriers, Boeing also makes what they call a "combi" model, with the after-part of the fuselage rigged for cargo, with rollers for pallets and all sorts of ingenious devices. Given the requirements, they can modify the airplane almost any way the customer wants, provided the proper weight-and-balance ratios are maintained. Engineers and designers had worked out this custom model for the prince, and it had become a two-thirds luxury, one-third cargo airplane.

Ken put a troubled look on the door to the cargo compartment. "She couldn't be in there, could she?"

"With all those corpses? I don't think so."

Neither of us said what we both knew the other must

be thinking. If she was in there with the corpses, maybe she was one of them.

Ken sprang forward and I came along close behind him. He jerked the handle and pushed the door open.

From the dim interior of the cargo compartment, with all its shadowy crates, we heard a gasping scream of terror.

CHAPTER ELEVEN

Ken and I threw ourselves into the gloom, stumbling across the floor of metal ridges and perforated tracks. I tripped over a protuberance and almost lost my balance. Only when I had regained it did I realize that what had almost sent me sprawling was the blanketed shape of one of the corpses near the door. Ken led the way around a big container on a pallet that was on the fore-and-aft midline of the fuselage. By that time, only seconds later, our eyes had become better adjusted to the dimmer light and we could see the edges of things more clearly.

As we circled this container on one side, I had the curious feeling that someone was scrambling in the opposite direction on the other side of it. If I heard footsteps, I heard them very faintly—the kind of sound that makes you wonder whether you really *did* hear something. Maybe I didn't actually hear anything; maybe it was the kind of sixth sense that sometimes tells you there's another presence nearby, unseen. Or maybe all this is a false memory of the details, supplied later by imagination to explain what must have happened. Everything was going by in such a blur that there is no sharp, unmistakable recollection to hang on to.

Whatever impressions I received from that brief, stumbling run around the pile of crates were immediately wiped out by the sight of what we found behind them.

Lisa Garcia's lovely form, in the smart white slacks suit she'd worn for traveling, was sprawled on its side on the corrugated floor, with one arm outflung, and with her blouse ripped apart in front, as though she had been in a struggle. Her creamy white breasts were partly exposed. What would have been sexy under any other circumstances wasn't under these.

Ken was bent over her immediately. "Lisa!"

Her head moved slightly, as though she were trying to turn it, and a great wave of relief washed over me. Her long eyelashes blinked upward as her eyes opened. For a moment they were blank.

"My God, Lisa! What happened?" Ken was darting his own eyes over her and touching her here and there as he searched for injuries.

"Ken," she said softly and a little hoarsely.

"It's all right, darling. It's okay now. We're here. How do you feel? Does anything hurt?"

"My neck," she murmured. She brought her left hand up and touched the curve where her neck began to meet her right shoulder. Ken immediately put his finger to it and said, "Nothing wrong. A little swollen, maybe. Did you fall or what? We heard you scream—"

Her eyes widened. "I think he wanted to kill me!"

"Who? My God, Lisa—"

"He came up behind me. Got his arm around my neck—"

"Maybe you shouldn't talk." Ken looked up at me. "Do you think you could get that doctor here?"

"I'm all right, Ken," said Lisa. "A little shaky, that's all."

"Better get looked at first. You were blacked out when we got to you."

"For a moment, maybe. I didn't exactly feel the blow." She was trying to rise now, and Ken was gently pushing her back again.

"Your head?" Alarmed, Ken began to run his fingers over her scalp. "That could be serious. You stay right where you are, and don't move."

"Not my head. My neck. It's all numb. Going away now, though."

I frowned. "Sounds like some kind of karate chop. They catch a nerve or something."

"The doctor, huh, George? Please?"

"Right away," I said.

I didn't have to pass any of the passengers on my way to the stateroom, so I raced there, more like a charging buffalo than a fleeing gazelle, because that's the way God made me. I hammered on the door. Eventually this produced Dr. Fayez, who looked at me with his big dark eyes as though to say, "Not again!" I blurted out an explanation of sorts and led him back to the cargo space.

Dr. Fayez, in his wild, Madras-patch pants, as fussy as a brightly plumed bird pecking for seed, went over Lisa thoroughly, shining a little penlight into her pupils and stroking and poking her here and there. He rose again, frowned, and said, "She seems all right. If we could run a few tests—"

"I'm perfectly all right!" said Lisa. "All I want to do is get up and get out of here!"

Ken helped her to her feet. "You've got to rest. And don't worry, I'll be with you. For a long time. Do you know what I mean?"

"Lisa," I said, "before you get too rested, we'd better know more about how you were attacked. Did you see who it was?"

"It all happened so quickly!" Anybody else's face would have been contorted with the thought she was putting into this, but somehow Lisa managed to retain her usual look of poise. She had pulled together her torn blouse to cover her breasts, but with a completely casual, unembarrassed series of movements. "I came back here, I don't know, to be where it was quiet and I could think. To be someplace different, anyway. All I was going to do was take a look, turn around, and come back again. My mind was actually on something Ken and I had been discussing—"

"George knows about it," interrupted Ken.

"Yes. Well, there I was, and it was kind of dark, and I had already turned to go back. Without any warning, this arm came from behind and around my neck, and something hard was pressed against my head in back. Without thinking, I tried to twist away, and I guess that's when I must have screamed. This person—whoever it was—shoved me forward a little and the next thing I felt was this numbing blow between my neck and shoulder. It didn't make me black out entirely, but I know I fell down. It was more like being stunned than knocked out."

"And you didn't see him at all—not even a glimpse?"

She shook her head. "Nothing. The only thing I know about him is that he must have been pretty strong. When I tried to twist away, he clutched at me, sort of, for a moment, and that's how he must have ripped my blouse."

I looked at Ken. "Sounds like he heard us coming and had to drop her—maybe started out to use that weapon we've been looking for. According to Dr. Fayez, the damn thing has to be pressed in exactly the right place to kill instantaneously. That would take some fumbling around, and explains why he didn't just shoot her right away."

"Oh, God," said Lisa, shuddering and losing much of her composure for the first time, "he *did* want to kill me, didn't he?"

"Come on, Lisa," said Ken, putting his arm around her. "Let's go where it's safe. We've still got a lot to talk about . . ."

"Karate blow, huh?" said Mike. We were in the executive office again, and this time we had it to ourselves. I was in an easy chair, almost having given up the notion that I might miraculously catch a few moments of sleep, and Mike was pacing like a bulldog in the pound wondering when its owners are going to show up.

"That's what it sounds like. I never believed all that crap about karate until I saw it actually work in Japan. They've got pressure points and things like acupuncture which Western medicine is starting to accept now."

"It figures," said Mike.

"What figures?"

"It fits the psychological profile of our murderer. Not that we've got much of a profile, with no files or experts to help us out, the way they would in some decently equipped homicide office. But one of the first things you always ask yourself when the perpetrator is unidentified is, well, what kind of a guy would do it this way? We already have a strong idea the murder weapon is some kind of special-purpose job—maybe even made for these particular murders by some private gunsmith who takes his money and keeps his mouth shut. They're all over the place, in Europe as well as in the States. In North Africa, for all I know. Your average NRA sportsman doesn't order things like that. Nor do law enforcement officers. Only one kind of guy would—someone bent on assassination. A professional hit man? Well, not the kind we ordinarily think of in the U.S.A. They usually use ordinary weapons that can't be traced. So what we can assume, from the use of this weapon, is that the guy must have had some sort of training in assassination methods, like they give in these camps where they train terrorist guerrillas. Libya has them; Syria, Bulgaria, and of course the Soviet Union. There must be some in the Caribbean."

"Or the U.S. itself? Like Camp Perry, where they teach CIA agents dirty tricks?"

"I'm not ruling that out entirely, George," he said. "But I happen to know something about CIA methods—more than most outsiders, anyway. We had a seminar once, senior homicide cops from all over the country, where they gave us a real behind-the-scenes look. It was pretty fascinating, especially their technical development lab. You know what crazy thing they were working on when I was there? A fold-up airplane that could be carried in a suitcase so the agent could make a penetration or a getaway. I don't know whether the idea ever got off the ground or not. But the strong impression I got was that they weren't concentrating on assassination techniques. In fact, one of the agents I met told me privately that when they wanted somebody knocked off—and, let's face it, they do, once in a while—they encourage some kind of local national to do it, or, at the very least, don't stand in his way. The Soviets tend to use cat's-paws, too. It makes sense from the standpoint of the government and keeps them from being caught red-handed.

The upshot of all this is that, contrary to popular belief, agents aren't really trained in assassination techniques. I can't say that for certain, mind you, but the probabilities are very strong that these murders are not the direct work of either a Soviet or U.S. regular intelligence operative."

"Which leaves somebody like Lowell Hibner out of it?"

"Unless he's overseeing somebody else's work. And I doubt that more than anything else. It may sound like flag-waving, George, but we really are the good guys. Besides, what possible interest could the U.S. have in terrorizing the prince, let alone encouraging his assassination?"

"Would they be protecting his highness? Would they be icing all these people to keep *them* from making an assassination attempt?"

"Rod Larrabee? John Larkin? Lisa Garcia? Are you kidding?"

"I'm just trying to untangle knots. All I seem to be doing is making new ones."

"But here's something interesting," said Mike, halting in his pacing and bringing his head around. "The victims. Those I just named. Plus the finance minister, Kebir, and Rita Schmidt, and the bodyguard, Muhanna. Let's scratch Rita from the list right away—we're pretty sure she accidentally walked into something. That leaves these others, and Lisa Garcia as probably an intended victim. What do they all have in common?"

"Not much." I shrugged.

"Think, George. *They all knew the prince intimately.*"

I lifted my head and gave voice to my favorite private cussword. "Jeepers!" It sounds pretty mild, but anytime I say it I'm either sore as hell or astounded. I was astounded this time.

"Let's check this out," said Mike, excitement glowing in his hard cop's eyes as he held out the fingers of one hand in order to tick points off on them. "Larrabee. According to him he'd been real buddies with the prince when he was doing his thing in Las Vegas. Kebir—a trusted aide, very close to the prince, before he dipped into the sugar bowl. Jake Larkin—the prince's flying instructor when he was training in Tucson. Muhanna—always curled up on the prince's doorstep. And finally Lisa Garcia. You couldn't get any closer to Prince Ibrahim than she got!"

"But why would this make them candidates for assassination? Did the prince tell them all some deep, dark secret that was dangerous for them to know? I could see it in Kebir's case, maybe, or even with Lisa. But the others? Would anybody actually confide anything in an alcoholic clown like Larrabee?"

"Details," said Mike impatiently. "We've got the pattern, and that's what I was looking for all along. The reason for this pattern is, as you suggest, probably political. Which is more in Hibner's department than mine. Let's go find him and see if this pattern gives him any ideas that might be helpful."

I came out of that nice soft easy chair reluctantly and tagged along behind Mike as he went down to the lower deck. Hibner was in a seat far to the rear, with no one else sitting near him, and as we approached I noticed, with the sounding of a distant alarm in my head, that he looked kind of funny. At first glance, he merely seemed to be sprawled comfortably in the seat that was tilted back for catnapping, with his hands folded in his lap, his short-cropped beard resting on his collarbone, and his eyes closed. But to me he looked more relaxed than he should have been—especially if he was supposed to be keeping an eye on Bernard Fourrier.

Mike leaned over the lanky professor (or agent—take your pick) and put his hand on his shoulder to wake him up.

Does that strike you as familiar? If you've seen or been in as many movies as I have, it does. It's one of the great cliché scenes of all time. The detective shakes the guy's shoulder to wake him up and he falls straight forward and stone dead. For a flashing moment, and with a sudden tight feeling in my throat, I honestly thought that was what was going to happen.

Instead, Lowell Hibner slowly opened his eyes, blinked

several times, and then stared at us stupidly. We could see his pupils trying to focus.

"Hey! Lowell!" said Mike. "You okay?"

There was a dumb beat of time. "I—I don't know," said Hibner. His voice was dry. He licked his lips.

"You got a medical problem or something? We do have a doctor aboard, you know."

Hibner shook his head and then put his fingertips to his temples. "A mickey!" he said. "Somebody slipped me a goddamn mickey!"

"*What?*"

"That pineapple juice. I thought it tasted funny!"

"What pineapple juice?"

"I'm trying to remember. Give me a chance—"

"You'd *better* see the doctor."

"No, no! I'm okay!" He straightened himself in his seat to prove he was. "I don't think it was your average chloral hydrate mickey. Some kind of barbiturate, for a guess. I just couldn't keep my eyes open." He looked around him, glancing at the daylight outside the windows. "How long have I been out?"

"I don't know," I said. "It must be a good hour since the last time I saw you."

He groaned. "Somebody caught on. Fourrier? I was sure he hadn't spotted the surveillance."

"Did he bring you the pineapple juice?" asked Mike.

"No. It was one of the stews."

"Which one?"

Hibner blinked again. "You may not believe this," he said, "but I didn't notice."

"I thought you guys were supposed to be observant," said Mike, and I knew immediately he wished he hadn't said it. This was no time for one-upmanship.

"We are, but we play roles of characters who aren't being observant. You know—low profile. Maybe George, who is an actor, will understand this." The implication was that Mike was *not* an actor, so I guessed we did have a little game of one-up going on here, after all. "I play 'em from the inside out; when I'm making like an absentminded professor, I go all the way."

"What's that supposed to mean?" asked Mike. "You stand at the urinal, open your vest, take your tie out and let fly?"

"Mike, please," said Hibner. "I'm trying to put this together through a goddamn headache. I was sitting here, trying to be inconspicuous. Fourrier was down the aisle, serving juice with the other attendants. My eye was on him. Some stew came by with mine and I just grabbed it from her without looking. Those young and pretty stews *do* look all the same, come to think of it."

"Fourrier was the one in your sights." Mike turned his head to look up and down the aisles. "I wonder where he is right now?"

"You'd better find out," said Hibner, grimacing. "If he wanted me out of the way, he must have some reason for it. And he must have had plenty of chance to lace that drink before it got to me."

"How could he be sure you'd reach for that particular drink? Or any of 'em for that matter?"

"How the hell do I know? It worked, didn't it? That's what counts. You'd better locate him and see what he's up to. In fact, I'll go with you."

"You sure you're up to it?" Mike watched Hibner struggle to lift himself out of the sleeper seat.

"I'll grab a gallon of ice water on the way. That ought to help," said Hibner.

I don't know what the rest of the passengers thought about the three of us rummaging through the airplane like winos in an alley. We tried to be casual about it, but they must have sensed that something was going on. We went forward to the bar area and worked our way aft again. In the bar, Hibner got his ice water, with Abdul looking disappointed as he served it and saying no, he hadn't seen M'sieur Fourrier. Mary Lou Carmichael and another stewardess were in the main galley. They hadn't seen Fourrier, either, and suggested we try the crew lounge. We headed for the crew lounge, but on the way we looked into wash-rooms and knocked on stateroom doors.

Bobby Troup opened his door and whispered, "Yeah, George . . . what's up? Julie just got to sleep."

"Sleep? What's that?" I asked.

From the darkened room I heard Julie's deep, familiar voice say, "It's what I don't do very well when I think the next person who knocks on the door is going to air-condition the back of my head."

Anyway, they hadn't seen Fourrier.

At her stateroom door, Candy Vandermeer, hairbrush in hand, and clad in a kimonolike robe—looking like the sexiest female basketball player ever—said, "You mean the little French steward with the eyes that pop out of his head?" She giggled, remembering. "No, he hasn't been here."

Jabala responded to our knock by peering through the crack as he opened the master stateroom door a few inches. "How many times must I ask you not to disturb his high-ness?" he said.

Fourrier hadn't been there, and Jabala seemed ready to swear it on the Koran.

At last we came to the crew lounge. The door was shut. It occurred to me that it ought to have been placed off-limits after we'd found the copilot and Rita Schmidt murdered in there, but with everything happening so fast and unexpect-edly nobody had thought of that. Mike rattled the knob of the door. It was locked.

He hammered on it. "Anybody in there?"

"One moment, please!" sounded Fourrier's voice from the inside.

One moment? There were a number of moments—I lost count. Mike hammered again and said, "Come on. Open this door!"

When it was finally opened, Bernard Fourrier, his jacket off and his shirt open at the collar, stared out at us through unabashed liquid eyes. I noticed that one of his shirt tails hadn't been stuffed all the way into his trousers. "What is it, m'sieurs? Do not tell me someone else 'as been *abba-trai*—eh—murdered?"

Behind Fourrier was a cute stewardess, a little on the plump side, with nice blonde hair that was clearly mussed. I had only vaguely noticed her before, and seemed to remember that she'd had some kind of European accent, possibly Swedish. And she wasn't wearing a nameplate. I guessed she hadn't been wearing her blouse a moment before either, because it was as rumpled and hastily put on as Fourrier's shirt. And she was blushing. Fair, Scandinavian skin takes on a very special color when it blushes, a little like lox on a bagel.

"Sorry to interrupt," said Mike, scowling.

"Interrupt? Why, m'sieur, we were merely 'aving a little discussion!"

"Uh, huh," said Mike. "How long have you two been in here?"

"M'sieur," said Fourrier, stiffening, "that is a crude question!"

"I'm accounting for people's whereabouts," Mike said. "Sometimes that calls for crude questions."

"I protest, m'sieur! My 'onor, and that of Miss Lundquist, is at stake!"

Miss Lundquist straightened out her blouse and looked out of cerulean-blue eyes as she managed, "Vee haff been in here at least half an hour. Ve are entitled to a rest period, and as acting purser, M'sieur Fourrier is the one who authorizes it."

"Yeah. Sure," said Mike.

Hibner touched his arm. "Let's pull in our horns, Mike, and start all over again."

He had reason, as the French say. There was nothing else he could do.

CHAPTER TWELVE

L.A. was still many miles away, but I knew enough about the airline headquarters there, and its chairman of the board, to imagine what must have been taking place. Later I found out I'd come close.

Carter Dilworth was in flight ops, monitoring the progress of WIA 300, the designation the flight had been given. In his shirt sleeves, he was wolfing down cold hamburgers and drinking stale coffee from Styrofoam cups just like all the people whose job it was to be there. Every time he called Captain Fowler for more information, Fowler bit his head off and asked him for Christ's sake to let him fly the airplane and stop bothering him—maybe not outright like that, but that was his meaning.

By mutual consent, Carter Dilworth and Secretary of State Edward H. Sutherland taped the phone conversation they had with each other, and I heard it later. It went like this:

"How are you, Carter? This is Ed Sutherland."

"Hello, Mr. Secretary. I'm fine. No, let me take that back. I'm in a damned uproar."

"I can understand that, Carter. We all are. We've got a very sticky situation here, and I'm grateful for your co-operation. I just want to make sure you understand all the nuances, so you won't make the wrong unilateral decision. The first and most important thing is that we've got to accommodate Prince Ibrahim, who is the keystone of our entire policy in the Middle East."

"I know all about that, and WIA has as much of a stake in Qram as you have. But I'm also an airline operator, Mr. Secretary, and to us the safety of passengers means more than anything."

"Quite true. And I agree with you. On the other hand, the safety of one particular passenger—Prince Ibrahim—is tied in with the ultimate safety of the entire country. I'm advised that a landing short of the original destination may well endanger his life. I even have opinions here from several leading neurosurgeons who say that is a definite possibility. But now we hear that the airplane's short on fuel and may have difficulty making it. It is very difficult for me to gauge the degree of risk from a technical standpoint. I want to hear it from you—your honest assessment of the situation."

"Let me explain something, Mr. Secretary. On instrument flights, the FAA and the airline itself operate under certain minimums. They always leave a margin of safety, like the forty-five-minute fuel reserve any aircraft must have on reaching its destination. If we observe those minimums Flight 300 might make San Francisco or Reno. But Captain Fowler—one of our most experienced pilots—has made us aware of the fuel situation from the start and is doing everything he can to fly the airplane at minimum fuel consumption. That particular aircraft is great; it can make a cat three landing—that's hands off—all by itself if necessary, but it's got to get to its destination to do so. Fuel consumption is a tricky thing when you start to get down to the very bottom of the tanks. You can calculate it within minutes—yes. But in just one minute, on final approach, that airplane can travel three or four miles, but three or four miles short of the runway is disaster. And more than a hundred lives could be lost instead of just Prince Ibrahim's."

"I want to hear the bottom line. Can he make it?"

"I don't know. Neither does he. His instructions are to use his own judgment. But I want to give you my *own* bottom line. I'm inclined to risk the prince's life instead of all those others. A life is a life, peasant or royalty, and I'd best remind you that some of those others are world-famous celebrities, one helluva lot more beloved by the citizenry than some Arab prince."

"Look, Carter, I called you to see if I could get a solution—not more problems. I'll talk as straight as I can. If anything happens to the prince it could be World War III. I sincerely believe the chances of that to be considerable. I pray that I'm wrong, but I don't think so. All I can do is ask you to bring that airplane to Los Angeles if it's at all possible. Cut that forty-five minutes down to ten, or five, or whatever's necessary."

"You're asking an awful lot."

"I know. I know. It's in your hands, and I'm confident you'll get that plane to L.A. if there's any way it can be done."

"I will, Mr. Secretary. But under these circumstances, if in my judgment or Captain Fowler's it can't be done, I'll without hesitation land it on Interstate Five."

I poked my nose into the flight deck.

"We're busy as hell here," said Captain Fowler.

"I know you're short a man. I thought I might help."

"Thanks. But O'Malley and I have everything under control. I'll be making an announcement to the passengers as soon as I decide where we're going to land."

"It won't be LAX then?"

"Depends on the fuel. If it looks safe to me I'll request a straight-in, unrestricted approach. I've double-checked what I'll need on final descent, and O'Malley's doing the same calculations now to double-check mine." He looked at the flight engineer, who was working one of the navigation computers built into the console and making entries on a payload-range capability graph. "You get anything different?"

O'Malley's freckles were clustered in concentration. "The maximum brake gross release weight I get is the same as yours," he said, "and maybe we can cut down a little by staying at point eighty-five as long as possible, then making

157

a sharp descent. We'd better get a reading on the adiabatic temperatures. They could make a small difference."

"Okay," Fowler said gruffly, possibly because he hadn't thought of it himself. "We'll crank that in, too."

I left them to their calculations, wondering whatever happened to seat-of-the-pants flying in helmets with goggles, and long, white scarfs that you didn't need a computer to learn how to tie. It went out with hand-cranked motion-picture cameras. It's a marvelous world we live in, but more and more we're becoming enslaved in a microchip, data-bank environment, without which nobody aboard this plane would ever live to find out if the murderer hadn't gone to an awful lot of unnecessary grisly effort.

There wasn't much point in advising Mike and Florence about what I'd learned on the flight deck; they might become unduly alarmed, and perhaps inadvertently communicate some of this to the rest of the passengers. The last thing we needed was panic in the aisles. They were seated in the executive office with Mike behind the paper-strewn desk. He was jotting notes to himself on a yellow, legal-size pad, part of the stationery in the well-equipped office, and he was wearing a very businesslike scowl. Florence was sitting very quietly, evidently contributing to his mental efficiency just by being there, even though she wasn't saying much. I wondered about this romance of theirs. You can say all you want about the spiritual, but any romance worth the name ought to have *some* sex in it. As far as I knew, neither one of them had yet gotten as far as playing doctor. For each of them, it was a little like buying a used car without even kicking the tires.

"George," said Mike, looking up, "I'm glad you're here. I've been mulling this over, and calling on Florence's knowledge of Qram politics to see if I can't bring some of this into focus."

"Well, I can help you mull, but I don't know anything about Qram politics."

"Let's put it this way. Two sounding boards are better than one."

"All right. Shoot," I said, wincing to myself as I realized the inappropriateness of my comment.

"You know about the pattern," he said. "Everybody was close to the prince. I've already mentioned it to Hibner, but he doesn't think much of it. Just coincidence, he says, and he still likes his terrorist theory, and he's still suspicious as hell of Bernard Fourrier. But a terrorist, in my estimation, wouldn't be taking time out for a quick roll in the hay between victims. Of course, he might be doing something like that just to throw us off, but that's really stretching it. I think Hibner's still a little fuzzy in the head from that mickey he got. He was a big help running interference for us with Interpol, but there's not much he can do for us now. I told him to keep on watching Fourrier, but that was just to get him out of the way."

I frowned. "You don't think there's any danger *he* might get knocked off, do you? The fact that he got a mickey strongly suggests that somebody already knows what he really is."

"I mentioned that to him," Mike said, with a slight smile. "It wounded his pride. 'I can take care of myself!' he said. I guess he can at that."

"Lisa's the one I'm worried about," I said. "She knew the prince intimately, like the others. There's already been one attempt on her life, and there might well be another."

Mike nodded. "I've put her with Ken Dilworth, in the 'A' section with a lot of other passengers around them. He has instructions not to let her out of his sight. He doesn't want to do that, anyway."

"That's great—as long as Ken himself isn't the murderer."

"Why should he be?" Mike looked at me sharply and I knew he was wondering if I'd found out something and was holding out on him.

"No reason," I answered. "I'm just doing it your way. Until we know more in the way of facts, everybody's a suspect. You know. Policeman's paranoia."

"That isn't my way at all," Mike growled. "And I don't know where the hell you got the idea. Maybe you've been acting in too many detective movies." He sighed. "God knows, I have."

"Could I get this back on the track, gentlemen?" said Florence sweetly. "If there is one?"

"Yeah," said Mike, nodding. "And the reason I keep getting off the track is that I don't like where it's going. Let me lay this out again for both of you. The victims were close to the prince. He must have confided something to them, possibly not realizing it, or maybe even deliberately—a message he hoped they might carry to someone in the outside world. At any rate, a very dangerous secret. It could be something that even his closest advisor, Jabala, doesn't know about. What could that possibly be? This is what Florence might be able to tell us. What issues were going on behind the scenes in Qram? You were there, Florence. You must have heard all sorts of rumors and speculations."

Florence shook her head. "They were mostly the kind of gossip you get about movie stars. Bedroom-oriented. There was a lot of talk about the prince's escapades when he went abroad, and some about how he—uh—kept himself entertained in Qram. It wasn't with his fat wife, we all knew that much. We heard he used to fly out to his lodge in the mountains pretty often, sometimes just overnight, and we never had any actual proof of it, but we all assumed they'd bring girls there for him to play around with. Oddly enough, nobody ever tumbled to Lisa Garcia's actual function at the palace. Any observers we had were tuned into politics, so they never even bothered looking into his love life. I don't like telling about it now. It makes me feel greasy."

"Just the same," said Mike stubbornly, "there has to be a connection. Like they say: '*cherchez la femme*.'"

"Your French is atrocious." Florence smiled.

Mike allowed, "My English ain't all that hot, either."

I got into it. "Mike wanted to go to London once and I told him he'd better take me along. As interpreter."

"Well, in any language," said Mike, "it boils down to girls. What was Rod Larrabee's connection with the prince in Las Vegas? Girls—at least the way Rod told it. Then Jake Larkin, his flying instructor. If they were buddies in Tucson, they must have spent their evenings chasing broads. Kebir, the finance guy? Well, maybe he handled the little presents the prince gave out as tips to hookers who gave him good service. Minks, sables—that sort of thing. Muhanna, the bodyguard. He'd be the one who admitted ladies into the bedchamber. Lisa Garcia's connection with girls is that she *is* a girl. You see how all this fits?"

"Frankly, I don't," I said, shaking my head.

"I don't think girls were any more important to Prince Ibrahim," said Florence, "than all his other playthings. And, as a matter of fact, he'd apparently been attending to business quite diligently in the past month or so, while that movie was being shot. He seldom appeared at public functions, the way he used to. He didn't throw any parties for the cast, which I think everyone expected, especially with the H-bomb girls you had on this picture. Larrabee complained that the prince wouldn't see him. At the embassy, we knew that he was busy conferring with a whole string of Arab leaders almost every day, or consulting with his advisors about the continuing problem of maintaining his country's sovereignty. Even the ambassador couldn't get to see him the way he used to."

Mike cocked his head to one side, like a bulldog hearing sounds humans can't hear. "If there's some sort of secret all the victims knew, and had to be killed, there's one witness we haven't thought of yet who could tell us what it is."

"Don't make me ask who," I said. "Just say it."

"Prince Ibrahim himself."

Florence looked doubtful. "He's not in shape to talk to anybody at the moment, I'm afraid."

"So we've been assuming," said Mike, "largely because Jabala won't let anybody disturb him. But when George and I were in his stateroom, the doc said he wasn't under sedation—just sleeping. That means he might well be able to talk when he's awake. And, for all we know, he could be awake this very minute."

"Jabala would never go for it," I said.

"We don't know that for sure, either," answered Mike. "There's one way to find out." He picked up the desk phone, which was connected to the airplane's communications system, and punched out the digits for the master stateroom.

A moment later I could hear the electronic gabble in the receiver that meant the phone was being answered, though I couldn't make out the words on the other end.

Mike said, "Mr. Jabala? This is Mike Corby. Look, I know the prince has to rest and that his condition is grave, but it's vital that we talk to him. Very briefly. Just a question or two. It has to do with the investigation."

The phone crackled with a reply.

"I realize that, Mr. Jabala," said Mike. "But what we want to ask does have to do with the prince's safety and well-being. It could lead us to the assassin who's obviously still aboard the plane. His next attempt might be directed toward the prince himself. If not on the plane, afterward."

More crackling.

"Wake him up, then," said Mike. "Believe me, it's that important."

After Jabala had evidently replied to this, Mike put his hand over the phone and said to us, "He's asking the doctor about it." A moment later he spoke into the phone again. "Yeah. Yeah. Got it. I understand, Mr. Jabala. Just a minute or two. That's all we need . . ."

The master stateroom was as dimly lighted as it had been before. Dr. Fayez stood in one corner, looking worried, and Jabala interposed himself between the bed and where Mike and I stood. He looked ready to take a bullet in his fat little body, if that was what we had in mind, and the way his rosebud lips were trembling I thought he hadn't dismissed that as a possibility. At that all his blubber might have absorbed a bullet, like a self-sealing tire.

"Don't come any nearer," he said. "Do not say anything to excite him."

The prince was stretched out on the bed, as before, but an extra pillow now raised his bandaged head slightly. I

162

could barely detect the movement of his eyes as he looked toward us out of the slits in the bandages.

"Your highness," said Mike, "if you can hear me, would you please move the index finger on your right hand up and down?"

There was a wait, and then the right index finger moved.

"The people who have been killed, as I'm sure you know by now, were all close acquaintances of yours. We think they may have known some secret that got them killed. Something you may have told them in confidence, maybe even unintentionally. If we knew what this information was, it could point to the murderer."

Jabala drew himself up. "That, Mr. Corby, is an improper question! We cannot reveal affairs of state to outsiders!"

"Is it an affair of state? Is it something *you* know about, Mr. Jabala?"

"There is nothing I am aware of. I am merely advising his highness not to respond if there is something that touches on national policy."

"I'd rather hear it from his highness," said Mike. "How about it, prince? Was there anything like that?"

After a long pause, the index finger moved again—from side to side.

"There!" said Jabala. "You see? You have wasted his highness's time, Mr. Corby. And you have disturbed him quite enough. I shouldn't have agreed to this interview in the first place. We've been more than cooperative."

Mike sighed. "Okay, your excellency. But I hope you understand that this had to be done. We're conducting a murder investigation and we can't afford to overlook anything."

"It would be better, I think, if you drop this investigation. You don't seem to be making any progress, and all you're doing is upsetting his highness. I must ask you, Mr. Corby, to confine your police activities to standing guard until we land, which should be very soon now. After that, someone who is more competent can take over. This is more than a polite request, Mr. Corby. It's an order."

"Maybe it is," said Mike, stiffening. "But I don't take orders from you, Mr. Jabala."

When we left the stateroom, Jabala was still standing there by the prince's bed, trembling like a rubber duck in an earthquake.

I poked my head into the flight deck again. I was the only passenger, with the possible exception of Ken Dilworth, who knew that Captain Fowler was contemplating a landing on a couple of eyedroppers' full of kerosene. I was anxious to find out whether or not he'd made his decision yet. I was a lot more worried about this than I was about Mike catching a murderer.

As I entered, Fowler was in the midst of a challenge-and-response check with O'Malley.

"INS switches," said Fowler.

"Previously completed," O'Malley answered smartly.

"Voice recorder."

"Tested."

"APU."

"Complete module tested."

I shouldn't have interrupted, but it came out before I could stop it. "Are we landing already?"

Fowler turned to look at me with annoyance. "This is for descent. But, yes, we'll be landing in twenty minutes. At Los Angeles. Better go on back there. I'll be calling for seat belts before long."

"Los Angeles? You do mean LAX, don't you?"

"Get the hell out of here!"

What I didn't like was the way he hadn't answered my question.

I went back to my seat. The one Mike and Florence had chosen to sit next to. They were there. Up to this point, they'd only been gazing into each other's eyes and holding hands, but now they'd become more daring. They'd allowed their knees to touch. I wished they'd get a chance to hop into the sack together, find out about each other and get it over with. At least they weren't chattering, for all the good it did me, because with a hairy landing coming up I had no intention of trying to sleep.

The "Fasten Seat Belts—No Smoking" signs went on. I heard Captain Fowler's voice on the loudspeaker.

"Ladies and gentlemen, we will be landing at Los Angeles International Airport in about ten minutes. Please fasten your seat belts and—uh—as a routine precaution, the flight attendants will be passing out extra pillows. They will instruct you in their use and point out the location of the emergency exits."

Mike looked up. "Routine precaution?"

"That's what the man said," I answered, trying to look calm. That was one of the hardest acting jobs I'd ever undertaken. In my mind's eye, I could see the scene that must have been taking place at LAX now, with other air traffic on hold overhead, with the taxiways cleared, and runway zero-seven left, all twelve thousand feet of it, stretched out and waiting. Approaching from the north, Fowler would be making a very gradual let-down and a wide turn over the water for a long straight-in approach. That would minimize the fuel consumed, and were we to run out anyway, we'd plop in the ocean instead of wiping out a few acres of homes and occupants. Meanwhile, ambulances and crash trucks would be all but paralleling the 747 as soon as we touched down. The only question was whether it would touch down on its wheels or the tip of its nose after losing lift if even one of the engines died on short final before Fowler could compensate. Knowing the exact nature of the danger we were in was of little comfort. I may have had a stiff upper lip if anyone looked at me in my seat, but there were a lot of wobbly feelings in my stomach.

Lowell Hibner came loping up to our seats, squeezing past stewardesses who were passing out pillows and showing people how to lean forward and hold them in front of their faces. Some must have warned him to go back to his seat, but they'd been too busy to enforce it.

"Mike. George," said Hibner quietly, looking down upon us as though we were students in one of his classrooms.

"Yeah? What is it now?" asked Mike, clearly annoyed.

"You'd better come back to the prayer room with me."

"Now?"

"Now! And let's make it quick."

I'm sure that Mike and I both guessed another body had been found, but we didn't have time to ask him about it. He swung around and cantered back down the aisle like a giraffe going across the plain, and we scrambled in his wake. He led us to the prayer room. Its gaudily decorated door was open and the light had been turned on in its interior.

On the same wine-colored rug where Rod Larrabee had died lay the crumpled figure of Acting Purser Bernard Fourrier in his smart blue uniform. There was a fresh pool of blood on that rug where his cheek lay. There was, as there had been with the other corpses, a powder-ringed hole in his head. But this time it was at the temple. And in one outflung hand was a slim-barreled pistol—evidently single-shot—with a long cylinder that must have been a silencer fitted to its muzzle.

A piece of airline stationery—the kind supplied on request to any of the passengers—was near the body. We could see that there was writing on it, and Mike started to lean over it in order to read.

"I've already read it, Mike," said Hibner. You could hear the tight control he was exercising on his own voice. "It's a suicide note. He says he's sorry he killed all those people, but he had to. *'Vive Unite Arabe!'* It means—"

"I can guess what it means!" snapped Mike. "What the hell did they have to do with Arab unity? And why did he have to kill himself, too?"

"Twisted thinking," said Hibner. "Who knows with fanatics? I tried to keep an eye on him but he gave me the slip. He must have had a key to the prayer room. I passed it and never knew he was in there. Next time I looked at it, I saw it was partly open. And there he was."

"Jesus!" said Mike. "What a way to close the case!"

"Well, it's closed," said Hibner, "and that's the important thing. You didn't exactly solve it but you can take whatever credit there is. In fact, I'm insisting on that. Not

166

a word, please, about any assistance I gave you. I'm still undercover, and if it's blown I get blown away with it."

"We'd better get back to our seats," I reminded both of them gently.

"There's something screwy about this whole thing," said Mike, gimleting his eyes at the corpse.

"Mike," I said. "This *could* be a crash landing—"

I pulled at his arm, and finally he reluctantly broke away.

I wasn't there, on the flight deck, as we came in, but I wished I had been. There would have been enough to see and hear to divert me and diminish the scared feeling that filled me. It was like an attack of indigestion to which a slowly expanding balloon has been added. I knew enough to imagine quite vividly what the pilots were going through.

The procedure, on the face of it, was routine, with all the steps of a normal landing, which are so precisely laid out that even the computer and the automatic pilot could have brought the airplane in without human assistance if that had been necessary. The only trouble was, the computer couldn't respond to a sudden loss of power quickly enough to restore the delicate balance needed to keep the airplane exactly on the curving flight path. When I say exactly, I'm talking about a matter of inches. It took almost magical anticipation of the slightest deviation—a sixth sense, if you want to call it that, and experienced pilots will know what I'm talking about—and that's something the marvelous human mind and nervous system still have on any computer.

The starboard inboard engine *did* quit, just before the airplane was ready to level off. In my seat, I heard its roar go down to a murmur—a faintest difference in sound I don't think any of the other passengers detected. They must have felt the airplane wobble, as I did, though.

The expanded balloon inside me seemed to burst. I was thinking: *This is it—I wonder if it will come real quick.* No pain or anything—just sudden nothingness. That would be the best way to go.

And then the airplane righted itself, flared out, seemed

to hang still for a sickening moment, and an instant later one set of its eighteen wheels went vmp! vmp! on the concrete, and after that the wheels on the other side did the same. I heard the engines howl as they were slammed into reverse. They held their roar for several seconds as we rocketed down the runway, and suddenly another of them, fed all that fuel, went silent as the airplane continued its rolling motion at well above a hundred miles an hour.

We came to a halt at almost mid-point on the field, and wouldn't you guess that fussy and much maligned Captain Fowler, rolling out with four dead engines, used his forward momentum to clear the active runway, sliding off diagonal taxiway thirty-two-H and creaking to a stop nicely out of everybody's way.

I wanted to shake his hand, so before whatever furor there was to be, I made my way once again to the flight deck just in time to see what was probably Fowler's first real smile in twenty years. It was aimed at O'Malley as he said, "You did okay, kid."

CHAPTER THIRTEEN

And so it was all over but the—

I was going to say "shouting," but there wasn't any. A great deal of confusion, maybe, but no shouting. The passengers debarked when the airplane came to a halt. Ambulances and crash trucks raced up while stretcher bearers waited for a boarding platform so they could take the prince off. As soon as we'd been hustled away from the airplane, all of us were surrounded by officials and police, police, police.

But nobody really shouted. Maybe because it wasn't really over with. Which none of us knew at the time.

It was so chaotic that I can remember only the highlights. Ken Dilworth taking Lisa to meet his father . . . Carter Dilworth glowering down at her for so long it almost broke her marvelous composure, then breaking into a smile and gathering her finally into a great big hug. All I could assume was that Dilworth was so glad to see everybody alive— including his son—that he couldn't get mad at anything.

I noticed Ted O'Malley and Mary Lou Carmichael sticking together, arm in arm, and figured they were ready for a starry evening as soon as all this clearance and questioning were done.

Mike wasn't with Florence Haverman, because the FBI men had whisked him off to one side, while the State Department representatives had done the same with Florence. But I was quite sure they'd find each other later on.

Then, somewhat surprisingly after just an hour or so, we were all free to go, to run the gauntlet of the press.

TV cameras were glaring like monstrous, one-eyed insects out of some horror flick. Jimmy and Gloria Stewart were being very patient with innumerable interviewers who couldn't get enough of them. He kept telling them that he was in his stateroom practically all the time when everything happened, but they didn't want to accept that and kept firing questions. Nobody seemed to care where Blossom and Candy had been as long as they posed for pictures.

My wife, Joan, who is terrified of flying anyway, came out to the airport with Grandma and picked me up at customs. I got a big kiss from both, and then Joan said sharply, "Are you all right?"

"Huh," I said, yawning. "No, not really," I said, thinking of our delicious big bed, "and I won't be until I crash."

I love Joan's mom, "Grandma," more than people who write mother-in-law jokes could possibly comprehend. She's our beautiful and fluttery Billie Burke, but her hearing ain't what it used to be.

"Where did you crash?" she asked.

In the several days that followed, I didn't exactly forget what had taken place on that airplane, but I did manage to shove it aside in my mind. First, I was busy with all the matters that had accumulated during my absence and now needed attention. They ranged from straightening out the kids' scholastic affairs, to cleaning my Koi fish pond, to getting reacquainted with my airplane. It worked great, and my new Texas Instruments Loran C let me punch in the lat-long coordinates of where I wanted to go, and I could make an absolutely accurate beeline for that spot. I was smiling a lot.

My agent called about doing a commercial for somebody's coffee. I told him I didn't drink coffee. He said, "Who cares! Take the money and run." I said I would if I ever started drinking coffee again.

And my next-door neighbor reported that a coyote had gotten into his yard and killed his little dog during the night.

That sickened me. We've lost two dogs and a cat to coyotes, and if they're going to get one of our animals at night anymore, they'll have to break into the house to do it.

Life, good and bad, picked itself up and went on.

Via the news, I kept tabs on Prince Ibrahim of Qram, Son of the Prophets, etcetera, etcetera. He had been shielded from all interviews and rushed to the hospital with a protective escort of U.S. marshals. Jabala and the doctor, after swiftly getting cleared through customs and immigration, had stuck by his side. The media tried to get follow-up stories at the Pilgrimage Hospital, but, probably because the prince owned it, they had to be satisfied with simple, daily handouts from its public-relations person. The operation, performed immediately, was reported as successful, and the surgeon who performed it miraculously eluded the reporters and dropped out of sight. Suddenly, the prince himself was spirited away. They wouldn't say where—just that he was in a safe and comfortable place, convalescing and doing nicely, thank you. As soon as he was strong enough he'd undergo some minor plastic surgery made necessary by some bomb fragments that had caused some slight facial disfigurement. By this time the screaming-headline excitement of the story had died down and the reporters had lost interest, so they stopped pushing.

I didn't see Mike and Florence in all this time, and presumed they were busy getting around to what they had been trying so hard to get around to. Everything must have been okay in that department, because Mike didn't come around to moan on my shoulder. I did hear—and, frankly, I forget where—that Florence had been granted a leave before she returned to Qram and was in a housekeeping motel somewhere.

What I was most interested in was the progress of the film we'd shot in Qram. Jennings Lang was delighted with the publicity it had now received, though this delight was somewhat dampened by the tragic killings that had brought it about. On the phone he said as much and added, "Unfortunately, we're not out of the woods yet."

"Oh? I thought it was clear sailing." To me, mixing metaphors is even more fun than mixing drinks.

"All these post-production costs," he said, and I could visualize his nervous scowl as he spoke, "and I can't get to the prince to countersign the checks. I've taken a hell of a chance and borrowed a big chunk so I can pay current expenses. If the prince doesn't come through eventually I'll be stuck with it, and God knows how I'll ever pay it off."

"You're not the only one who'll be stuck," I said. "I'm working for a percentage of the gross, remember?"

"George," he said, "don't even put your troubles in the same basket as mine."

"Outside of that," I asked, "how's the post-production coming along?"

"Great," he said. "I signed Henry Mancini to do the score, and he gets nominated for an Oscar every time he moons at a river. And all the takes we've got really look good. I was a little worried about that in Qram, because we never got to see any dailies there. Just too damned far to fly 'em back and forth. But, no sweat. The photography's superb. Fine performances, too. We've got a winner, if we're ever able to put it together now. Look, George, how would you like to see a rough cut?"

"Very much. Have you got one already?"

"Well, it's as much a string of dailies as a rough cut, but I had it put together to show some of the people who are supplying interim funds. There's a screening tomorrow morning. Mike says he'll be there, and you're welcome, too."

"Reserve me a seat on the aisle," I said.

Now, I prefer people who are punctual, and I always try to be on time myself for any appointment. I have a way of leaving early for wherever I go, to allow a cushion. But when I'm ready to go there's always somebody delaying me, sometimes at the front door. It's a conspiracy.

This time it was Lisa Garcia. She drove up in a sports car of racing green, which perhaps she'd borrowed or rented. She stepped out of it all smart and glamorous in a poplin jacket and a tweed cap, to say nothing of perforated driving gloves. I wondered if Ken had taken her shopping on Rodeo Drive, using his old man's American Express card.

"George," she said. "I'm so glad I found you in!"

"I'm not in. I'm already ten miles down the freeway, mentally. Got a screening. What is it, Lisa?"

"I've *got* to talk to you."

I looked at my watch. "Okay. Ten minutes. Inside, where there's quiet."

We sat in a corner of my living room. The two Cairns and two Maltese came to the patio door and wagged their tails, and Lisa said weren't they darling and wanted to pet them, but I reminded her that there wasn't time for that. Besides, the two cats, Panther and Kook, were already climbing all over her.

"I'd have talked this over with Florence," said Lisa, quite poised, and yet with a soft sincerity in her eyes, "but I couldn't get hold of her quickly enough. I've just got to have someone else's opinion. Someone I trust. I hope you'll forgive me."

"I probably will, if I know what for."

"Prince Ibrahim wants to see me," she said.

"You're kidding."

"No," she said, "but the point is, do I want to see *him?*"

Somewhat taken aback, I said, "I don't know. Do you?"

"Let me explain this, George. I'm right in the middle of all the wedding plans now that Ken's father has given us his blessing. He softened up so much with relief when he saw we'd both landed safely that we didn't have to come clean with him. Ken was right—his bark is worse than his bite. So I've been putting my past behind me—all of it— and just when I thought I was succeeding in that, here comes this call from Jabala. He and Ibrahim are in some mansion or villa or something up around Big Sur. Casa Madrona, I think they call it. Another bit of real estate they own. The prince, he says, has just *got* to see me again."

"What for?"

"Apparently not for what you must be thinking. I say apparently, because that's what I thought at first. As far as I can understand it, he's bored sitting there and convalescing and wants me to see him briefly just to cheer him up. He wants to find out what I'd like for a wedding present, and if I say the Taj Mahal I might get it. But that's not why I feel I ought to go see him, nor is it that he was very good to me—very understanding—and he's an all-around nice guy. If all he needs is a little cheering up, I guess some people would say I owe it to him."

"Not me. Anyway, what's the problem?"

"Don't you see? Ken, who knows I was Ibrahim's mistress, may very well think the worst, and if his father starts putting two and two together, this whole new life of mine has a good chance of ending before it gets started."

"Right. Make some excuse and don't see the prince."

"That's what I thought, too. Until Jabala started dropping subtle hints. Maybe they weren't hints; maybe he was just making conversation. But what he said was that his highness was certainly looking forward to continuing co-operation with World International's chairman of the board, Carter Dilworth. He thought it would be a good idea if I kept the prince in his mellow mood. Now, I know Ibrahim, and he can be impulsive—sometimes even unreasonable. He may be a nice guy, but he's also, in many ways, a spoiled brat, and you and I would be, too, if we'd been brought up with all those millions. I'm afraid if I don't go see him, I'll queer the whole deal for WIA, and Carter Dilworth may find that the most unforgivable sin of all."

"Okay," I said, "if you have to go see him—take Ken with you."

She shook her head. "Jabala was firm about that. Alone, he said. Which makes me think Ibrahim may want to talk me into coming back again."

"Would you, if he made the right offer?"

"Not for the sun and the moon—and I think he owns a piece of them, too. George, I've been building up to this new life of mine for a long time, and I'm not going to lose it now. And not the least of it is being in love with Ken in a way I never thought I would be with anybody."

"Good for you. Good for both of you," I said. "But what *are* you going to do about Ibrahim?"

She frowned for a moment, then nodded slowly. "I think I'll just go there and tell him, in complete honesty, how I feel about Ken. I know how to handle him, and I think I can make him accept that. If he hasn't already. Anyway, this is the one sure way to close the final door to the past and make a really fresh start."

"You'll have to be strong," I said.

"I've always had to be strong."

"Fine," I said. I looked at my watch. "Now, if you don't mind—"

Lisa rose. "I'm sorry I took this much of your time. I'll drive up to the villa right now; I can make it by late this afternoon, I think. Ken's out of town for a day, so this would be a good time to do it, get it over with. And thanks for your advice, George."

"I didn't give any."

"You didn't? I thought you did. Well, no matter. You listened, and that helped me decide."

That sounded familiar. Mike Corby always thought I was giving him advice when all I was doing was listening. It's the secret of being a successful uncle, and it covers you against any chances that your advice, if you gave it, might be dead wrong.

The screening room Jennings Lang had for the occasion was like a small theater with only a few banks of seats. It was actually a sound-mixing studio with an open space for the actors in front and a bank of sliding controls forming the first row. In the rear was a glassed-in control room, and above that a projection booth. As usual, a few shirt-sleeved technicians wandering around had mysterious things to do before we could start, so Mike Corby and I were able to sit by ourselves for a few moments and bring each other up to date.

As a lieutenant of detectives on the New York Police Department, Mike had been noted for his rumpled suits. He bought them at large discounts from reject racks in the Garment District; now, as an actor, he'd turned to sports clothes, all of them expensive, but still looking cheap and rumpled two minutes after he'd put them on. He had a sure instinct for making designer items look like something off a Salvation Army pickup truck.

His brow was rumpled, too. "She got to a phone," he said.

"Who?" I asked.

"Meredy. Who else? There weren't any in that Mexican village she was holed up in, so she took one of those buses with the roosters and bicycles on top to the next town and finally got hold of me."

"That's nice," I said.

"Nice? I was in bed when the phone rang."

"So she woke you up—"

He shook his head. "She didn't. I was in bed, but I wasn't alone."

"Oh," I said.

"Very embarrassing," he said. "I couldn't talk with Florence listening. I mean, I'd told her about Meredy, and how we'd sort of separated, and how she'd gone to Mexico to paint, but, Jesus! This was a conversation that had to be private! Meredy even asked if somebody was with me, and I said no, and she said, 'You're lying, aren't you?'"

"Well, what did she expect? And, come to think of it, what do *you* expect?"

"I don't know!" He seemed in agony. "Florence ducked out for a moment and let me finish talking to Meredy. Meredy said she'd been thinking about getting together again, but now she wasn't so sure. Then, after I hung up, Florence came back in and said she'd been thinking about getting together permanently, but now *she* wasn't so sure."

"Mike," I said, "you got yourself into this and you're going to have to make up your mind one way or the other. Unless you want to spend the rest of your life shuttling secretly between L.A. and Mexico."

"Remember Midas the Greek?" said Mike, sighing. "Everything he touched turned to gold? With me, it's manure."

"I wouldn't say that. You handled things pretty good on that airplane. You didn't exactly solve the murders, but

176

you got a lot of credit for keeping them from getting worse. And all the publicity didn't hurt your career, or, for that matter, the picture itself."

"I've been wondering about that," said Mike, shifting his frown into a lower gear. "Did the way Fourrier committed suicide really wrap it up?"

"Everybody thinks so. What else could it have been? We went through all the possibilities."

"It still bugs me," he said. "For a lot of reasons, some of which I can't put my finger on. I think the biggest one is that Fourrier just wasn't the type. The worst crime he was capable of committing was adultery, and if that in itself were a crime there'd be more people in the clink than there are in the Russian Army."

"Let sleeping dogs lie," I said.

"Maybe. But when I do a job I have to finish it right. You must feel that way about your work, sometimes—it can get very important. Besides, if, for some reason, Fourrier wasn't the murderer, there could still be some world-shaking conspiracy going on that we don't even know about. Maybe we didn't avoid World War III after all."

"Oh, come on now," I said. "If Fourrier wasn't the killer, why did he kill himself? Why did he write that note? It was in his handwriting—they checked."

"He could have been forced to write the note. Somebody else could have killed him and put the gun in his hand. I checked the results of the autopsy, as a matter of fact. No powder deposits on his hand, the way there usually is when someone fires a gun. They figured it was the single-shot weapon, which doesn't have apertures outside the barrel. They also kinda shrugged in every other way—a natural reluctance to open it up again."

It was my turn to frown. "I don't know, Mike. Are you sure you're not being oversuspicious?"

"That's possible. But it's more than just these loose ends. I told you before I had the feeling something very significant had slipped by me and I hadn't picked it up. I still have that feeling. I woke up a couple of times thinking

I'd just dreamed the answer, and then I couldn't remember what it was I'd dreamed."

"You're just feeling mixed up, Mike. Probably on account of Meredy and Florence. You've got to solve that one before you try to solve anything else."

"How come everybody but me can straighten out their love life?" he grumbled. "You'd have thought Ken and Lisa had three strikes against them, but it looks like they worked it out fine."

"Maybe they've still got some problems," I said. I told him what Lisa had said when she'd called on me earlier.

"Well, at least they both know what they really want," he said. "Oh, hell. Let's watch the movie."

It wasn't exactly a movie, like one you take in while eating popcorn. The sequences had been strung together according to the story line, but they hadn't been finely edited with close-ups in the right places, and with some of the more repetitive footage cut, and, of course, the opticals hadn't been put in yet, so there were no dissolves or fade-ins or anything like that. The big thing it lacked at this stage was the background music, which nobody does like Mancini, and some of the sound effects, like crunchy footsteps that didn't actually register when the scene was shot, still had to be dubbed in. But, for all this, the sense of the film as it would eventually appear was there, and we could get a very good idea of the performances. I thought they were great—especially that of Jimmy Stewart, who played a retired airline pilot with a terminal disease taking one last sentimental journey. The part had some depth, and he brought it out in his deceptively effortless way. I was the cigar-chomping engineer, Patroni, again, and I played it straight, without any histrionic tricks, which was exactly how the director had wanted it. Blossom Foster was better than ever. I liked to think that the coaching I'd given her on the side had something to do with it, but in the last analysis it was her own growing maturity that made her performance. What all this added up to was a very gripping sense of reality so that you really believed all this was actually happening and that you were part of it. I didn't think we had an Oscar-winner, like *The Godless*, which we'd shot in Mexico, but it was damn good and I couldn't see how it would fail to turn a profit eventually, if Prince Ibrahim would come out of his shell, up there on the northern California coast somewhere, and fork over the funds needed to finish it. Mike thought he had problems, but on a scale of one to about ten million they were nothing compared to what Jennings Lang had on his hands.

This viewing gave producer Lang another chance to see it as a whole and clean up any little glitches that might have crept in. He was in a huddle with Andy McGlaglen, the director, and they were muttering to each other, picking the thing apart with fine tweezers and making notes for the film editor, who was contributing his own suggestions. The public is impressed by the stars, and sometimes by the director, but the unsung hero of any really good motion picture is the film editor, and I sometimes wish there were a way to put his name in lights, too.

Several times Jennings had the projectionist stop the film and roll it back a little so that he could get another look at a scene that had just passed. One of these was a long shot where a stunt man, who was supposed to be Jimmy Stewart, was falling off a racing camel. The airliner had made a forced landing in the desert, and one way to get help was to ride for it on this camel a wandering Bedouin had brought to the scene and—

But never mind all that. I don't want to spoil the movie for you in case you ever get to see it.

"Take a close look," said Jennings, running the scene again. "Right there—just as he falls. It's only an instant, but we get a pretty good look at his face, and we can see it's not really Jimmy Stewart. Somebody with sharp eyes in the audience just might pick it up. We've got some other angles on the fall, and we'd better use one of them instead, even if they're not as spectacular as this one."

The film continued to roll.

I thought I had sensed Mike stiffening in his seat beside me, and now, suddenly, he grabbed my arm.

"George!" he said. "That's it! That's *gotta* be it!"

He'd raised his voice and, annoyed, I said, "What's gotta be what?"

"Would you guys mind quieting down a little?" called Jennings.

Mike rose. "Outside, George. Where we can talk."

"What the hell's bugging you, anyway?"

"Don't ask questions. Come on."

I followed him to keep him from embarrassing me further, ready to bawl him out good once we reached the corridor. There I drew myself up, aware once again of how much we looked like Mutt and Jeff together. Mike squared himself in that bulldog stance of his and said, "It all came in a flash when I saw that double! What's really going on—and why those murders were really committed! I also remember now what's been bothering me all along!"

"This better be good," I said. "And make it quick—I want to see the rest of that movie."

"George, we haven't got time for that. We don't even have time to stand here gabbing about it."

"Will you please tell me what in hell you're talking about?"

"I want you to trust me, George—maybe like you've never trusted me before. I know about the murders now. I know it wasn't Fourrier—he was just a patsy. But there's something else I know, and this is something we've got to take care of right away. Lisa Garcia's in real danger, George, and we've got to stop her from seeing Prince Ibrahim!"

"Have you blown your cork? Now, look, Mike—"

"The chances I'm right are ninety-nine percent, or more. That's enough to act on. Did you say Lisa figured on getting there by late afternoon?"

"The way she drives that sports car, I can imagine she will."

"We can't have the cops intercept her—by the time we explained everything she'd be there, and we have no way of making them believe us, anyway. There's only one way to do it. Your airplane!"

"What?"

"You keep it at Van Nuys, right? We can get there in half an hour."

"Now, look here, Mike—"

"Every minute we waste here is bringing Lisa closer to getting killed herself! Get that into your head, George, and believe me! Now, come on, move that big carcass of yours and I'll tell you everything on the way!"

"Mike, if this is another of your wild fantasies—"

"It's not. And if you don't fly me up there I'll charter a plane and go myself. Do you want to be in on this or don't you?"

I wasted another moment staring and then I said, "All right, goddamnit, let's go!"

CHAPTER FOURTEEN

To Mike, an airplane ride was only a means of getting from one place to another fast, and so it is, coldly speaking, but the esthetics of it escaped him entirely. Maybe *I'm* wrong; maybe winging free a mile above the earth in the clear ocean of the air, with the landscape spread out below you like some model of the place where people dwell isn't the most breathtaking and beautiful situation a man can put himself into, and maybe those who fly are the odd ones for seeing it this way. At any rate, Mike and I saw it differently.

Mike kept glancing at the ground nervously, as though wondering when we'd plunge toward it, and at me nervously, as though wondering when I'd make the mistake that would bring that about. He was beside me in one of the two forward seats and I'd had to tell him several times to just sit there and for Pete's sake relax, and don't do anything to keep me from flying on course and straight and level. I'd placed the destination airstrip coordinates in the Loran, and with no restricted or prohibited zones between us and it, I'd bypassed the auto-pilot and was hand flying us there as steadily and directly as possible.

He tried to cover his nervousness by talking, and I didn't mind that because what he talked about was how he'd guessed the truth about the murders. He'd given it to me in bits and pieces on the way to the airport, but now he tried to put it together into a neat package.

"It hit me when I saw the double who was supposed

to be Jimmy Stewart fall off that camel," he said. "You know how they do with doubles. They pick somebody with the same build as the star and sometimes, if they can get it, a strong resemblance. They usually photograph the action with a long shot so the face is blurred, or in shadow, or, anyway, not seen clearly by the audience."

"I seem to have picked up this much about the motion picture business along the line somewhere," I said dryly. "What else is new?"

"Well, you gotta remember that what came to me wasn't as sudden as it seems. I'd been kicking the whole schmeer around in my mind ever since we got off the prince's airplane. Everybody else figured the murders were solved with Fourrier's suicide, probably because they wanted it that way, but I just couldn't buy it entirely. I'd had a good look at Fourrier, and that gives you a different impression than just reports of what the guy was supposed to have been and what he'd allegedly done. I just couldn't see him as either a terrorist or a mass murderer. I realize that the instinctive impressions of one cop don't stand up in court or anything like that, but they've been a help to me before in the course of an investigation."

"You're the one who always says everybody's a suspect till proven otherwise," I reminded him.

"I never said that. Or did I? Anyway, don't confuse the issue. The pieces seemed to fit, but when you looked hard at the cracks, they didn't. Take the motive. The killer was all wrapped up in some cause that had to do with Arab unity, and Prince Ibrahim could be said to be against that, but not so damned much he had to be killed for it. Besides, Fourrier had never taken a shot at the prince himself. He knocked off all the others, Hibner theorized, just to spread terror—maybe as a kind of warning. Now, an assassin might sacrifice himself to get to the main target—Prince Ibrahim—but what's the sense of killing a few people who knew him and then resorting to suicide when he'd practically gotten away with it?"

"He was a fanatic," I said. "What he did wasn't supposed to make sense."

"Fanatics act on impulse. It's all emotional. They don't cook up elaborate schemes and carry them out as coolly as this murderer did. They might be cat's-paws, and get the plan from somebody else, but the people behind an assassination attempt know they're nuts and wouldn't trust them with anything that wasn't fairly simple and direct. Now, as I say, Fourrier wasn't this kind of a nut but he had a background that could make some people think he was, so they used him not as a cat's-paw but as a red herring. In fact, he was the one who made the real murderer's getaway possible. With his suicide, the case seemed solved, and there was no reason to hold everybody else aboard the plane and investigate them thoroughly."

"This still doesn't explain why the murderer went after Larrabee and the others and not the prince himself."

"That's the part I'm trying to explain, if you'll stop interrupting. No attempt was made on the prince, because that guy in the stateroom, flat on his back, and with his head all wrapped in bandages, wasn't the prince!"

"Are you sure of that, Mike? Really sure?"

"It's the key element. Once we assume that, the rest falls into place. You saw what pains Jabala went to to keep somebody like Lisa Garcia from getting into that stateroom. How Larrabee and the copilot got the brushoff earlier when they wanted to see Ibrahim. They all knew the prince quite well—any one of them might have spotted the so-called patient for an imposter if they'd had a close look at him. My guess is that he was somebody who looked like the prince at a distance—the way Jimmy Stewart's double passes for Jimmy himself. But, the way things were, and with the double bound to be exposed to public view, even briefly, once we'd landed, there was just too much chance one of these people might make him and blow the lid off the whole scheme. Even the stateroom wasn't completely secure; Jabala was running out of excuses to keep them from poking their noses in and was worried as hell they might do it by accident. There was only one way to prevent exposure, and while it sounds drastic as hell to us, it was perfectly natural to the conspirators, who have always looked at human life

184

as something pretty cheap. It's the way of the desert, I guess, or something in their culture. We see it among certain groups in the Middle East all the time. If somebody gets in your way, what the hell, kill him."

"But what was the whole scheme? Why an imposter in the first place?"

"I don't know exactly. Maybe the real prince is dead and they can't afford to let that be known because it might bring about a revolution. The way Florence talks, that would be inevitable. Maybe he got killed in the bomb blast, or, more likely, died recently in some other way. We know he hadn't been making many public appearances for a while. When he did show himself it was from a distance. They didn't want him photographed at the airport and they tossed my hotel room when they thought I'd taken some pictures. What this suggests, is that the bomb at the airport was actually part of the plan. It gave them the excuse to fly the double out of the country where he didn't have to be seen by the populace for a few weeks. Time enough to pretend to give him plastic surgery, which would explain his changed appearance. It's also why Jabala was so insistent on a non-stop flight—any landing would have increased chances of somebody getting to the prince and seeing him."

A few thermals, coming up from the ground, were making the airplane fishtail a little and I made like a yaw damper with the rudder pedals, lessening the slight insta-bility. "It's still got a lot of holes, the way I see it," I said. "We know Larrabee and several others might have blown the lid if they'd had a close look at the prince, and it seems to figure that Rita Schmidt was killed when she caught the murderer doing away with Larkin. But what about that big eunuch, or whatever he was, who was always curled up on the prince's doorstep? Sure, he knew the prince intimately, like the others, but he was evidently completely loyal to him and he'd be squawking about it if anything had really happened to the prince. Long before they got around to killing him, too."

"I'll admit that's a hole," said Mike, frowning, "but I can think of several explanations for it. Maybe he agreed

185

to go along with the scheme and then changed his mind. Maybe they managed to keep him from seeing the prince closely at first, and then he accidentally got a good look at him and started to object. Exactly how it went isn't important—just that he was a potential danger is what really counts."

I nodded thoughtfully. "Okay, what you're saying is that Jabala, and, of course, the doctor are behind all of this. And that one or both of them may be the murderer."

"I'm saying they're in on the scheme. It could be one of their secret police or some hired hit man who did the actual dirty work. And they may not be alone in trying to put some figurehead in the prince's place. Some of his other advisors may well be taking part in the conspiracy. Remember, whoever gets the prince out of the way runs the country with a free hand, and whether he—or they—are on the right or on the left or in the middle is beside the point. It's one hell of a prize, with billions of dollars and all kinds of power that's up for grabs, and, from their standpoint, is worth all kinds of trouble, including a few murders."

"They could have just knocked everybody off back in Qram, if that's what they wanted."

"They could have, but they didn't. It would have made an awful stink and there would have been too much demand by U.S. authorities for an investigation. By doing it on the plane they had their patsy, and once he was thought to be the murderer that would be an end to it. This was why Jabala seemed to have a sudden change of heart and allowed us all to fly out on *The Star of Qram*. If they'd singled out Larrabee and not the rest of the cast it would have looked too suspicious. Somebody would have started poking into it—some damn gossip reporter, maybe—and found out Larrabee and the prince had laid all those whores together in Las Vegas, and the whole thing never would have been laid to rest."

"I don't know," I said, frowning. "All this seems as far out as the theory that Fourrier did it."

"The murders themselves were far out," said Mike, "and any explanation for them is going to be just as bizarre.

186

To our way of thinking—not to these characters to whom deep and dark conspiracy is a way of life. We may never even be able to prove everything I'm saying—Jabala and his friends might be able to stonewall it if we come up with any accusations. But that's not our immediate concern. The attempt on Lisa Garcia's life failed because you and I stumbled into the cargo compartment at the right time. That warned her, and they never got another chance. She still might run into the prince sometime and know he's an imposter. In fact, if she's going to marry Ken, and if WIA is going to do business with Qram, the chances of that are pretty good. They've got to get rid of her now, while they still can. We've got to stop her from sticking her nose into that villa, where they can do it."

"What if you're wrong, Mike? What if it really is the prince up there in the villa?"

"Then there's no harm done. We shortstop Lisa and it all gets straightened out afterward. But the chance I'm right is very, very strong, and we'd never be able to live with ourselves afterward if she gets killed when we could have prevented it."

"One more thing," I said. I looked down at the rocky coastline, made out the shape of Morro Bay, checked my time, and saw that we were right where we were supposed to be. The Loran showed we were five-point-five nautical miles from the small airstrip near the prince's villa. I'd checked the current NOTAMS to be sure it was still there with all its facilities. "If Jabala and the doctor didn't personally kill all those people—and somehow I can't see either one of them in that role—who did?"

I had dipped the wing sharply in order to look down. Mike had grabbed the side of the seat. "Do you have to do that?" he asked.

"Yes. Come on, Mike—who did the actual dirty work?"

"I think I know," he said, "but for the time being I'm not going to tell you."

"Why not?"

"Just fly this thing flat, will you, George?" he said, "and let me do this my way . . ."

I was rather proud of the smooth landing I made on the little airport's single dirt runway, but Mike, who wasn't interested in airplanes, knew only that he was *down,* and that was good enough for him. Not so much as a grunt of approval. It was like an actor giving a good performance and not getting any applause.

The A-36, flaps down, settled squarely on its main wheels, more than nine feet apart, holding firmly to the strip in spite of a brisk crosswind, and finally resting on its nosewheel as, losing momentum, it coasted to a halt. The runway was bumpy, and I didn't like that, but Mike did. He was ready to like the ground no matter what condition it was in.

I taxied to the low, metal-sided building that was the airport's only structure. Several light airplanes were parked around it, dogged down by cables to rings sunk in the ground, but there wasn't any sign of human beings around either the aircraft or the operations shack. I'd come in carefully, which you always do with a strange airport, flying a pattern to give it a good inspection before making a final approach, and I'd seen that it was well off the highway and the nearby town it presumably served, with a winding road of several miles leading to it through rough, wooded country. The next problem was to get to town, which wasn't much more than a gas station, a tavern, and a couple of stores, but through which Lisa Garcia would necessarily have to pass to get to the turnoff that led to Casa Madrona. Trouble was, I didn't see so much as a bicycle to get us there.

The NOTAMS—notices to airmen put out periodically for the benefit of pilots—had neglected to mention that this so-called airport was virtually abandoned. Maybe it wasn't supposed to be; maybe everybody was down at the tavern killing the lovely afternoon. Anyway, we peered through the dusty windows of the operations shack and saw that it was empty.

I looked at my watch. "Goddamnit, she ought to be getting here about now. Might take us almost an hour to walk to town."

Mike had his nose to the window. "There's a phone in there," he said.

"Yeah. If we could get to it."

He moved to the front door, which had a cylinder lock, and rattled it to confirm that it was locked. "Ever hear about cops and robbers? They get to know about each others' work. Got any tools aboard that crate of yours?"

"Certainly. And don't call it a crate—that went out with the Spads and Jennies. It's an airplane. Not a bus or a kite or even a plane. Airplane. And say it in a hushed voice, with respect."

"Costs that much, huh?" he said, grinning. "Come on, George; the tools."

Mike got the door open with a screwdriver and a vise-grip. We pushed inside. At the jerry-built operations counter there was a wall phone with a printed list of numbers stapled next to it, and one of these numbers was for Don's Taxi Service. I called and a woman answered. Don was somewhere around, she said; she'd see if she could find him. What were we doing at the airport, anyway? I said we'd flown in and she said, oh, yeah, she'd thought she'd heard an airplane. Sit tight, she said. Implicit in her words was the local philosophy; everything will happen sooner or later if you just simmer down and wait for it.

I looked around the inside of the prefab building as I waited. There wasn't much to look at—the counter, a few forms on it, a two-way radio, and an aeronautical chart of the local area on one wall. At one end of the room was a bank of large shelves and, stacked neatly upon them, were several packed parachutes. A poster on the wall near the shelf said CLIFFSIDE SKYDIVING CLUB and gave the date of an exhibition that had evidently taken place earlier in the year.

Mike used the men's room. Correction: there was only one, so it was the people's room. I sat on a chair of tarnished metal and ripped vinyl and leafed through an old aviation magazine.

It was twenty minutes before the taxi—a dusty old Chevy that looked as if it had served as a tank in the Korean

189

war—arrived, and Mike and I went out to meet it. Don, the driver—I presumed it was Don—was a beefy man in a checkered shirt and a straw cowboy hat. He didn't get out of the driver's seat and let us scramble into the back seat ourselves.

"It's six bucks to town," he said.

"Get there fast and it's ten," said Mike.

"You guys in a hurry or somethin'?"

"No," said Mike sarcastically, "we're just the last of the big spenders."

I don't know whether Don got it or not. He ground several gear teeth down to size to get the taxi going and headed for the road in a cloud of dust.

"How come nobody was at the airport?" I asked.

"Charley's got the flu," he said, and from that I had to deduce the entire situation. Don evidently wasn't one to waste words.

"Look, Don," said Mike, "where do you hang out in town? On the main road?"

"There ain't no other road," said Don.

"What I mean is, do you see whoever comes to town? We're looking for a young lady driving a green Datsun 280-Z."

"Oh, *that* one!" said Don. "She was a looker! What is she, some model or something?"

"She's already here?"

"I just said so, didn't I? She stopped at the gas station. That's where I hang out. Wanted to know where the turnoff for Casa Madrona was."

"How long ago?"

"I don't know. An hour, maybe."

"Did she go there?"

"How do I know? We told her where the turnoff was and she took off. How come you guys are so all-fired anxious to find her?"

"It's an emergency, Don," said Mike. "We've got to get her back to L.A. A close relative just had an accident there." That was as good a lie as any, I reflected.

"I guess them Arabs up at the villa will have to be

190

disappointed," Don said. "I figure she was goin' up there to—uh—entertain 'em, sort of. That's it, ain't it?"

"You've got a dirty mind, Don. No, that's not it."

"Well," said Don, shrugging, "no skin off my ass. They keep to themselves up there, and that's okay with us, though you'd think they could spend some of all that money they got in the town. So what do you guys want to do? You can't call the villa—number's unlisted. Unless you know it."

"Take us to the villa, Don," said Mike.

"That'll be twelve bucks."

"Okay. Just drive. And if you want a tip, don't ask so many questions."

Don didn't ask any more questions, though I could see he wanted to. Mike and I lowered our voices as we talked, and Don kept angling his head around, trying to hear. We muttered out of the sides of our mouths, the way guys in the slammer do, and I think that foiled him.

"Now, look," Mike said to me, "we can't just walk up to the front door and ring the bell. If they see us looking for Lisa, they're bound to guess we know something. What we've got to do is get in some other way and surprise them."

I frowned. "Doesn't sound easy."

"I don't think it will be, but we'll know better when we get there and see what the layout is. I've got to find some excuse to have Don let us off before we reach the house, so they won't see us approaching."

"How about: 'It's such a nice day, I think I'll walk the rest of the way'?"

"Very funny. I'll just tell him to stop and let him wonder about it. For twelve bucks he'll do anything, no questions asked. You got twelve on you, by the way?"

"Yeah," I said. Part of being an uncle is picking up the checks. I made sure about my cash, anyway; I didn't think Don would accept my American Express card. I said to Mike, "Are you armed?"

"Are you kidding?" he said. "I'm not a cop now, I'm a damned actor."

"Well you're not a damned *good* one yet, so don't knock it."

CHAPTER FIFTEEN

Casa Madrona had been built by some guy who had made a fortune in real estate in southern California and had evidently decided to emulate William Randolph Hearst by putting up another San Simeon on a rocky promontory overlooking the rugged coastline. He didn't quite make it, except perhaps for the Arabs. It wasn't as big as San Simeon, but it was just as imported, except for his taste, which was California tacky. He'd gone to Switzerland itself for some of the boards and bricks that made it an authentic chalet, a little summer place away from home with umpteen bedrooms and gold-plated faucets on the bidets, and Keane paintings of saucer-eyed children in every room. No matter where you went in the house, you had the feeling you were being watched by old Stutz Bearcats with their headlamps on. If anyone ever told you the story of what the Arabs did to that mansion on Sunset Boulevard in Beverly Hills——for example, painting pubic hairs on all the full-figure statues—— you would understand why they must have considered Casa Madrona a regal retreat.

It was named after one of those twisty-trunked, reddish-barked trees you find up and down the Pacific coast, and the approach to it was through a thick forest of fir, so that I was sure nobody in the house could see us coming. Don, his ass already ours for twelve bucks plus a three-dollar tip, let us off at a place where he said we could walk to the house in two minutes, made a back-and-forth U-turn in the narrow road, treated us to one last puzzled stare, then drove off.

We had barely walked one minute before the house came into sight, and, in front of it, parked, was the green sports car Lisa had driven. To my surprise, no fence, no walls, no gate. Mike touched my arm, and I nodded, and then he led me through the trees toward the side of the house. I kept waiting for dogs to bark, but evidently there weren't any of those, either. Somebody who doesn't like dogs can't be all good, I thought, but that was only to cover up the tight, scared feeling in the pit of my stomach.

The windows on the side of the house were too high for us to raise ourselves on tiptoe and look into them. They were of stained glass, anyway—one featuring a Godzilla-size Coca-Cola bottle—so we might not have been able to see through them. We listened hard, but there wasn't a sound from inside the house. They really built houses tight in the old days.

"The back," whispered Mike, and pushed on in that direction. We passed a couple of flying buttresses and several dormer windows. The decoration on the eaves was all jiggly and colorful, like on any Swiss cottage.

Mike was making his way, in back, toward a jutting wing with a kind of porch and a door. I wondered if I'd be watching him pick a lock again, and also wondered what the penalties were for addictive breaking and entering, because Mike suddenly seemed to be making a habit of it.

Mike put his foot on the first step of the porch.

A voice behind us said, "Please be very still, gentlemen."

Even as I turned, startled, I knew I had recognized that voice. Yakub Seif al-Jabala, chief of staff to his highness, Ibrahim, Protector of the Faith and all that jazz, was his old roly-poly self with one major difference. There was a very efficient looking Luger-type pistol in his hand.

"Oh, hi there, Mr. Jabala!" said Mike, in ridiculous innocence.

"Stay right where you are." The Luger flickered. "And you'd better have a good explanation. In case you're wondering, there have been hidden cameras watching you ever since you got out of the cab." Ah ha, thought I, *electronic* walls and gates and fences. "You have approached the house in very suspicious fashion."

"Well—uh—you see," said Mike, ad-libbing desperately, "we weren't sure anybody was home, so we thought we—"

"As I thought," said Jabala, cutting him short. There was no blubber on those licorice eyes of his. They were lean, hard, and mean. He was wearing an embroidered, collarless Arab shirt that hung over his casual country slacks and gave him the look of a fierce desert sheikh, for all his dumpy figure. "You don't have a good explanation. May I suggest the truth as an acceptable substitute?"

"Now look here, your excellency," said Mike, "if you'll just put that gun down—"

"Hardly," said Jabala. "You followed Miss Garcia here, didn't you?"

"Well, yes, as a matter of fact. Okay, Jabala, I'll come clean. We had an idea the prince might try to seduce her or something, and we didn't want that to happen."

"Do you take me for a fool? There have been times when that was to my advantage, but this isn't one of them. You must have guessed quite a bit to take all this trouble in coming here. I'm afraid that makes both of you rather dangerous."

"What about Lisa?" I blurted out. "Is she inside? Is she okay?"

"Go in and see for yourself," said Jabala, with what may have been a faint smile. "And move slowly. I'll be right behind you."

We went through a large kitchen, and then down a hallway, and then into a richly appointed living room, with Jabala behind us, telling us where to turn. I had a feeling the eyes in the Keane paintings followed us, but I guess I've watched the Three Stooges too often. There was a thick carpet underfoot and all the upholstery looked expensive. There was a fireplace and there were potted plants. No TV set—other than the monitors for watching two clumsy idiots approach. They were roughing it out here in the country.

Dr. Fayez was standing by the window, where he'd evidently been peering through the curtains to note whatever was going on outside. Small and birdlike, in his country-weekend dress he was more brightly plumed than ever. His pants were Scottish plaid and his shirt was Hawaiian tourist. He was neatly shaven, as usual, to the razored edges of his small spade beard.

A trim man in full Arab dress sat on the couch and looked up at us indifferently. He had handsome, chiseled features and a hairline mustache, and for a moment I thought he was Prince Ibrahim. In the next moment, I wasn't so sure. I'd seen pictures of the prince, and this man's face seemed to be subtly different, though I couldn't say precisely what the differences were. He was about the same height as the prince, but, I thought, just slightly heavier. And he didn't have those snapping eyes that showed in photographs of the prince.

Mike looked around, then met Jabala's eyes. "Okay, where's Lisa?"

"In a moment," said Jabala blandly. "Gentlemen, may I introduce his highness, Prince Ibrahim of Qram, Lion of the Desert, Son of the Prophets, Protector of the Faith, Guardian of the Ancient Tribal Territories."

"Yeah?" said Mike doubtfully.

"His appearance has changed a bit following plastic surgery made necessary by his disfigurement in the bomb blast, of course, but he does bear a remarkable resemblance to his former self, doesn't he?" His sardonic smile would have done Basil Rathbone proud. "That's because he's actually a distant cousin of the former Prince Ibrahim. But no one will ever know that now, will they?"

Mike drew a deep breath and said, "You're right. We did guess. He goes back home, takes the prince's place, and does exactly what you say, which means you run the whole country. Is that it?"

"Very succinctly stated," said Jabala.

195

"So what happened to the real prince? Did you already kill him?"

"Not quite yet. We have to be certain everything's in place before we get rid of him permanently. He's in his hunting lodge in the mountains. Under guard and under heavy sedation, of course, but, under the circumstances quite comfortable."

"Nice of you to see to it," said Mike. "Look, Jabala, you don't really think you're going to get away with all this, do you?"

"And why not? It's worked out perfectly, so far. And it's really quite important for Qram. My country has been a puppet, jumping when the United States pulls the strings, long enough. It's time the Qramis people enjoyed the benefits of our oil for a change. With the prince removed this way, they can do it without a bloody revolution or a war that might be ignited. You can see how a few unimportant lives are nothing compared to that."

"What do you want from me, an argument?" said Mike. "I'm not into politics. But I know something about murder, and that's what you've been up to. I figured out how you replaced the prince with a lookalike—never mind how—and how you had to knock off those people on the plane to keep it a secret. So now let me ask you if you think I'm dumb enough to walk in here without some kind of insurance. The whole story's in somebody's hands and it goes to the cops if I don't get out of here."

After an almost imperceptible pause, Jabala said, "You're bluffing."

"Okay, if you think I am, call it."

"If you'd had time to do what you say, you'd have also had time to stop Miss Garcia from coming here. And I don't think you would have been pussyfooting around the house, either. If you were sure, you would have sent the FBI or someone like that. I have been fortunate enough, Mr. Corby, to learn many American expressions during my long residence in your country. The one that comes to mind now seems most appropriate." He did smile; no mistake about it this time. "You're batting out of your league."

Mike glanced at me and frowned. I thought he was asking what the hell I thought we ought to do now, but this time I didn't have an answer for him. He looked at Jabala again, and I could sense that he was trying to eat up time in the hope that the U.S. Cavalry or its equivalent would, at any moment, come riding to our rescue. "You said we'd see Lisa. Is she really here, or is that some kind of bluff of yours?"

"Come with me, gentlemen," Jabala said blithely. "And you, too, Dr. Fayez. I think we're going to need you."

There was a staircase, and more corridors, and then another, narrower staircase, rising through the musty gloom of the old mansion's interior. It's harder to get your bearings in a strange house than in the open sky, but by the time we had arrived at the door to an upper room I could sense that it was in the top of one of the structure's circular, crenelated towers. Jabala stayed slightly behind us with his gun pointed, and Dr. Fayez came forward, found a key in the pocket of his dress Stuart pants, and opened the door.

The scene was backlit because the windows of the tower room looked westward toward the sun and out over the wild Pacific Ocean beyond a steep slope and a rocky shore. I couldn't see clearly what was in the room and had to blink my eyes several times. There was a bed. Lisa Garcia was sitting on the edge of it. Her figure—why did it look a little different? I'll tell you why it looked a little different. She was naked.

The sight was a treat that many men, in the past, had paid a great deal of money for. The way things were, I had little appreciation of that. Lisa's large eyes fastened themselves on Mike and myself as we entered, and she said quietly, "Oh God, they've got you, too."

"A precaution, as you see, gentlemen," said Jabala, following us into the room. "Someone without clothes is much less likely to attempt an escape."

I stepped forward. "Are you okay, Lisa?"

"Stay where you are, Mr. Kennedy," said Jabala, gesturing with the gun. "She is quite unharmed. There is no point, after all, in being sadistic about any of this. We'll try to make everything as quick and efficient as possible."

Mike swung his eyes around the rest of the room. "Someone's missing, Jabala."

"Really? And who might that be?"

"The guy who does your dirty work for you."

Jabala nodded. "You've guessed that part of it, too, I see. Don't tell me you know who it is."

"I should have known all along," Mike said. "But it really hit me this morning. When I tumbled to the double you used for the prince, I remembered something else. It slipped by me at the time, but it was bugging me just the same. The murderer, right after Jake Larkin and Rita Schmidt were killed, knew that Rita hadn't been shot, but strangled. At that point, we hadn't told anybody. The murderer himself was the only other person who could have known."

"Very clever," said Jabala. "I'm glad you didn't realize it sooner."

"So where is he? You're not going to wrap this whole thing up all by yourself, are you? You don't like to get your hands dirty the way a good, honest murderer does."

"All this childish invective," said Jabala, without missing a beat, "really isn't going to help you a great deal, though I suppose you're rather desperately trying to put me off balance. Very well, Mr. Corby. The man who is going to kill you is out in the hall. You might as well meet him." He turned toward the door and called, "You can come in now!"

Lowell Hibner, lean and languid, appeared in the doorway and then stepped into the room as though he'd just been passing by and had become mildly curious about what was inside. In a loose tweed jacket he looked more professorial than ever. His half-smile was that of an instructor appearing in his classroom for the first time at the beginning of a semester. There was a gun in his hand, though he held it lightly and pointed off to one side instead of poking it toward us, as Jabala had been doing with his Luger. I sensed that Mike had been looking for an opportunity to take Jabala's gun away from him, and I'd almost been wondering when he'd make his play, but I saw now that we had a much more confident captor who knew how to keep himself from being overcome.

"At last you've blown your cover," said Mike, his eyes hard and flat on Hibner.

"Yes. Thought you might get it eventually. Had you fooled for a while, though, didn't I?"

"Got to give you that much, Lowell. You made a pretty convincing CIA man."

"That's because I used to be one. But the pay was lousy, frankly, and the chickenshit even worse. Free-lancing's a lot better. Jabala hired me to set up Qram's own intelligence agency—so secret even the prince didn't know. As you can see, he's getting his money's worth."

"I've been conned before," said Mike, "but I guess you get the blue ribbon. Offering your services so you'd know if we started to get close and could do something about it. Jabala's secret police probably knew Fourrier's background. It was likely Interpol would have a record on him. It made him a perfect patsy. How did you get him to write that suicide note?"

"Wouldn't you, with a gun in your gut? Everybody wants to live just a little bit longer."

Mike nodded. "Very neat. But don't let the fact that I admire your technique make you think I regard you as anything but a fourteen-karat sonofabitch."

"In my business," said Hibner, unruffled, "that's a compliment."

"Okay, Lowell," said Mike—and I had to admire *him* for keeping his voice straight and level—"what's the bottom line?"

"I'm surprised you ask. No, I'll take that back. You're trying to draw it out—put it off. Hoping I'll take an ego trip and recite all the clever details so maybe, just maybe, you'll get some last desperate chance to wiggle out of it. Well, everybody likes to show off a little, but I don't think I will this time. Let me just say that, as usual, I've extemporized and come up with a surefire way to cancel out the three of you."

"Come on now, Lowell," Mike said, "you can't just make us disappear. George here is a public figure. There are people who know we've come here. There'll be all sorts of questions."

"And the unfortunate accident you're about to have," said Hibner, "will answer all of them." He turned to Dr. Fayez. "I think it's about time now."

Fayez nodded nervously. He took a vial and a small plastic case from his pocket. He opened the case, slipped a hypodermic needle out of it, and, sticking it into the soft top of the vial, drew the plunger back to fill it. He tested it with a little squirt, looked at Hibner, and said, "Who is first?"

"It doesn't matter," said Hibner. "How about George? I think I'd like to get his *bigness* out of the way."

"If you think I'm gonna just *let* him stick that needle in me . . ." I blurted.

"But you are," Hibner said calmly. For the first time, he pointed his gun at a point just below my belt buckle. "You see, you've got a choice. If you don't roll up your sleeve and be nice and quiet about it, I'll put a bullet where it's most painful. You come across macho on the screen, George, but if you make any hostile gesture at all, you'll spend your last few minutes of life singing soprano."

If this had been a scene in a movie and I'd been acting it out I would have asked myself, well, just how would the character I was playing react to all of this? But it was happening to me, not some character, and I didn't have any control over the reaction. What finally happened, I think, was no reaction at all. I felt dumb, and I must have looked dumb. That balloon blowing up inside me had now reached the proportions of the *Hindenburg*. I was in a daze, and it was somebody else, not me, letting that little asshole of a doctor roll my sleeve up.

The bite of the needle. I hardly felt it. The faint pressure as Fayez pushed the plunger. And nothing at first—no rush of numbness or pleasure or whatever it is addicts are supposed to get from a needle.

"Jesus, George, I'm sorry!" said Mike, staring at me.

"Well. Some days are like that," I mumbled. Some exit line.

And then Hibner was saying something else, but suddenly I couldn't make out what it was. A buzzing sound drifted in from some far place and settled in my ears. Everything I was looking at began to take on fuzzy edges.

After that, blackness.

I was floating. The buzzing I'd heard just before the blackness had become the steady hum of an airplane engine. Heaven must have moved into the twentieth century, I thought; they take you there in an airplane these days. Like in *Here Comes Mr. Jordan*. If Claude Rains is flying this thing, I'll know I'm okay. It goes up and up and up, into the sunlight silence, and there are the pearly gates. Heaven? For the likes of me? That was a lot better than I'd expected.

But it wasn't heaven, it was just the sky. And the airplane I was in was my own. I was in the right-hand seat slumped down, with the seat belt and shoulder harness keeping me from slumping further. I turned my head as things came into focus again and saw Lowell Hibner, in the left-hand seat, flying the plane. He seemed to be taking up an awful lot of that pilot's seat, and when I blinked a few more times I understood why. He had a parachute strapped to his back.

Maybe I moaned. I thought I heard a moan, so it must have been mine. Hibner turned his own head and looked at me in surprise. "I'll be damned," he said. "You woke up pretty quick. That stupid doctor should have adjusted the dosage to your body weight. How do you feel?"

"I've had better days," I said quietly, testing my voice. "I've got a headache and my mouth is dry and I'd like nothing better than to stomp on your face so many god-awful ways that you'd have to *like* one of them. But outside of that I'm feeling fine."

"Don't try anything, George." Hibner picked up his gun from his jacket pocket and showed it to me. "My reflexes are pretty fast. I can see you out of the corner of my eye."

"What the hell are we doing here? Where are we going?" My words were still coming through the splitting headache, as though it had been a wall of foam. But everything was getting just a little clearer with each passing moment.

"Look in back, George," said Hibner.

I twisted around to look, and that was when I learned that in addition to being harnessed in the seat I was tied there with several coils of nylon rope. My hands were down at my sides, where they could do no more than fumble with the seat cushion. In the back, I saw Mike Corby and Lisa Garcia, seat-belted into two of the passenger seats. Lisa was fully dressed now, in her smart motoring outfit, but, like Mike, she was out cold with her head lolling to one side.

As I turned back again, instinctively struggling a little against my bonds, I wiggled my left hand a little in the process, and it brushed against the portable backup radio which was Velcroed between the seats. With all the nav-com units I have on the panel there was nowhere else to put it. It was quite compact—no bigger than half a cigar box—and not only didn't get in the way there between the seats, but sitting where it was, it was virtually unnoticed.

I'm not sure what prompted me to do what I did next. Part of it was a kind of instinct; pilots in trouble usually reach for a radio. Another part of it was foreseeing what would happen and latching on to an idea that was all but unfolding itself in my still fuzzy mind. The radio, I knew, was on the emergency frequency—121.5 kilohertz—and the talk button was on my side. By stretching just a little more, I got my thumb and forefinger to switch it on. I glanced at Hibner. His eyes were still straight ahead as he kept flying the airplane.

"Come on, Hibner," I said. "Where are you taking us? What have you got in mind?"

"Can't you guess? All right, George, if you insist on knowing I'll give it to you straight. Looks like I get a chance to show off after all."

By just a little extra slumping and stretching, my right hand, hidden behind me, grasped the unit, and I held the spring-loaded talk button down.

"We're at fifty-five hundred feet, as you can see, George," said Hibner. "Heading south, toward L.A. You're flying Mike Corby and Lisa Garcia back after a pleasant visit to his highness, Prince Ibrahim, in his elegant villa, Casa Madrona. All very normal, and exactly what anybody would expect, right? A few minutes ahead of us is the mountainous and inhospitable Gorman Pass. Planes have mysteriously crashed there before. Before we reach it, I trim her nose down a little, set the throttle, and jump. They'll wonder a little how an experienced pilot like you managed to hit a mountainside on a nice, clear day, but then they always do. I imagine she'll explode on impact, so they probably won't have much to go on. Mr. Jabala and Prince Ibrahim will express their profound regrets, I'm sure, when they hear the news."

"You've got it all figured out, haven't you, Hibner? Just like the way you murdered all those people on the plane from Qram. Don't tell me that whole conspiracy was off the cuff, too."

"I've got to share the credit with Jabala on that one. I'll have to say this for the blubbery little bastard. He cooks up a pretty good conspiracy. I guess it's in his blood."

"How did you ever get hooked up with him in the first place, anyway?"

"You really want to know? Okay, what the hell..."

Hibner talked. And kept on talking. In his business he didn't get much chance to brag about how clever he was—how fearless—how ruthless—how utterly depraved and amoral, and, to his way of thinking, all these were sterling qualities. He traced out the entire plot, from Jabala's desire to run the country his own way, to the virtual kidnaping of the real prince and his incarceration in his mountain lodge while his distant cousin and lookalike took his place at public functions, seen only from a distance by most people.

Quite a story. He told it to the world. Well, maybe not the whole world, but to the Coast Guard, the U.S. Air Force, the FAA, assorted hams throughout the country, and anybody else who happened to be monitoring 121.5, which has a bigger audience than a televised account of the Second Coming on all three networks in prime time.

I don't know how much time passed as Hibner told his story. I wasn't looking at my watch, and my mind wasn't keeping track of the minutes. All I was doing was sitting in place, frozen, thanking God I was meticulous about keeping the little Terra radio batteries fully charged, and hoping Hibner wouldn't notice my thumb locked on the talk button of the TPX-720. And Hibner, without realizing it, played right into my hands. The Japanese have a proverb that even the monkey can fall from the tree—meaning that any expert can goof once in a while—and this, in effect, was what Hibner did. He talked so much that he evidently passed the point where he'd planned to leave the airplane, and when he discovered it he said, "Oh, shit," and did a one-eighty to fly back and get on his original course again. That killed more time.

The moment of truth had to come eventually, however. He lined the aircraft up in a southeasterly direction, right toward that big pile of granite that springs from nowhere out of the flatlands south of Bakersfield. He got his bearings over Ford City below, then after trimming the plane and adjusting the creep-proof vernier throttle, he hurried himself out of his seat and started clambering over me to exit through the only front door in a Bonanza, which was on my side.

"Sorry it had to work out this way. Nothing personal—I hope you realize that—but this is where I get off."

"Lowell," I said quietly, "take a look out the window."

He said, "Huh?"

And then he looked and saw what I had just seen. Two Air Force fighters, throttled way back and with flaps way down, had fallen into formation on either side of us.

"What the hell!" said Hibner.

"The backup radio," I said, nodding at it. "You've just been on 'Candid Camera'!"

He understood immediately. He looked around a couple of times like a trapped wild animal, and then said, "They haven't got me yet!" He muscled the door open a bit, which wasn't easy, since the airflow was trying to muscle it shut.

"Lowell," I said, "that big secret of yours has just been declassified. You don't need us dead anymore. Go ahead and jump, if that's what you want, but, for Christ's sake, let me loose so I can land the airplane."

He stared at me for a moment, as though in shock, then suddenly shook himself and said, "What the hell. As I said, George, it never was personal."

The oddity is that he'd tied me with a lengthy slip knot. He'd never expected that I'd wake up, and was intending to yank it free as he jumped anyway, so that my body would be found in a more natural position after the crash—if there had been anything left of me to find. The two in back weren't tied at all. With a single yank and then a mighty shove on the door, both he and my binding were gone.

I leaned forward and eased in some power, rolled back the trim wheel, and settled down to the business of flying the dual-yoke airplane from the right seat, exercising my right thumb, which was numb from holding the radio talk button down for so long.

The Bonanza is normally a pretty quiet airplane, but not with the door open, and you can't close it in flight. I banked a bit to see Hibner's red-and-white parachute far below floating earthward. The din in the cockpit could have drowned out a full house at Dodger Stadium at the moment of a Valenzuela no-hitter, but it sounded like the Philadelphia Orchestra string section to me.

Epilogue

My home was full of joyous people.

The long private road leading to our house was packed with cars, ranging from Blossom's new white Rolls-Royce Corniche to a Volkswagen beetle of Stubby's with a heavy chain hanging out the front window, attached to a chunky anchor lying on top of a sign in the road which said, "The Bug Stops Here!"

Bobby Troup favored my Lowery organ with a touch the poor instrument, having been hammered daily by my ham fists, thought only existed in paradise. Jennings Lang never stopped smiling once he got word that the prince, long before the unpleasantness, had put funds in escrow to cover the film's unforeseen expenses. In any case, Ibrahim had been released unharmed and, as far as we knew, Jabala had taken up residence in a condo just north of where Jacques Cousteau did the program on Arctic seals.

My six-foot son Chris did his share of smiling as Blossom, in cardiac-arresting white halter and shorts, favored him with singular attention for a while. But from the moment Candy Vandermeer came in the room in flat sandals and shook hands looking him straight in the eye, he found it more difficult to smile because his mouth was open all the time.

Jimmy Stewart never stopped hesitating, and it got even worse after he tasted our housekeeper Sherry's lemon meringue pie. People have been known to bargain their souls for less, and the only real problem she had all day was turning down offers of people who wanted to steal her.

At least I hope she turned them down.

But it was Mike who was the most honored and sought-after guest. He sat with Florence, and I noticed their knees weren't touching. The romance, it seemed, wasn't *off*, exactly, but they weren't racing each other for the bed anymore either. Surrounded by my teen-aged girls Shannon and Shaunna and four million of their intimate group, he mesmerized a flock which I would have thought only had ears for MTV.

". . . the one last piece of the jigsaw was missing," said Mike. "On the plane, where had he stashed the gun?" He paused. "That was the one loose end. Our search had been most thorough, and granting there were lots of hiding places on a 747, we had scrutinized every one we could think of, again and again, with the concentration of a forty-niner panning for gold."

Gloria Stewart looked at the rapt expressions and whispered to Julie London that she thought there was a law against teen-agers paying that much attention to *anything*.

Mike went on. "I was allowed to see Hibner after he was captured, and though he wasn't thrilled to see *me*, I know it gave some measure of satisfaction to see the crestfallen expression on my face when he gloated how simple it had been."

He hesitated. Somehow, like in an E. F. Hutton commercial, not just the young people, but all of the people in the whole house quieted. All eyes and ears were riveted on him.

The guesses started as simply as the first tremors of a snow slide, but the excited voices soon built it to an avalanche.

"The john! In the john on a string where he pulled it up when he needed it!"

"Under the carpet!"

"The radar range!"

"Inside the piano!"

"Above the movie projector!"

And, from Stubby, "Under Blossom's sweater! Nobody'd ever notice it there!"

There were some wise guesses and some long shots, some well-thought-out and some just made to get a laugh. All fell tumbling one after the other until, like the spent avalanche, the roar became a rumble, the rumble a murmuring, a murmuring which shortly dissolved into a silence made more pronounced by the preceding din.

Mike may not have considered himself much of an actor, but he took a pause that would have done credit to Jack Benny. When it got just beyond unbearable, his quiet voice had only the barely audible ticking of our brass wall clock for competition.

"It was in front of me in the computer room all the time."

Mike went on and no one even breathed. "Each time he came upstairs and tamped out his pipe, he palmed it, and slipped it under the stack of already digested messages on the corner of the desk. We were finished studying them, so they sort of became invisible. He had access whenever he wanted, and we never even looked."

So, Mike wasn't perfect. But then again, true perfection may only exist in the hereafter.

And by the way, I was told that the party almost went on until the hereafter. A few times in this story I've given you an accounting as it was repeated to me, for those portions where I wasn't actually present. I have to do it again, about this very party in my home. I'm sure I've accounted for everything correctly, but I just wanted you to know I missed a lot of it myself.

I fell asleep.